KONSTANTIN ZUBOV

The Last Portal Jumper

Welcome the challenge!

K. Zubov

BOOK TWO

MAGIC DOME BOOKS

The Last Portal Jumper
Book 2
Copyright © Konstantin Zubov 2025
Cover Art © Linni 2025
Designer: Vladimir Manyukhin
English translation copyright © Celia Alexandra
Gonzalez 2025
Published by Magic Dome Books, 2025
All Rights Reserved
ISBN: 978-80-7702-137-1

This book is entirely a work of fiction.
Any correlation with real people or events
is coincidental.

All Books
by Konstantin Zubov:

The Last Portal Jumper
A LitRPG Progression Fantasy Series
Books 1-4

How I Built a Magic Empire
A Portal Progression Fantasy Series
Books 1-3

The Afflicted
A LitRPG Apocalypse Adventure Series
Books 1-2

Table of Contents:

Chapter 1

THE MOUNTAIN OF DEBRIS continued to grow, my nerves along with it. Come on out already, bastard! At least then I'd know what to be afraid of.

It did. It was the beetle. It was 10 feet long, five feet wide, and six feet tall. Six thick, hairy legs extended from what looked to be an iron-strong shell, and long antennae protruded at the front. My biggest concern, though, were the two sturdy horns and huge mandibles capable of slicing me in half.

It had no eyes, and I'd been counting on starting the fight by blinding it. I'd even gotten my bow at the ready. Well, since it was already in my hands...

I pulled the bowstring back and shot the monster in the jaws. I missed the mark a bit, and the arrow bounced off the hard shell. But the scarab turned sharply. It paused for a moment, let out a long, raspy sound, and charged at me.

"Help!" I shouted, as I rushed along the cave walls.

How?

Viz laid flat on my shoulder and made no attempt to take off.

How should I know how he could help? I didn't know much about what he could do yet.

Meanwhile, the beetle turned around, surprisingly deft for its size, and ran towards me. Maybe I could wear it down?

I glanced at its powerful, tree-trunk legs again and realized it would be a bad idea to rely on that approach. The same went for shooting it with the hope of hitting its jaws. It wouldn't let me get far enough away for a well-aimed shot. And even if I hit it, the arrow wouldn't make much of a dent.

Maybe the terrain was the key?

A quick look around the relatively smooth walls revealed nothing. Even if I turned into a hobbit, it was unlikely I'd be able to climb high enough fast.

My gaze fell on the mountain of stones in the center of the cave, and I turned around sharply to rush towards it. I ran to the top and down the other side, nearly falling twice. The scarab scrabbled up behind me, scattering large stones in its wake.

Hm. The maneuver gave me a slight advantage, but considering the risk of twisting an ankle, it wouldn't be smart to repeat it unless absolutely necessary.

The monster's head appeared over the heap of stones. I bent down, grabbed the nearest bit of rubble the size of a volleyball, and launched it at the clicking mandibles.

The beetle recoiled and shrieked. I repeated the move, but the second stone didn't land, instead just bouncing off the monster's shell. The scarab got over the hill, and I had to hurry away.

Stressing, running, and thinking, and acting simultaneously was hard, but the one successful hit I'd gotten in reassured me a little and helped me rethink.

I'd wanted to gouge its eyes out, but it had none. But it did have antennae. And since it had antennae, that meant it needed them for something. This was clear from the way it was waving them around. I had to cut them off. Aha!

"Viz," I called, having somehow trained him to respond to that name in the past week. "We need to cut its antennae off, preferably at the root!"

Have you seen what it has? Those... On its mouf... its... Manbibbles?!

"If I die, you'll starve to death!"

But... You has lotsa bwud. And den maybe someone else would come along. I do love caves.

"Damn it, Viz!"

Fine, I'll twy.

I thought I heard him sigh. I felt his sharp claws dig into my jacket and a shove, and he flew off. A loud screech filled the cave, drowning out the scarab's gnashing and scuttling feet, and then the bat took a sharp turn, his wings shimmering.

I followed his trajectory, which almost made me crash into the wall. Viz was flying high above the head of the monster, but suddenly dove and came within inches of it.

"Attaboy, Viz!"

He had a wide enough wingspan to chop off both antennae simultaneously, and the scarab's reaction immediately confirmed that the plan had worked. It shrieked, reared up on its back legs, and lunged at the place I'd been standing just seconds before. There was a loud crack, and the horn that had plunged into the wall ripped apart.

The beetle shrieked again, and I quietly started moving further away. The beetle had become permanently disoriented, and it turned and scuttled towards the center of the cave. It dove onto the stones and started tossing them around, but then came to its senses and froze.

I took a few steps. There was no reaction. I took out the helmet I'd used to hatch Viz (who, having completed his task, immediately tucked himself into my inventory with a sense of accomplishment), and threw it at the wall 30 feet away.

There was a thud, and the beetle turned its head. Which meant it could still hear. Just worse than before. I wondered why it didn't lunge at the helmet. Did it know it was a trap? It didn't matter. I knew what I had to do next.

"Hey, ugly, come here!"

You talkin' to me?!

Viz appeared on my shoulder.

"No!" I shouted, and started stomping on the cave floor with my heel.

Okay den.

The weight on my shoulder disappeared, and the scarab turned and scurried towards me. Everything inside me tightened, but I didn't need to hurry to get out of the way. If the scarab knew I was trying to trick it, it would be more careful now.

So I kept stomping, looking with a mixture of horror and disgust at the huge, bare maw drawing ever closer. I could even see deep into its black throat. Now!

I crouched slightly, channeled all my strength, and leapt back.

Thanks, Nikos! All week, he'd made us practice this exercise, almost more often than we did push-ups, and now I understood why: the ability to dodge at the right time was priceless.

I tumbled across the stones. Behind me, I heard a deafening thud, then scraping, a crack, and a howl that turned into a wail. The scarab literally killed itself against the wall. Well, almost... It was still jerking madly and trying to get up, but it didn't work.

I took out my spear, then changed my mind and pulled out my sword again. I changed my mind again, put everything away, and ran to the center of the cave. Keeping at a safe distance, I started chucking heavy stones at the monster's beat up head.

After about 20 of them, the beetle's movements had become much weaker. After 10 more, they stopped altogether. But I remembered rule number one, which had been drilled into me first by Visilius, then Nikos: don't let your guard down until the system tells you the enemy is dead.

It took 10 more stones.

Congratulations! You've killed a level 15 Scarab Warrior (mini-boss).

ATTENTION: Quest completed!

Your vision has improved.

The cave seemed to get brighter.

That was a mini-boss?

I threw another stone with a sigh and dropped to the floor of the cave. I just sat there for five minutes, then suddenly felt a fierce hunger. Fatigue and body upgrades made themselves known. Since I was aware of my new dietary tendencies, I'd fortunately brought some spare provisions.

"Come on out, hero."

Viz appeared on my shoulder, immediately swooped down, and swallowed an egg in the blink of an eye.

"I could have done without the needless arguments," I chided.

He froze and turned slowly to look at me. He wrapped his wings around his body and gave me a guilty look.

My bad. I was a Nervous Newwie.

"No more of that. If we're in a serious battle and I tell you to do something, you do it immediately."

Okie. Especiawwy since I'm a level 4 lady now.

I thought Viz was just using an expression the

first time, but this time, he was definitely talking about himself in the feminine.

"Wait, are you a girl?"

What awe you, a woman-hater?

"Of course not, I was just surprised." I bit off half a meat pie, lost in thought. "Why didn't I know that until now?"

Maybe you need your heawing checked.

"Maybe you should speak more clearly."

Between you 'n' me... Viz seemed to lower her voice in my head. *I'm your bat and can't actuawwy speak, so you just look like a schizophwenic talking to yoursewf from the outside.*

It took me three tries to swallow the pie that got stuck in my throat. I looked around for the wineskin filled with water to wash it down.

That was the longest I'd heard Viz talk since he'd h — since she'd hatched, and it was hard to wrap my head around. Sure, I was already used to the fantasy world I'd fallen into and was leveling up like in an RPG, but the fact that a magical bat was arguing with me telepathically and using words like "schizophrenic"...

Hm. Maybe I'd actually gone insane from the anesthesia and was still lying on the operating table, glitching? I mentally knocked on wood. System forbid!

I slapped myself on the cheek and poured the rest of the water over my head. Better. The ludicrous thoughts rushed off in an unknown direction, but were immediately replaced by another...

"Your name doesn't suit you, then," I sighed

sadly.

I mean, I don't reawwy care. Call me a vampi-wess if you want.

"I'll think on it. I wonder if there are any other rewards around here?"

I glanced around the cave.

No-ope. Lotsa info. Now I can find all kinds of stashes.

Oh! That was a helpful ability.

"Is there anything useful to cut out of that bug?"

Dunno. I only know what I've seen, heard, or read in this world, and the very last things that happened in the other one.

Ah! That was it! Before I'd gone in for the operation, I'd been reading books for leisure about the background, life, and evolution of gangsters. Now I understood where Viz was getting the slang from.

"Okay, I'll see if I can get anything from it."

Good luck. Don't fowget about the antennae.

"Can you help?"

She pretended not to hear me and disappeared into my inventory.

*   *   *

For the next two hours, I meticulously dissected the scarab. I collected all the internal organs I could extract, as well as all the parts that had been cut, torn, or broken off: the antennae, horns, and some nondescript pieces.

Once I'd finished, I sat down to rest and argue with my inner Scrooge.

"Take a nap, then keep clearing out the cave!" he said, squeezing my neck in his long, bony fingers. "You saw a lot of veins on your way here. There was rare ore! And the ants and beetles are freebies. Kill another hundred or two, and maybe you'll level up 10 times!"

"No! We were taught not to sleep here alone," I shot back. "The boss could respawn, or spiders could come crawling, shoot a web, and then it's over! And anyway, this place'll be available to me for another month. I can farm plenty."

"Coward!" he said, trying to provoke me. "While you still have the strength, you should at least go clear a few more caves and collect the moss."

"Fine!" I agreed, and stood up.

Contrary to what I'd feared, the monsters didn't go into a frenzy outside, and I was able to choose a direction and move on in peace.

Scrooge had overestimated me. Having killed less than 20 cave dwellers and scraped off two more moss beds, I realized I was on the verge of collapsing and passing out. My legs were shaking, and I was having a hard time raising my arms.

"Wuss!" Scrooge croaked, but I ignored him and activated the return portal.

The Last Portal Jumper

* * *

It was already starting to get dark. There were hardly any students at the portal, but there were two guards and a team of medics. One of them came up to me hurriedly.

"Are you hurt?"

"No, just tired."

"That'll go away on its own," the mage said, grinning. "Go hand over your loot."

He turned around and walked casually back to his group.

He'd reminded me about the loot for good reason, since many students who weren't planning on staying tied to the guild in the future preferred to hang onto it and sell it later at the city market, where the prices were about 20% higher. You could earn a good reputation as a champion for handing over loot here. Reputation wasn't earned just from loot, but also from quests, clear-outs, special missions, winning tournaments, years of service, and so on.

I hadn't decided on my future career yet, but it wasn't worth being greedy, especially because after you reached a certain reputation threshold, you would get a special color-changing bracelet. It was said that the bracelet opened many doors. If it was the right color, of course.

I trudged to the building I had to go to and found the door I needed. There had probably been a line here during the day, but there was no one around now.

The inside of the room reminded me of the S.T.A.L.K.E.R. games. There was a table in the middle, where a portly man was sitting, a bunch of shelves behind him. He looked like he was about to open his mouth and ask, "You got the loot?"

"What're you standing there for? Hand it over!"

His voice was even similar.

I nodded and started pulling out containers of monster parts, ore, and vials of moss.

"Hm." The inspector looked me over, his appraisal seeming to change. "Not bad."

"That's not everything," I said with a sheepish smile. "But there's nowhere else to put it here."

"Hm..." The man stood, graceful for his size, quickly weighed and measured the loot, and wrote the results down on a chalkboard. "Go on."

I took out the rest — everything other than the scarab warrior parts — and the table was almost full again.

"Not bad at all." The man nodded, openly reverent, and quickly counted up the rest of the loot. "Anything else?"

"Do you take scarab warrior parts?"

"Over there," he said, pointing towards the wall. There were diagrams of various monsters that could apparently be found in the guild dungeon, as well as a list of loot each one dropped.

"Could've shown us that in class..." I mumbled to myself.

"Self-teaching!" the inspector laughed. "Everyone has to figure out the first rule of loot mining themselves."

"What's the first rule?"

"I told you, you gotta figure it out!"

"Grab everything that's lying around?"

"That's more like the first rule of being a rogue, but close." He nodded approvingly and stopped picking on me. "If you kill a monster and you don't know what parts of it are valuable, take everything."

"I almost guessed it," I said, smiling, and pulled out the scarab's antennae, horns, and heart, the items I'd seen on the list.

"Did you take anything else?"

"Yeah..."

"Let's have it."

I dumped everything out, including chitin fragments and maybe even random stones from the cave.

"Well done!" The inspector leaned across the table and clapped me on the shoulder with his thick hand. "You won't get any money for this garbage, but I'll toss in a little extra reputation for savvy."

He put away anything of value and added a note to the board. He added everything up and wrote the total on the board first, then put his hand on the ball that was sitting on the table and said it out loud.

"Now you put your hand on."

Oh! It was like an electronic signature.

I touched the ball and immediately felt a sharp pain on my palm. I pulled it back and saw a green

triangle with a sword and shield in the middle —
the symbol of the Champions' Guild.

You've received First Rank in the Champions' Guild.

You've received a skill point.

"Congrats, kid!" The inspector smiled broadly
and held out a hand. "You got the highest marks
out of everyone who passed the exam today!"

"Thanks!" I shook his large hand. "What about
reputation?"

"If you keep going like this, you'll get your
bracelet in no time!"

"And money?"

"A champion shouldn't be materialistic," he
said with a stern look, but dropped the act quickly
and laughed. "Kidding. Here."

Holy shit! Almost 1,800 gold! I hadn't tussled
with that huge fucker in vain. And most importantly, that gold wouldn't be lying around collecting dust in the bank. I knew exactly where I
could put it to good use!

Thanking the inspector, I left the warehouse. I
took a couple steps in the direction of the barracks, then came to my senses and looked up at
the clock on the tower.

9:25 PM.

I could make it!

My fatigue retreated in horror, driven away by
my empty stomach, and I almost sprinted into the
canteen, where a little surprise was waiting for me.

Griselda, Russel, and Brun were sitting at a
large table, and judging by the pleased look on

their faces, they were celebrating getting first rank. With kombucha. I waved at them and hurried over to get some food. Of course, the variety so close to closing time was unimpressive, but I still filled up a tray to the brim.

"You've got to show me the kitten," the cook said with a smile as she took the gold coin and handed me two raw eggs.

"Of course," I said, smiling widely and grinding the Lying Through Your Teeth ability. "But he's really skittish and scared of crowds."

"I understand," she said, shaking her head, and I walked over to my friends, ears burning.

"Did you give up?" Russell asked, flushed, as he cleared some space on the table.

"What a weird question," I said with a grin as I sat down.

"Then here!" He handed me a mug.

"Oh, I got — "

"Take it!" he insisted, changing his tone and winking. "You'll like it."

Hm. It looked like there was a reason they were so cheerful.

I took the mug and sniffed it cautiously. Aha... The smell of kombucha was clearly mixed with the distinctive scent of liquor.

"Well, to first rank, then!"

I held out the mug, and we toasted.

Chapter 2

"HURRAH!" RUSSEL AND BRUN SAID in unison, and the normally stoic Griselda giggled.

Knowing they'd kick us out soon, I dug into my meal while listening to stories of my friends' heroic feats. I was especially surprised by the perpetually cantankerous, sarcastic Brun. He'd chosen the medium difficulty (or rather, distance) in the dungeon, and managed to make some good money (400 gold). Everyone else had gotten about 200, which they were also delighted with.

On top of that, Russel and Griselda had gotten level 3 during the exam, and Brun had gotten level 4, which really surprised me. I kept quiet about my own level, as always, but I'd already seen to that issue. I'd told them I'd supposedly been initiated almost a year ago, and my grandfather had been training me ever since to prepare me for the guild.

"Maybe we can go as a group to the farthest part," said Russel, who was much more drunk than the rest. "It's basically the same there, just with a few more monsters."

"There are bats and spiders there."

I put the last piece of chicken in my mouth and washed it down with the spiked kombucha.

"There shouldn't be too many of them," Russel said, brushing it off.

"Have you been there?" the astute Brun asked.

I quickly bit off a piece of cabbage pie, thinking things over as I chewed slowly.

In theory, going together didn't sound like a bad idea. Chiefly because you could only go into the dungeon once every five days. Something about the negative effect the portal's energy had on an underdeveloped body. If I went alone, then I'd have to leave when I got tired, like I had earlier in the day. But if all four of us went together, we could sleep in shifts, which would give us the opportunity to get further in, and we could also collect more loot.

Secondly, it was generally safer to be in a group. Five bats could attack instead of three, and then you might take a good beating on your own.

And quests could be split up among the group. I'd gotten worn out today more from hacking at the wall for ore, but that was something, say, Russel could do. It'd be good for him. He could lose weight that way.

Overall, I couldn't see any personal drawbacks, financially or otherwise, to going as a group, and my friends would be able to grind levels and make some cash. The stronger they were, the better. Especially considering that all my baron rivals were always with their buddies.

"Yeah, I've been to the far part," I said, answering Brun's question. "I'll go with you all, as long as at least one of you can shoot well, and you follow all my commands to the letter."

"I'd go with Ilya."

Griselda turned to me, and her hand brushed my knee (accidentally?).

"Me too," Brun nodded and took a sip from his mug.

"We'll take down all the monsters there!" Russel shouted happily, clapping me on the shoulder.

Not long after, we were told the canteen was closing, but to celebrate the occasion, they let us take some food and another mug of kombucha with us. We decided to take our little celebration to Brun's room.

*   *   *

Generally, I liked everyone in the group. They were all good people. There was just one thing that bothered me: we were all champions, which meant that our versatility in tough battles would be severely limited. After all, even someone who wasn't knowledgeable on the subject would know that every party should ideally have at least one mage.

Of course, at some point, I'd have to become

one myself... But everything that was going on around here unequivocally indicated that a sorcerer would be needed much sooner, and I had to find and befriend one no matter what.

And, as it turned out, there were places where I could do just that.

"We could also do group quests!" Russel continued to throw out ideas as he paced around the room.

"What, clear cursed areas?" I asked, doubtful.

"Well, no," he said with a wave of his hand. "Who'd let us go there?! In the places where there are anomalies... You know. Where you killed those spiders." I'd told them about that, but left out the part about the mini-boss. "If you go in a group or find partners there, you can get a quest for everyone at the same time. Like, it'll tell you to kill mutant rats if you're alone, but dogs if you're in a group."

"Poor puppies," Griselda lamented, sitting next to me on the bed.

"Well, not dogs..." Russel turned to her and zoned out for a while, apparently trying to think of a more appropriate animal. "Hmm... A horse!"

"Poor horsey..."

"One with fangs and horns!"

"Now it's scary!" Griselda shuddered and pressed herself into me. "I'm not going!"

Not wanting to get the tipsy girl more worked up, I tried not to move and changed the subject.

"What was it you said about partners? Are there just people looking for groups there?"

"Of course. There are always people like that near areas where you're highly likely to get a quest."

Interesting. I'd need to keep an eye out; I might get lucky enough to find a mage. Of course, I could leave it up to fate and wait until I happened to run into one or become one myself... But why? First of all, one thing didn't preclude the other, and secondly, if you just waited for food to find its way to your mouth, you'd die of hunger. And if you asked me, it was better to put yourself in the middle of the buffet.

"Are there only quests to kill things there?"

"Mainly, yeah," Brun said, sitting on the only chair. "But you can come across any kind anywhere you go. For example, yesterday I was walking from... Basically, I was on a walk, and I got a quest to deliver a bouquet offered to me. Except the reward was unreasonably high, and the address to deliver to was somewhere at the port, by the river... I didn't risk it. The quest was probably a bunch of steps or had some complication, like the bouquet had to be delivered to someone with a big brute of a husband."

Hm. The quest system here was definitely interesting. It was definitely worth studying thoroughly and figuring it out. In fact, we had two days off before the next course started, so I could start looking into it immediately. Actually, tomorrow I'd go on quests, and the day after I'd find the Linda Visilius had mentioned in his letter to me.

"Want to walk along the waterfront tomorrow?"

Pushing back her light hair, Griselda turned her sweet, drunken face to me.

Woah. She'd spent the last week working hard — studying, training, and carrying out her prefect duties with care. She was extremely shy, and she'd look away as soon as you glanced her way. But now... She clearly had no poison resistance, which could easily be taken advantage of, if desired. But why would I?

"We'll see," I smiled and stood up, moving her carefully. "Thanks for tonight, guys, but I'm exhausted. I need to go to sleep."

I shook their hands and turned around to see Griselda already standing at the door.

"I have to go too. Night, everyone." She smiled and left the room.

It looked like a second round of the battle for my honor was coming, and I wasn't sure I was strong enough to fend off a powerful attack.

My apprehension turned out to be in vain. Even with the alcohol, she took my hint and didn't take further initiative.

"Good night," I said, standing at her door and smiling gallantly. "Congrats again for getting your first rank, champion!"

"Thanks! You too."

She stood on her tiptoes, gave me a peck on the lips, and went into her room.

When the door had closed behind her, I felt all my energy leave me, and I walked back to my room, supporting myself on the wall. I somehow managed to get there, and I opened my door with a sigh of relief. Viza immediately flew over and swallowed an egg. I don't even remember my head hitting the pillow.

* * *

I was awoken to the sounds of morning warm-ups starting. I shot out of bed, imagining what Nikos would do with me. But as soon as the cold water hit my face, I realized that it was the first day of our two-day break. Hallelujah!

But a break was no reason to relax! I finished my morning routine and started my exercises. I called Viz out for some company.

I didn't know if she was following my example, happy to be progressing, or that our bond was growing, but lately, she'd been goofing around less and flying earnestly around the room, practicing various moves (whatever she could, given the limited space), and even occasionally working on her Wings of Death attack.

Whenever I proposed a new name to her, she always answered, "I don't give a shit," "Whatever you say," or "I'm sick of this!"

I practiced for an hour and a half, then headed over to Brun's. I'd agreed to help him carry our plates from last night to the canteen.

Russel was already there, looking a little rough, and Griselda showed up right after me.

Taking advantage of the fact that everyone else was in classes, we got to the canteen before it got busy and took the best table by the window.

"So, are we going to an anomalous area to-gether?"

Judging by the expression on Russel's face, he regretted suggesting that last night.

"Definitely not today," I said, digging into my fried eggs." I want to look at the solo quests on the notice board."

"You have to get there in the morning," Brun said, making a face. "The slickest guys take all the best stuff as soon as the quest giver posts them."

"What are you scaring him for?" Griselda looked at Brun with reproach. "The requirements are all different. He can find something better an-other time. And anyway, he can at least see what things look like. Want me to go with you?"

The last part was addressed to me. I didn't re-ally mind. I liked her. And unlike me, she'd been to the Central City twice before, so she could help me. I didn't want to go with a crowd, but I didn't know how to politely get the hint across to the oth-ers.

While I was mulling it over, the issue resolved itself.

"I'm going to the market to spend some cash from yesterday!" Brun said, downing the rest of his zoka. "Russ, wanna come?"

"Of course," Russel answered with a smile, ap-parently worried I was going to drag him along on my quests.

"Sure," I said, belatedly answering Griselda's question.

"Then meet me at the gates in 20 minutes!"

She grabbed the last two pies from her tray and got up from the table.

"What bad short-term memory some people have," Russel mumbled, watching her (ass). "She was the one who read the sign out to us a week ago about not taking food from the canteen."

"We need to get her drunk more often," Brun said, and he got up from the table smiling.

* * *

I'd been imagining the notice board as a stand with papers pinned to it, like something out of *The Witcher*. That was not the case.

It turned out to be a 65-foot wall with six rows of ads. As was customary, the two lowest rows were intended primarily for hobbits. The middle rows were for dwarves, and the top two rows were for humans, since there weren't really any other races represented in the city.

We got there around 10, and there were a lot of empty spaces on the wall, quests taken by earlier risers. There were also at least 30 not-so-early risers walking along the wall and reading the offers closely. But they were doing so in an odd way, touching the ad and freezing, often looking off to the side.

"Everyone's handwriting is different," Griselda explained. "Or rather, by and large, what's written on the paper doesn't really matter. Like, that one over there just has a house drawn on it and nothing else."

Some kinds of quests did just have drawings, the quality of which could be compared to cave paintings, and there was just an X on some.

"So, the people giving the quests do it through a system," Griselda continued. "They take something that can be hung on the wall, touch it, and add text through the interface. Then, whoever touches it sees the details of the quest, the reward, and whatever else the quest giver wanted them to know."

"Smart," I said, nodding approvingly.

"What, have you never even written letters?" She lifted her blue eyes to me.

"I don't remember," I said, giving my usual excuse. "Though I'm not sure writing even existed in the sticks I lived in."

"But they taught you how to fight well there." She smiled and took me by the elbow, leading me over to the notice board. "Try it out!"

I extended a hand and touched a piece of paper with "Daredevil needed!" written on it in large letters.

Quest: Take out the rabid elk in the forest to the west/southwest of the Central City.

Reward: 200 Gold Coins.

See Gnira for more details at...

Accept/Decline

It wasn't a daredevil they needed, but someone with a ton of free time. The vagueness of the unfortunate animal's location indicated that the hunt would take quite a long time.

"And while you're reading an ad, no one else

can see it," Griselda continued. "Here, try it."

She touched a pink piece of paper in the shape of a heart. I repeated after her, but I didn't get a system message.

"Try now," she said, taking her hand away with a sly smile.

"Dreamboat needed." Hey, that was me!

Quest: Water the delicate rose grown specifically for a looker like you. Your race doesn't matter.

Reward: 50 Gold Coins.

Note:

Jerks who are prejudiced against women over 70, please drown yourselves in the river!

See Mila Bretta for more details at...

Accept/Decline

Shit, why did I read that?!

"Okay, I get the idea," I grumbled at Griselda. "I suggest we split up. It'll take less time to find something useful that way."

"If Mila Bretta's ad is gone by the time we meet up again, I'll know who took it," Griselda said, laughing, and she touched the next sheet of paper.

Oh, shit! Maybe I should stand guard to make sure no one could take it accidentally? Ah, the hell with it. If that were to happen, I'd drag Griselda over and show her I wasn't going to see the old woman.

"Hey, wait!" Griselda called out. "I forgot to tell you, the quest giver's address is dynamic."

"What does that mean?"

"What a hick!" I heard several voices mocking

me at once.

Go on, then, pick on the noob. We'll see how you change your tune once I become an invincible outsider!

"It means," Griselda said, coming closer to me, "that the address written isn't a stationary place, but just wherever the quest giver is at the moment."

Interesting... I'd have to remember that if I was ever on the run (which I could never rule out as a possibility), it would be a bad idea to post any ads on the notice board.

"Thanks!"

I smiled at her and turned around, walking slowly along the wall and touching any ads that caught my eye or that didn't have any text written on them.

"Kill an oversized moth" (the reward was too low), "Find a lost boy" (too far away), "Looking for a drinking buddy" (the reward was a bonus bottle), and so on.

Having read over 40 ads, including ones for hobbits, I came to the conclusion that either quest givers really thought people were idiots or they were just unable to offer adequate payment for hard work.

Although, out of the corner of my eye, I noticed that there were people willing to take those quests, including the ones I rejected. Maybe it was because I already had a good bit of money. I still had what Visilius had given me, and the 1,800 gold I'd earned the night before gave me the confidence to not rush into anything.

"Hey! I found something!" Griselda called over to me. "Will you be offended if I leave?"

"Of course not. Are you going to tell me what you found?"

"I'll tell you later." She was getting ready to leave, but then stopped, remembering something. "And thanks for what you did last night. Or... didn't do."

She kissed me on the cheek and left. I watched her (ass) and thought that after she'd kissed me on the lips, another peck on the cheek was a step backwards. Well, whatever. I didn't need to be tying myself up with a burden, or ropes, anyway. I needed to grind.

I turned back to the notice board and saw a hobbit standing a few feet away who'd just put up an ad. Remembering that the competition was tough, I took two quick steps over and touched it, noticing out of the corner of my eye that another halfling was coming towards.

Quest: Act as the mediator in negotiations between two families.

Reward: 500 Gold Coins if successful, 1 if not.

Note:

You must be a human or hobbit.

See Clifford for more details at...

Accept/Decline

It wasn't a bad one to start figuring out how the whole system worked. In any case, I'd be able to grind my communication abilities. I could practice those on more than just women.

"Hey, move your hand!" someone rasped from below.

Ah! It was the competitor I'd seen scurrying towards the new ad behind me.

"I got here first."

"What are you, big guy, blind?! A hobbit posted that, and it's hanging on the bottom row! It's mine!"

The halfling had apparently seen a young, unfamiliar face, assumed I might not know all the rules, and decided to bluff me. Like hell, idiot.

>>Accept

"Ugh, you bastard!" the hobbit shouted, and he slammed his fist into my stomach with all his might.

Or rather, he started to, but I was expecting the attack and turned my body so his blow just brushed my side. It was still unpleasant, though. I grimaced and give him a shiner in return. He flew back against the wall, and miraculously avoided a broken nose or teeth by putting his hand out at the last second.

"It said it was for humans!"

I wanted to hit him a few more times as a lesson, but I saw two guards coming our way and restrained myself. I'd already been to the local police station once. I wasn't in a hurry to see it again.

"No fighting!" one of the guards shouted.

"I was just kidding around with my friend!" I grabbed the hobbit by the collar and turned to the soldiers. "Right, buddy?"

"Right!" he shouted, while simultaneously putting all his weight on my foot.

"I'll break your arm, you little bitch," I hissed, continuing to smile at the guards.

"I hope you break your dick on a woman, eunuch!" he shot back.

"Split up! The hobbit to that side of the notice board, the human to the other one."

"I'm done here anyway."

I smiled widely and left, shoving the unlucky hobbit's shoulder.

"Prick!" he finally decided to throw at my back. But I ignored him and hurried toward the address in the ad.

Chapter 8

CLIFFORD, THE QUEST GIVER, was probably the hobbit I'd seen hanging the ad. In all the commotion, he could have just given the details at the notice board rather than hurrying home. Although, like Griselda had said, I could see his changing location in the quest menu, so I could follow him easily. Or I could pick up the pace and catch up to him, which I quickly did. Although, that wasn't so much a result of speeding up, but the fact that the hobbit had decided to go into one of the taverns.

I wanted to follow him inside, but there were two things that made me hesitate. Firstly, the tavern was clearly high-end, and secondly, I couldn't shake the feeling that I was forgetting something. Something important about quests and this halfling... Ah! What an idiot I was. I had to turn into a hobbit!

It wasn't clear yet what I'd have to do, but while Clifford could easily reach the second row on the notice board, he'd hung the ad on the bottom row instead. Which meant, I assumed, that he wanted another hobbit to take the quest. Probably... It didn't matter. I had to change my appearance. But where?

The street was full of people, and the alleyways between the houses were too narrow to squeeze into. I walked slowly along the road, searching for an opening. After another quarter mile, I realized the most discreet option would be to crawl under a cart as a human and out the other side as a hobbit. I wasn't seriously considering that option, of course, but the others were even worse.

But I didn't give up, and finally, I found what I was looking for. Oddly enough, in the most crowded area: a massive hole-in-the-wall slop house for the not very well-off. I'd been to a similar place in Brinth, and I remembered that there'd been a pretty spacious bathroom there. Most importantly, the stalls had been separated by partitions, albeit thin ones. If it was the same here, then it was exactly what I needed.

I slipped in and, elbowing my way through the tight rows of enthusiastically imbibing guests, pushed open the bathroom door. There were five individual stalls. Two were open, and most importantly, there was no one nearby. No one would see me go in as one thing and come out as another.

Trying to ignore the odor, I darted into one of the stalls, closed the door, and turned into a hobbit.

Phew! Done. I was certain no one was outside monitoring who was going into the bathroom and how long it took them to leave. I'd have to keep this place in my back pocket for future use.

I didn't linger to take in the local aromas, but headed outside and hurried to the tavern Clifford had gone into.

* * *

"What do you mean, you didn't get it?!" At first, the man thought he'd misheard, but once he understood that was exactly what the hobbit had said, he slammed his fist on the table so hard that the glasses on it shook and fell. "Fucking idiot! Do you have any idea how hard it was for me to get him to post that ad?!"

"I'm sorry, sir! It's all my fault, sir! I got distracted, sir... I was just a few seconds late and..."

"I don't give a shit about your problems! God damn it!" The man pounded the table again, then stood up, sweeping an arm across the table to make everything on it go flying. "You stubby-legged buffoon! I ought to — "

"W-well, when he fails the quest," the hobbit stammered, "the ad will be posted on the notice board again."

"What good is that?! It won't be as persuasive the second time!"

"He's a human! Even if Clifford talks to him, he'll still be prejudiced. I can get him to trust me after that.”

“Shit!” The man huffed and sat down in a large armchair. “Go to the notice board right now. If you miss it a second time, get out of the city immediately.”

“Yes, sir!” The hobbit left quickly, bowing his head and backing away.

* * *

“Mr. Clifford?” I walked up to a small table, where the hobbit was eagerly tucking into a vegetable medley. “I’m here about your ad.”

Funny — I was a hobbit now, but I still had no desire to eat vegetables or grass. I still loved meat and potatoes as much as I had before!

“Ah, hello!” Clifford nodded and indicated the chair across from him. “I’m glad one of us took the quest.”

“It said humans could take it, too,” I said, offended at the racist statement despite myself.

“Yes, but still.” Clifford thought for a moment and didn’t pursue the subject further. “Is the general idea of the quest clear?”

“The general idea is, but I was hoping for the details that were promised.”

“By all means. Here’s the thing...” He began to fidget. Tellingly, he didn’t offer to treat me to some zoka or kombucha; he didn’t even ask my name. “My family is in the beer business. We’re comfortable enough, but... As it happens, we had a somewhat unsuccessful collaboration with a certain powerful person. He took offense, and is now meddling in our business. I need you to go try to smooth things over with him."

"Why can't you go yourself?" I asked, reading the menu board hanging on the wall in my peripheral vision and reeling from the prices.

"He doesn't want to see anyone in my family. Can you help me?"

I shrugged. "Why not? What can I promise him as a peace offering?"

"Our most sincere, heartfelt apologies!"

I waited for him to continue, but he didn't.

Hm. There was something like a blood feud going on here, and this asshole knew he'd dropped the ball, but was only willing to offer apologies. Well, not quite... The "most sincere, heartfelt apologies!" That was completely different. On top of that, he would only pay one gold coin for failure. Maybe I should have given the quest to that douchebag at the notice board after all.

"Okay, I'll try."

Clifford "suddenly" remembered something. "Ah, right! You'd better bring a human partner."

"Why?"

"The gentleman in question is a human, and... Well, after that incident, he doesn't speak to hobbits."

God damn it! What a cunning snake. He'd specified 500 gold, but had known in advance that it would have to be split between two people. It wasn't a big deal for me, of course, but it didn't speak very well of him.

"What was the incident, exactly?"

The hobbit made a face. "What does it matter? We just need to agree so I can send my most—"

"—Sincere, heartfelt apologies, I remember." I paused, pretending to think it over. "Mr. Clifford, the ad didn't say the money would need to be split in half..."

"So what?" the miser said, looking at me.

"I'd like to raise the price."

"No!"

My skills were nowhere near his, but I kept at it and eventually got him to add on a bonus of 50 coins. It was practically nothing, but I could sense my trading ability progressing.

Finally, he told me who I was going to see and where I could find him. There was no nav system here, though, so if I couldn't find the house, I'd have to either wait or look around for it.

"Deal," I said as I stood up.

"I'll wait for the good news from you," Clifford said, an unnatural smile spreading across his face. With that, he immediately forgot about me and went back to his vegetables.

* * *

Damn it. I wished I hadn't turned into a halfling! I tramped quickly over to my "secret room" and turned back into a human.

I went back out to the main room and was going to just leave, but I decided there was no hurry. There was something fishy about this whole thing, and I needed to ask around. What better place for that than here?

I pushed through the crowd to the bar.

"Beer, a large roll with sausage, and an interesting story!" I shouted, having difficulty making myself heard above the din.

"Two gold for the beer and roll, but I got no time to chat." The fat, short-haired guy behind the bar took the money and immediately started pouring the beer.

"What kind of story are you looking for, handsome?" A blonde woman, who'd been standing behind me, turned around, pressed her heavy chest into me, and smiled widely. "I know plenty of them and could tell you for a gold coin. For 10, I'd even play all the roles."

Her bright, clownish makeup, minimal clothing, and behavior suggested she wasn't particularly high-society.

"I'm curious about the dispute between Mr. Clifford and Mr. Phillips."

"Oh! There's still someone left who doesn't know about those assholes?!" someone shouted behind me, causing half the room to roar with laughter.

"Kid," the blonde said, smiling even wider, "that's a story I'll tell you for free, with the help of all these guys."

"It's my favorite!" a hobbit passing by guffawed. "When the boss is fucking me over, or I don't have enough money for fucking women, I always think about it and everything feels easier."

Book Two

About 10 people spent the next 20 minutes telling me the peculiar story. In a nutshell, Phillips was a wealthy and extraordinarily powerful man by Central City standards.

In the fall nine months prior, he'd thrown a birthday party for himself. He'd invited some of the most important members of the local high society and, naturally, thrown a feast. The birthday boy prided himself on his unconventionality, and instead of the standard pompous ball with exquisite dishes and century-old wines, he'd decided to throw a theme party of sorts, à la "drinking in the countryside."

He'd rented a park within the city limits and had mock cottages and other elements of rural life built. The food was prepared there over campfires and in ovens, and Phillips chose beer as the main drink. Much to his misfortune.

No one knew whether what came next was accidental or orchestrated by someone (all of the guests had their fair share of ill-wishers). The beer tasted perfectly normal, but the gastrointestinal consequences were furious.

Basically, all the guests gathered, changed into rural villager clothes, toasted the birthday boy, and within an hour, almost everyone was sick. Violently so. The entire rented park stank to high heaven.

How Phillips patched things up later with his afflicted guests, disgraced in front of the whole city, the story didn't say. The only reason he didn't put a hit out on Clifford was because it would be obvious who'd done it. And because Clifford was far from the only hobbit in the Rogues' Guild and the local halfling diaspora (many also believed there was an unwritten rule not to fight with other races because of the escalating situation with the orcs at the border).

Of course, after the incident, Phillips came to detest Clifford, and did everything in his power to ruin his life. If it weren't for the support of other hobbits, he would have been sent across the River Styx a long time ago.

"Everything's settled down a little now, of course," the blonde ended. "But they say that all words related to 'shit' and 'caca' are now banned at Mr. Phillips's estate."

An eruption of laughter filled the previously silent room.

"Thanks," I said with a grin, and I drained the last of my beer. "It's been fun."

"Come back again soon. I have plenty to show and tell you." The woman winked and took advantage of the fact that I was walking past her to smack my ass.

* * *

I left the tavern and headed for the king of assholes, Mr. Phillips.

The map was extremely helpful. My new target was about a mile away, and I would have been searching half the day without it. Using the map, I got there in half an hour. Although, the closer I got, the more I was tormented by my looming doubts for a successful outcome. It was one thing to hear about the big shots at the event. Seeing the most affluent neighborhood of the city for myself was another thing entirely.

Officially, private property didn't exist here, but everyone was well aware that for a certain (huge) amount of money, you could rent a place for a very long time, then rebuild it as a house to live in. The map was leading me to one of those houses.

In front of the richly adorned stairs were two guards armed to the teeth. They cast a disdainful look my way (and I'd changed into my best armor for this, too!) and didn't even bother to ask why I was there.

"I'm here to see Mr. Phillips."

"Reason?" one of the guards asked lazily, scowling.

I'd thought long and hard about that answer. Obviously, I couldn't tell the truth. They'd throw me out, maybe even beat me. What I needed was a half-truth.

"I know that shithead Clifford stabbed him in the back."

I was taking a risk by deliberately using the taboo word. They would either shoo me off immediately, or it would pique their interest.

One of the guards turned sharply and took a step towards me.

"What did you say that for?"

"Say what?"

"Well... You used a word that starts with an 's'..."

"Hang on, Firmin." The second guard reined him in and looked at me. "Stay here."

He turned around and walked quickly into the house. The door slammed behind him so hard that I could feel the vibration on the ground.

Hm. Something about this was making me uneasy. It seemed fine, but also not fine... I went back through what had happened in my head as Firmin looked at me like I was a shit stain on his shoe, and I realized that his behavior was completely understandable. But the one who'd run into the house seemed somehow softer and like he'd been waiting for me. It was probably just paranoia.

The second guard reappeared a minute later. "Enter!"

A wide marble staircase led from the opulent parlor to the second floor. We climbed the stairs and went through the open doors of a sprawling room.

Behind the desk was a man of about 45 with a huge black mustache and his hair combed to one side. His expensive suit and the signets adorning his fingers left no room for doubt: I was standing before Mr. Phillips himself. The guard positioned himself behind me, blocking my escape route.

"Speak," Phillips said languidly without taking his eyes off the papers he was reading.

"I have information and a plan for how to get back at Mr. Clifford."

"Go on." He still appeared to be highly indifferent.

While I was on my way here, I'd thought the hardest part would be getting into the house and talking to Phillips, but that wasn't how things had gone, and I wasn't prepared for this turn of events. There was nothing I could do about it, though, so I had to continue.

"Mr. Clifford wants to make amends." This caused him to wince, as if he had a major toothache, but he didn't say anything, and he kept his eyes on the desk. "He's looking for a mediator and posted an ad on the notice board."

"And?"

"Well, my hobbit friend accepted the quest, and he's ready to help punish that bastard."

Phillips finally set the papers aside and turned his hazel eyes on me.

"Not interested."

The fuck do you mean, "not interested"?! I thought. I'd come up with a brilliant, complex psychological long con that would force them to make up, or at least ease the tension a little, and would let me shake both Clifford and Phillips down.

"Don't you want to hear the details?" I mumbled, losing courage.

"Kid, do you know the saying, 'Let bygones be bygones'?"

With this, he opened a desk drawer and began rummaging around.

"I've heard it."

Well then... It's old history, and personally, I'm not interested in recalling and discussing it further."

Phillips took out a pouch and threw it at me.

You've received 100 Gold Coins.

"So forget about it and discard the quest now. You can't get us to make up anyway, and I no longer want revenge. It's too costly. Do we have an understanding?"

"Yes, of course. I'll give it to my friend, and he'll discard it..."

"Discard it right now!"

The mask of indifference fell from his face and anger flashed in his eyes. I could sense the guard approaching behind me.

Menu > Quest:

Act as the mediator in negotiations between two families.

Do you want to discard the quest? There is no penalty for doing so.

What choice did I have? Whatever was going on here, it smelled fishy, at the very least.

Quest discarded.

Remaining discards for today: 2/3.

"It's done," I said.

"Klim, escort the young man out."

Phillips's face became neutral again, but I could clearly see the vein pulsing in his forehead, and the paper in his hands was trembling fiercely.

As I descended the staircase, trying with all my might to portray myself as a simple fool, I could sense with every fiber of my being that this was not the end of the story. And I was very curious to see what would happen next.

Chapter 4

AS IF THEY WERE just going to let me go...

About 20 minutes later, I noticed I was being followed, and only because I was constantly on my guard. My tail clearly knew what he was doing. He kept his distance and almost didn't give himself away.

"Thanks!"

I handed a silver coin to a merchant in exchange for a meat pie.

It was my third, and I didn't really want it, but talking to merchants gave me the opportunity to look around seemingly at random. Which, praise Lady Luck, is exactly how I managed to discover my pursuer.

Irritating, of course, but I still had an ace up my sleeve. I could always turn into a hobbit or dwarf and lie low, or even leave the city completely.

But it hadn't come to that yet.

I took a bite of the pie, looking idly at the stalls, and walked along the busy street.

I had to remember what had looked suspicious in the first place, and why I hadn't liked this whole story from the beginning for seemingly no reason. So, what were the facts?

First, there was the hobbit who'd been gunning for the quest. As far as I knew, there were rules at the notice boards, and the latecomer shouldn't have acted that way. He'd started shouting immediately, and then picked a fight. And he'd generally looked highly distressed. Sure, his wife could have just given birth, and he needed the money urgently... But in that case, he could have just gone to see Mila Bretta.

Then there was the guard... Oh! If we assumed he'd been warned that someone was on their way from Mr. Clifford and needed to be allowed in, then his behavior made sense. Otherwise, like the first guard, he would have just thrown me out, or even attacked me.

The same went for the offended rich man, who had put all his effort into pretending he'd forgotten the whole thing, but was grinding his teeth the whole time I was there. The bastard had known a human took the quest, too! This part was important when taken together with the rest of the information I had. And it brought me to an interesting conclusion...

The hobbit had been expecting the quest, and he had clearly been sent by Phillips himself. The hobbit had screwed up and told his boss, who'd alerted the guard that, contrary to standard procedure, he should let the suspicious young man from Mr. Clifford through.

Hm. Everything fit together perfectly, without paranoia in play. And the last piece of the puzzle was the stone-faced guy pretending to just be strolling around the city rather than following me.

But then, why had he been sent after me if the matter was settled? There was no reason for it. It would only make sense if there were more to this story. Could I keep tabs on it? Easily.

As soon as I discarded the quest, it would have appeared on the notice board again, and most likely, the hobbit I'd encountered earlier would snatch it up immediately. Which meant that whatever Phillips's original plan (that I'd accidentally thwarted) had been, it would be carried out.

And I could only think of one reason for why I was being followed now: eliminating the witness. The witness to what? Unfortunately, the most logical answer to that was to assume that they wanted Clifford killed.

Okay. So, now what?

Kill my tail?

Maybe, but that would only provoke the quest giver.

Just turn into a hobbit, get away, then turn back into a human and lie low at the Champions' Guild?

A workable option, but it would be a good idea to let the guards know... Actually, better to report it to the guild. If they believed me there, then maybe, given my achievements, they would contact Phillips and ask him not to kill me. Ha! Not to kill me, or not to kill Clifford? Damn it. The more I thought about it, the worse this scenario became.

Maybe I should just turn into a hobbit and go to the Rogues' Guild for now?

Ehh... I could, but I was starting to make friends, not to mention getting used to my current routine.

Laughter erupted up ahead, and I was surprised to discover that my feet had led me back to the inn where I'd changed my appearance earlier. Well, great! Regardless of which plan I decided on, this was a necessary step.

There was a fight going on outside, and almost all the guests had poured out of the inn, surrounded the participants, and were now loudly cheering on their favorites. I slipped past them into the inn and went directly to the bathroom. All the stalls were open, and there was no one around. I didn't even bother going into a stall, but just turned into a hobbit right there.

Then the door flew open, and I turned around to find myself face to face with my pursuer, except now he was wearing a mask. Shit, he'd been right behind me! He must have seen the crowd outside and thought he could finish his job there.

His gaze slid along the empty stalls, over my face, and landed on the baggy clothes I hadn't managed to change.

I couldn't be sure if he'd put the pieces together, since I immediately sunk my dagger into his throat.

You've killed a level 27 Human.

Your inventory has increased by 28 pounds.

I caught the black box mid-spin.

I didn't want the blood to splatter, so I left my dagger in his throat and just turned the body, grabbed him under the arms, and dragged him into the nearest stall. I locked the door behind me and considered whether the body would fit through the hole in the floor and whether there was enough space.

It would fit. If I had to, I could cut his arms off and dispose of them separately. And there was plenty of space down there. It looked like it was just a big pit that drained into the city's sewer system.

"Fucking Sano!" a drunken voice said, and the bathroom door swung open. "I thought he'd kill that sissy! I put two gold on 'im!"

"They were in cahoots, I'd bet my life!" another voice answered.

"Assholes!"

One of the idiots pulled on the door to my stall, even though all the others were free. The latch rattled pitifully and didn't give the impression that it was secure at all. Fuck! If he'd pulled a little harder, it could easily have broken. I was also anxious that people were now coming back in from outside, and there'd likely be a mob in here soon.

On the other hand, the noise would be helpful. Wait, what was I doing?!

Okay... Just lift it a little... Shit! I wasn't tall enough, and the corpse's legs were separating...

I turned back into a human, lifted the body, directed his legs into the hole, and started to lower him.

The door was pulled on again, and I turned back into a hobbit. It'd be better to get busted in this skin, since I was already wanted as a hobbit anyway.

The latch held, and I lifted the dead man's arms and leaned into the body, trying to push it through the hole.

The body got stuck around the shoulders, but I had a feeling it would fit. I stepped on the head and put all my weight into it. Yes!

The body slipped through, and I heard a muffled splash from below.

I exhaled and checked to make sure I hadn't left any evidence. There was blood, of course, even though I hadn't pulled out my dagger, but in the low light, it could easily be mistaken for traces of human waste, of which there was plenty. I straightened my clothing and went to leave, when—

"Jesus, did you get stuck in there or what?!"

The door was pulled hard, and the latch gave with a crack.

"Motherfucker," I muttered, shoving my shoulder into the drunk guy hopping around by the door.

"Meet me outside, jackass!" he shouted after me, and he rushed into the stall.

I had nothing better to do than start a fight near my crime scene.

I left the tavern and joined the crowd outside.

* * *

At this rate, I'd find all the seedy places in the city in no time. On the one hand, there was really nowhere else to change my appearance, and bathroom stalls were perfect. I'd just need to wash my things more often to keep them from reeking.

Overall, everything went as usual. Fate, having spat on my plans and objections, walked to the beat of her own drum, and now a major figure in the city had become my enemy. That was something to consider.

Of course, the canteen was cheaper and more filling, but there were people there, and right now, I needed solitude.

I chose a mid-range establishment and, having cleaned myself up a bit, sat alone in a corner by the door.

The young, dark-haired waitress in a short blue dress called over to me. "What'll it be?"

"Umm..."

I short-circuited for a second, an image of the body disappearing into the wooden hole of the shitter flashing before my eyes. I caught the distinct odor of blood and excrement. Damn it...

"Do you have krinch?"

That was what the mixture of water and liquor was called here. It smelled just like vodka. I hadn't tried it myself, but the men in the village drank it all the time.

"Of course."

"Half a pint of that, two servings of boar, two potatoes, pickled vegetables, and a big piece of bread."

"Anything to drink?"

"Oh! Beer, please."

The waitress left, her wide hips swaying, and I leaned back in my chair and started looking around at the patrons.

Was it possible I had more than one tail? Not likely. The second one would have come in already. And even if he was waiting in the hall, he wouldn't be able to pick out a hobbit from the crowd. In any case, Phillips had lost a man. Even if he wasn't found, it was obvious what had happened.

Would he look for me? Probably. Would he find me? Not necessarily. Only two of his inner-circle guards and that hobbit at the notice board had seen my face, and the city was a big place. Would he carry out his plan, knowing there was a living witness? That wasn't guaranteed, either. After all, when Clifford died, only a fool would be left wondering who was behind it. It would just be a question of evidence and the manner of death.

Maybe I should go warn the hobbit? No. Firstly, it was too obvious, and they could be waiting for me. Secondly, I was a murderer now. If I wormed my way deeper into this affair, the guards would come after me. That was why I couldn't say anything to the Champions' Guild. Or could I?

No. Not worth it. Until I started accusing Phillips of plotting Clifford's murder, he was unlikely to put himself in the spotlight and hang his dead man on me.

What other options were there?

Kill Phillips himself.

"Your beer, marinated vegetables, bread, and krinch. Hot food'll be out in 10 minutes."

The waitress placed everything on the table, being sure to show me the hefty contents of her plunging neckline, then scampered away again.

I poured myself a glass of krinch, drained it in one gulp, and took a bite of cabbage. Not bad. It was a little weaker than vodka, but basically the same.

Anyway, where was I? Ah, right! The idiotic idea to kill the rich man, who was protected by soldiers of God knew what level. No, better to head for the capital and get level 2 as a champion. I might get lucky enough to see an elf... Although Visilius had told me not to. It could accidentally trigger an exclusive quest. Which would probably be something like the hit I was considering, only more cold-blooded... Screw it. It was better to sit here for a while.

All in all, then, there was just one thing I needed to resolve. Or rather, one thing I needed to come to an agreement with myself on. Now that I knew about this murder plot, did I have the moral right to stay out of it?

Considering the fact that Clifford was clearly a piece of shit himself, it was perfectly... Damn it, it still didn't sit right with me.

"Your meat and potatoes." The waitress pushed the other plates aside and set down the new ones. "Anything else?"

"Um..."

There was a thought spinning on the edges of my awareness, trying to break in, but it couldn't find an opening. Maybe the girl's luscious figure was distracting me.

"One sec... Ah! Just a quick question, off-topic. I lost my memory, and I've forgotten how to send letters. Could you help me?"

"The post office..."

The eyebrows on her pretty face lifted.

"Is it far?"

"It's on the next street over, that way," she said with a wave of her arm.

"Thanks so much! Here's a tip."

"Thank you!" She smiled widely and left.

I poured and knocked back another glass, took a bite of the meat, and started on dinner. It couldn't be past six yet. State institutions were open until seven or eight, so I'd make it. If only there were a way to send letters anonymously.

* * *

There was a way. Actually, I was pretty surprised by the post office. It essentially consisted of a stationary access point to email, or rather, system mail.

People could go to the nearest office, then go

into a booth, as was standard in these situations, and put their hand on the ball to open the system interface. The sender could then configure various settings to find the recipient, dictate the text, and sign if needed.

The letter would go to the station closest to the recipient, who would get a system notification. You could also send letters to another city, but that took longer, about the same amount of time it would take a mounted courier to get deliver the letter physically.

But finding the recipient wasn't so easy. There was no directory or phone book here, and the hardest part of ensuring your letter got delivered correctly was describing the recipient as accurately as possible.

Name: Clifford. Race: Hobbit. Place of residence: Central City. Occupation: Beer merchant. The input window was still glowing red. According to the hint, that meant that the information entered matched more than one person, and the letter couldn't be sent.

Personality traits: Cheapskate. Social relationships: Animosity with Phillips. Damn it! It was still red. Age: 40–70.

Yes! The field was glowing green.

Subject (up to 30 characters): They're going to kill you!

Message: You are going to be murdered in the very near future by means of a setup using your ad on the notice board.

Signed: Anonymous.

Send!

There. Whatever happened next, my soul could rest easy. The letter would get delivered in a few hours, and if Clifford wasn't a moron, he'd hurry to the post office and read it.

Now I needed to cover my ass and keep my mouth shut, at least in the areas of the city where Phillips lived and by the notice board where I'd met the hobbit. Which... Where was I now?

I opened the map and checked the address. It was just under 2 miles to the guild. I didn't have to hurry. What was that icon nearby? Oh! It was Ngiza's jewelry shop. The one Visilius had sent me to in his dying letter. I'd found out the shop address a week earlier, but I wasn't able to get there. But now it was almost on my way.

I knew I couldn't go in, but I had to at least go by it and make sure it hadn't closed down.

My common sense sighed reproachfully. *Haven't you had enough adventures for one day?*

I brushed it off and left the post office. I'd just go past it and take a look.

*　*　*

The shop was still there. And the sign made it clear that the person I was looking for was still there: "Ngiza has the best jewelry in the northern mountains!"

I felt a force nudging me at my back and my chest at once, one urging me to take a few steps forward and go into the shop, the other driving me back. I wavered for a few minutes before deciding to leave my visit to Ngiza for another time. If it turned out that what Visilius had said about overthrowing the emperor was true, it would make today's adventures look like a walk in the park.

To make sure no one was following me anymore, I zigzagged through the streets, glancing around inconspicuously, and went into a few shops. I didn't see another tail, but I still breathed a huge sigh of relief as I went through the gate at the Champions' Guild.

My friends and I usually met at the canteen around 8:30. I still had time, so I went up to my room, took out Viza, and started my evening exercises.

The intense exertion drove all unnecessary thoughts from my mind, and once I'd washed up fully and changed my clothes, I felt like I'd been reborn.

A handsome, fit, dark-haired man looked out at me from the mirror (a well-polished piece of plastic) and smiled. I considered giving myself a clean shave. Phillips and his lackeys wouldn't recognize me. Although, it'd be easier to just wear a hat and different clothes.

I heard a thud. It was Viza, who'd overestimated herself and knocked over a chair with her wing. She was growing rapidly, by at least 2 inches every day, and soon there wouldn't be enough space in the room for her to turn around.

"Train hard," I said, throwing one egg to her, then another, "and you'll eat well!"

She caught both eggs and swallowed them in flight.

Not enough!

"I'll be back with more."

I know you bought 20 of 'em today!

"That doesn't mean you need to wolf them down all at once."

You know, there've been cases in your world where starving cats have eaten their dead owners.

"Well, you're not a cat, and I'm very much alive."

But we're not in your world.

I grinned and threw her another egg.

"You'll get the rest tonight!"

* * *

My friends had already gathered, and we started on dinner. Brun and Russel had come into a bit of money and made the acquaintance of a few women. Griselda was smiling mysteriously all night, but kept her quest to herself.

"Did you get up to anything?" Russel asked, putting down his third empty plate.

"Nah, I didn't find anything," I answered.

"Are you coming with us tomorrow morning?"

"I don't know yet."

"Well, if you want to, we're meeting here right when it opens."

Russel spoke calmly, but I could see the worry in his eyes.

"Okie doke."

"What?"

"I said, sounds good!"

* * *

I went to bed early, and slept surprisingly well. And since I didn't have any plans for the day yet, I got up early for breakfast.

"Morning!" Brun greeted me, moving his tray a little. "Russ got cold feet. He said he'd be here in an hour."

"What did you expect him to do? He also goes running to Nikos at the last second, and there's much more incentive there."

"That's for sure," Brun said, grinning. "You heard the news?"

"How? I just got up."

"I also just got up, but I've already caught snippets of it three times. It's all anyone is talking about."

"What is it?"

"There was this funny thing that happened last year... A bunch of bigshots got poisoned at some event and shat themselves in public."

My fork froze mid-air, the skewered piece of egg just inches from my mouth.

"Anyway, the guy that delivered the tainted beer was found dead this morning. Drowned in a big barrel."

"Of beer?"

"And then some..."

Chapter 5

WELL, IT SEEMED HIS HEART couldn't bear it. Or rather, Phillips's trampled pride couldn't. He couldn't just stand around waiting for a report from the man he'd sent after me, who probably hadn't been found yet, and decided to take matters into his own hands. Brun didn't know the details, aside from the fact that in the beer was a large amount of... the products of human life, so to speak.

There were just two questions left.

The first was impractical: why did Phillips wait so long if he was going to leave a signature anyway? There was an ironclad excuse there: they set me up and left this clue specifically so people would think I did it. But the answer could be a simple one, too. Maybe Phillips just considered murder by, for example, a shot through the window to be insufficient for the offense, and waited for the ideal moment.

The second question was as practical as it gets: what now?

I couldn't go to the guards. They'd ask me why I didn't tell them sooner. And on top of that, Phillips would find out about me much faster that way than by waiting for me to make myself known again. Hm. I might as well turn into a dwarf and go to the jack-of-all-trades guild and do some bullshit there.

Ugh, no! The most I was prepared to do was to wear a hat pulled down over my eyes for a while, and maybe shave off the stubble. It was still pretty thin and not exactly a woman-magnet. Other than that, I'd just act like nothing had happened. Maybe the system was giving me a secret exclusive quest. In that case, it would work itself out. The important thing was to be prepared to waste someone else in the shitter.

"Ilya! Anyone in there?" Brun was snapping his fingers in front of my face.

"Hm? What?"

"I said, are we going to the notice board?"

"Give me a minute to think."

"Fine, smarty-pants, think on it." Brun smiled and pulled a piece of pie towards himself.

I had to push the whole thing away and remember what I'd come here to do before getting that quest.

Mainly: get second rank at the Champions' Guild.

And enlist mentors in a variety of disciplines like archery, knife fighting, and so on to help get to that goal. Try to learn the simplest spell. I could grind some important abilities on my own, like stealth (in the city), walking quietly (in the forest), lockpicking, and so on.

Find a girl for a no-strings relationship. Maybe two at once, twin sisters preferably. Grind and get loot in the guild's dungeon, and try to complete various quests.

I was also interested in going to the casino and taking part in a combat tournament for newbies (under level 20). Oh! And when I went to the forest, I'd have to see what my wight could do. We'd finally found a common language. She was unlikely to cause mischief now. On the contrary, I'd noticed a couple of times that she seemed to like showing off for me.

Ah, and I couldn't forget about reading the system bible. I had access to it now.

That was my incomplete list for the near future.

Of course, my legs were itching to head over to Ngiza's jewelry shop, but I had to abide by at least some of Visilius's precepts, and there was no need to rush. Moreover, my intuition (that jerk) was telling me that this quest could easily lead me out of the city, probably very far away.

Which of these things could I do today without exposing myself too much in case they were looking for me?

Almost all of them, really, if I was smart about

it. But the item I was really interested in was finding out what magic was and whether I could do at least some while working on the champion's branch. Like Visilius had said initially, it was nearly impossible for a regular person of my age. But I was an outsider, and I'd drank that potion he'd given me. So I had a little bit of mana.

Alright, it was decided! That's what I'd do today. Especially since I could combine it with another point I'd forgotten about: making friends with a mage.

"Sorry, but I have to stop in at this one — "

"Attention students!"

A burly warrior came into the canteen in full combat gear. He was accompanied by two equally robust, strong-looking soldiers. A deathly stillness hung in the air.

"An emergency situation has occurred in the city," the champion started in a loud voice. "A prominent member of the Rogues' Guild has been murdered. The rogues have accused us of orchestrating this incident, and there have already been several attacks on members of our guild today. We recommend remaining on campus until the conflict is over. If you still want to go into the city, travel in large groups and avoid confrontation whenever possible. We believe these acts are of a planned nature. Thank you for your attention."

The warrior finished his speech, turned around without waiting for a reaction, and quickly exited the canteen.

"Actions..." Brun muttered.

If only you knew what kind... Though, apparently, I didn't know anything either. In light of the new information, everything that come before felt like even more of a setup. But I had no idea who was framing whom.

It was a good thing that my involvement in this whole thing was fading into the background. Even if I'd stayed out of it yesterday, nothing would have changed. I'd need to keep an eye on the situation. Maybe talk to Nikos. Although... What would I tell him? That Phillips was behind the murder? Everyone already knew that. But who was behind Phillips, and what did the rogues and champions have to do with it?

There was clearly something of a much higher order going on here.

One thing was clear: as I walked around the city today, I'd need to pay close attention to my surroundings and, if I needed to, hit the gas and get out. At least the woman Visilius had written about lived nearby.

*　*　*

Instead of the standard two guards at the gate, there were at least 10. One of them repeated the recommendation to stay inside.

"I'm only going two blocks," I said with a shrug. "I need to check in on my uncle."

"Aren't you the guy who killed the scarab and had fights with all those barons?" a second guard asked as I walked past. He was a strong, solid guy of about 25.

"Well, not all of them..." I was surprised he knew that. "How did you know?"

"It doesn't happen as often as you think," the guard said, grinning and turning to the first. "Let me escort him quickly."

The first guard nodded. "Okay. But come back immediately."

"Of course." The champion winked at me and indicated the direction. "Double time, march!"

He wasn't kidding. We did actually march.

"What is it that doesn't happen often?" I couldn't pass up the opportunity to shed some light on my popularity. "Killing the scarab or squabbling with barons?"

"Killing the scarab before getting first rank," he answered. "The instructors have their own competitions, something like a betting pool. Nikos told us last week that he had a fighter who could kill a monster boss."

"I didn't even know there was a boss there."

I slowed down and looked at the guard, even more surprised.

"That's exactly what I mean." He laughed and nudged me forward. "Everyone knows Nikos never gives his students any hints. But even without knowing whether you'd go to the far end of the dungeon, he just strolled in and said, 'One of mine is going to go after a boss. I hope it's not the spider.'"

"Could there have been a spider boss?" I asked, taken aback.

"It could have been any of the ones there." He waved a hand to indicate a turn. "After that, people started being interested in you and found out that you'd already made a name for yourself in other areas. I especially enjoyed your scuffle at the fair and when you killed the spider in the cellar."

What was this, a breaking action news report?

"How did you know about the spider?"

"A deal with the city guard. They tell us about all clear-out quests that members of the guild participate in. It counts towards your reputation."

"What about other quests?" I asked, trying to sound casual.

"Is it true what they say, that you hit your head?" The guard laughed and slowed down as we approached our destination.

"It was a long time ago, but yeah," I said, spreading my hands.

"Everyone should get a knock like that," he said, and stopped. "Generally, system information is all private. All the details of quests stay between the quest giver and whoever takes it. But in cases when the quest giver is the city, and that's who you get the reward from, then the guild can get information about it. Make sense?"

He looked at me with something like sympathy. Apparently, Visilius's story had worked again. Society loved cripples and holy fools, and this guy clearly came from a common family.

"Thank you for the info, sir, and for bringing me here!"

"No problem. And if you ever see me without

my uniform, feel free to drop the formalities. I'm Dromdir."

"Ilya!"

I shook the hand he'd extended, and then he ran back to his post.

Not bad! I'd only been in the guild for a short time, but I'd already earned some reputation. I'd have to fight more monsters and barons.

Pleased with myself, I took a look around.

The address was correct, and before me stood a flower shop called Linda's Dainty Home. The name matched, and Visilius hadn't mentioned his old acquaintance's occupation.

The bell on the door rang as I went inside.

"How can I help you, young man? Flowers, decorations, or maybe perfume for your lovely lady?"

Smiling widely behind the counter was a pretty woman who couldn't have been over 30. Her light hair framed a beautiful face with an upturned nose and fell over her shoulders. Her voluminous chest was barely contained by a tight, white sarafan, and white heeled boots on long, slender legs completed the pleasant picture.

"Hello, I'm looking for Linda. Visilius sent me."

The smile froze on the woman's face, and bitterness flashed in her green eyes.

"Do you mean that old geezer is in the city?" she asked slowly.

This didn't appear to be a cheerful meeting... But no one had promised me it would be.

"Unfortunately, Visilius is dead."

The smile finally faded, along with the hostile glint in her eyes.

"That's impossible..." she whispered, not taking her eyes off of me. "Are you sure?"

"I was there when he died."

She walked past me on stiff legs and turned the sign on the door around to tell any potential customers that the shop was closed.

"Come on."

She led me through the shop, and we climbed the staircase to the second floor. There was a study in one of the rooms.

"Do you drink?" she asked, opening a cupboard door.

"My poison resistance is level 2," I said, "so, nothing too strong."

"Better to have a strong one then. You'll get to level 3 faster." I heard a familiar tone in her voice. "I'll give you a nastoyka. You'll vomit, and then in five minutes, you'll feel like a new person."

"Are you a relative of Visilius's?" I blurted out. Even before I saw her back tense up, I'd realized I'd said something wrong.

The woman silently took a carafe with some kind of clear, brown liquid and two glasses from the cupboard. She filled them, her movements sure, and sat in an armchair.

"And who are you, exactly?" I sensed a threat in her voice.

"His student."

"How did he die?"

"Count Krunite's son, Brunhide, killed him."

"That brat could never..." She grimaced.

"There were 12 men. Visilius killed four and wounded four more."

"Where were you?"

"In the forest. Then I took out the rest, including Brunhide. He would have died anyway, to be honest."

"Sit."

She pointed me to a chair, then lifted her glass. I sat and lifted my own, and we drank in silence.

"Now, give me the details."

* * *

I spent half an hour relating the events of the last few weeks of Visilius's life. Of course, I omitted the fact that I was a portal jumper, and my fast progress as a result of that.

"There's something you're not telling me."

Linda (who the woman turned out to be) took the empty decanter away and pulled out a second. I'd only had one glass to her three, but I still felt pretty drunk.

"Why the hell did he take you on like that?!""

"I guess he liked me." I shrugged and drained the glass she'd just filled without waiting for her.

I'd asked her questions at least five times since we'd started talking, but she hadn't bothered to answer once. Frankly, while I understood that she was clearly on edge, this behavior was already seriously annoying me. I'd even say it was maddening.

"Visilius said you could help me. If you can't, then I have other things to do..." I said sharply, looking Linda in the eyes.

"Ah, now I see," she said, smiling for the first time since we'd sat down. "He found someone as bold as himself. So, the old geezer sent you to me and didn't even tell you who I was?"

"I told you," I said, leaning back in my chair, "he wasn't planning on dying. Or rather, he was hoping to avoid it... It was just bad luck that the wolves attacked when they did."

"And he gave you a potion worth, as far as you know, 10 million gold. And all of this along with some fucking note..."

"Alright, enough!" I went into my inventory, took out the empty potion vial and the note she'd just mentioned, put it all on the table, and stood up. "Whoever he was to you, I'm sorry for your loss. I have to go. They told us not to leave campus today."

I nodded at her and turned to leave.

"Stop."

Her voice was quiet, but it hit me like an electric current, and I quickly realized that I couldn't move. Not at all. Even the muscles of my face were frozen.

"Sit."

To my horror, I obeyed. This witch disguised as a pretty, 30-year-old woman was controlling my body. At least I still had control of my mind.

"Give me a nod when you've calmed down," Linda muttered, reading Visilius's letter.

Very fucking funny. Anger rose within me, and a demand/desire/need formed: I had to do everything I could to learn to resist these spells. These skills supposedly showed up after level 10, and they'd be the first ones I'd level up.

"What does he mean by 'Don't tell her too much'?"

Linda tore her eyes from the note and quickly filled and drained her glass. I realized in that instant that I could move again.

"Figure of speech, probably," I croaked hoarsely, thankful for the long-awaited freedom. "Something like, be clear and concise."

"I see..." She leaned back in her armchair and closed her eyes. "He was my father."

"I'm sorry," I muttered, and I took a drink.

"For my loss, or for the fact that he was my father?"

"For your loss. And I'm sorry you didn't get to see him again."

There was a long pause.

His daughter, damn it. And you didn't need to be a rocket scientist to figure out that their relationship was, to put it mildly, tenuous. Linda was clearly reliving that now. I knew I couldn't tell her I was an outsider. That would put both of us at risk. Visilius probably wouldn't want me to be seen around her too much, either.

"You wanted to give me something to sober up."

"Are you able to tell it apart from a mind-control potion?"

"No."

"Then remember: never accept food or drink from a witch or sorcerer in their home."

"They can slip you something outside their home, too."

"Really strong potions, aside from poison, have a very limited shelf life. Literally minutes. Witches can only create the conditions necessary to store them at home. Here's your sobriety powder, by the way."

She tossed me a small pouch.

"I've sobered up already, thanks."

"Keep it then. It's grengar poison. It won't go bad. A pinch would keep you on the toilet for a day. Two would kill you in an hour. It's tasteless and odorless. Antidotes only work if you take them within 10 minutes."

The longer I spent with the woman, the more I recognized Visilius's habits in her, although she annoyed me much more.

"Alright..." Linda sighed deeply, pushed the half-empty decanter aside, and look at me. "I'm obviously not in the mood, but we should get down to business. What do you want to learn?"

Chapter 6

MAGIC TURNED OUT to be fairly complicated. Or rather, it would be easier if I were a mage. Then a list of available base spells and passive skills would have appeared to simplify the process. I had to try to figure something out that didn't have the standard description.

"What was he thinking?!" Linda shook her head in frustration when I once again failed to make the simplest flame. "It takes folks months to learn this, even when they've chosen the mage branch..."

"Months?" I asked, surprised. "They get first rank in a week at the Mages' Guild."

"Well, they can use the spells that the system gives them by default, and they have all sorts of upgrades and whatnot there." We were still sitting in the office, and Visilius's daughter was leaning back in her armchair, desperately trying to teach me what, in her opinion, were the absolute basics. "To put it very simply, imagine a 17-year-old kid. He wakes up, puts on his pants, shirt, jacket, helmet, and rings, puts his boots on one at a time, and so on. And when he turns 18, he's already got some level 5 clothing and has set up his inventory so that now, he can put on all of that gear with a single thought command in a second. Are you following?"

"Yeah."

"So, with the magic that novice mages can use, it's the same as your acceleration. He just taps, and it works." Linda was gesturing enthusiastically as she explained. "The difficulty only starts when he has to come up with his own spells, ones that aren't in the book. And if you don't even have a book, and any spell, even the most basic spell, requires you to understand, sense, put together, and feel flowing through you... That's why it takes months."

"Then maybe there's no reason to rush...?"

"Meaning what?"

She raised her eyebrows, and I immediately realized that I'd almost given myself up under the influence of the alcohol. She didn't know that, sooner or later, I'd become a full-fledged mage.

"Well, I mean, you're explaining it now, and I'll practice at the guild. Once I get the basics down, I'll go — "

"You'll never be able to do it by yourself, not without a book! You have to at least do one thing in front of me. Come on, try it again. And sober up already!"

"Thanks... I'm already sober," I said, almost truthfully, and went to try again.

Okay... The first thing I needed to do was push the thought that I was doing unnecessary nonsense out of my mind. That wasn't true. An ordinary person, having become a champion, wouldn't be able to master magic. But I wasn't ordinary. I had to understand the basic structure anyway, so that at some point in the future, when I could study magic in earnest, I would actually be able to do cool shit instead of just mashing buttons. Like bringing a meteor shower down on enemies!

Alright. I closed my eyes and concentrated. I breathed deeply and steadily, pushing away all worries and doubts. Linda had said that eventually, everything would come automatically, and with the right ability, I'd be able to cast spells with juggling daggers and making small talk, but I couldn't do anything without full concentration to start.

Inhale, exhale... Inhale, exhale... I concentrated on the sensations around my solar plexus and imagined energy starting to gather there. Inhale, exhale... I needed to direct the energy there and feel it build up. It seemed like there was something there... Or was that just my empty stomach grumbling? Ugh, not important! Feel the energy! Become one with it!

I couldn't feel anything for a long time, but then suddenly, something clicked, and I felt warmth in my chest. There! Now, don't rush it. I needed to understand this feeling, its origin and structure. I had to try to handle and move it. A little to the right... Now left and up... Now in a circle.

Twice, I almost screwed it all up. The warmth dissipated and became barely perceptible. But both times, I managed to bring it back to the center of my chest, though it wasn't easy.

After a few dozen tries, I was able to handle it with more confidence, and I felt like I could try to move it into my hand.

Okay... I visualized my veins. The way they flowed from my chest to my shoulder, then along my arm to my palm. Then I imagined them as a road along which I needed to guide this cluster of warmth, trying not to let it spill. Let's do this! Careful now... No rushing. I needed the energy to remember the path, and I needed to figure out how to lead it along that path. Okay... *A little higher*, I instructed. *A little more. Now, stop around the shoulder. Just like that, good. Daddy's with you, daddy won't leave you... Slowly down now. A little more. To the elbow... Forearm... Okay, be careful! The road narrows here... You should compress yourself. It doesn't matter that you're getting denser and brighter. That's how it's supposed to be. Okay, now into the palm, and... Most importantly, let's imagine that you're not a cluster of internal energy, but a little tongue of fire... A hot, bright, all-consuming flame...*

Fuck! What was that?!

Book Two

My palm was burning. My eyes snapped open, and I instinctively clapped my hand on my knee. There was smoke billowing above me, and the distinct odor of burnt flesh filled the room.

"Shit, that hurts!" I croaked through gritted teeth.

"If you'd thrown that fireball you just made, I would have torn your head off." Linda watched me without blinking, then quickly remembered herself and ran over. "Give me your hand."

I held out my palm.

Motherfucker! I'd never seen a blister like that before. I managed not to lose consciousness either from the alcohol or, more likely, the shock of the pain.

Linda gripped my hand surprisingly tightly in one of hers, and with her other, she started treating me. I'd already been through a similar procedure when I was being treated after sparring with Nikos, but it was much more intense this time, and the blue light pouring from Linda's fingers was much brighter.

To my great joy, Visilius's daughter turned out to be a strong mage, and the pain began to subside without ever reaching a truly acute phase. The redness went away too, and the blister went down.

"Hold it like this!"

Linda showed me how, then quickly walked over to the cupboard.

"Is it wise to accept unfamiliar treatment...?" I asked, watching her come back carrying a vial of brown ointment.

"No! You need to carry these things with you." She scooped out a thick glob of ointment and started rubbing it into my palm. "So take the rest! It's terrific for relieving the effects of injuries like this. You'll feel good as new in an hour."

"Was it really that bad?" I asked, surprised. "Why is magic not enough to heal it?"

"Well, I'm not a healer," she said, surprised herself. "I just gave you a basic treatment. All mages know it."

"So, what kind of mage are you? A control mage?"

"Doesn't matter right now!" She skillfully placed a bandage on top of the ointment and turned to me. "When can you come back?"

"Umm..."

I couldn't immediately find the words to say, since until now, I'd thought this visit would be my only one.

"I have classes starting tomorrow. And there's still that commotion with the Rogues' Guild..."

"I'll expect you any day after 10 in the evening. I'll give you a toothbrush."

"Can you tell me what happened?" I nodded at my bandaged palm. "I was sitting with my eyes closed."

"How can I say this..." Linda went around the table and sank into her armchair. "How do you feel overall?"

"What do you mean?"

"You're not dizzy? No nausea?"

"Well, a little, but mostly likely from the pain.

I think it'll pass soon."

"Mm-hm."

She picked up the decanter that had been pushed aside earlier and took a large gulp directly from the spout.

"What the hell's going on?"

I was starting to get irritated again with her pattern of ignoring my questions, mumbling, and meaningful silences.

"It's just..." She paused before continuing on, her piercing green eyes on my face. "Even if we ignore your age and development path and pretend you're a level 5 mage, after that spell you did, you should have been passed out for at least an hour, and then taken a full day to recover. But... Shit, you're just a little dizzy. And it's not from the alcohol."

"Well, I am actually dizzy..."

"Cut the shit!" Her eyes flashed.

"And if I come back, can I count on a somewhat... warmer welcome?"

"We'll see."

*　*　*

I probably should have been looking around me on the way back to the guild, but, to be frank, my mind was elsewhere. Meeting Visilius's daughter had been too intense, and I couldn't think of anything else.

First of all, it seemed like I didn't get burned that badly. If I were anyone else, it would have been time to panic. But I was reassured by the fact that Visilius would never have sent me to her if she were completely inept.

Secondly, magic was cool! And I seemed to have a greater inclination towards it than strength training. Except if I studied it on my own, I'd either kick the bucket from an unsuccessful spell or reveal that I was an outsider to everyone.

What were the risks of that exposure, considering that I was still pretty low-level? Probably death. Whether that came in the form of a hired hitman or an insurmountable exclusive quest from the system was irrelevant.

Generally, in all likelihood, I'd have to tone things down and focus on the Champions' Guild for the time being. But... Damn it, how could I refuse an offer like Linda's?

Free lessons (though I knew that, sooner or later, I'd have to pay her) with someone who was clearly a very powerful witch...

Speaking of which, that control magic of hers was the stuff of nightmares! I had to study magic, if only to learn how to resist that. It didn't seem like she could control minds, otherwise she probably would have forced me to pay. But even just the ability to control someone's body was really something. And what if an enemy were to do that to me?

Hm. If a florist could do that, what was a truly badass mage, champion, or rogue capable of?

There was only one conclusion to come to: grind, grind, and grind some more. I couldn't hang out in the canteen and flap my lips. I couldn't slack off and enjoy myself (any more than necessary, anyway). I had to dedicate all of my free time to grinding levels and abilities, honing skills, and studying magic. With my 100% bonus and stubbornness...

"Hey, kid! Don't think so hard. It'll make your head hurt."

I lifted my head and discovered that I was already standing at the gates of the Champions' Guild, and the guards were looking at me, laughing.

"Oh, I was just trying to remember if I'd bought bread," I said, shrugging.

"Go buy some at the canteen," one of the guards said, cracking up and indicating the ball on its pillar. "And don't forget to put your hand on that, deep thinker."

* * *

I wanted to eat, of course, but I headed for the class schedule first. I wanted to see what Nikos's schedule was like.

He was currently running pre-dinner strength training with the students who'd already gotten second rank. There was still another hour and a half left. I considered the best course of action and remembered that because of the quest yesterday and my early rising today, I hadn't done my full training routine in a while. That was what I'd do, then. Even if I didn't get a chance to talk to Nikos, I wouldn't have just been wasting time.

My stomach protested this decision, but I ignored it and headed for the training grounds.

I spotted Nikos's silhouette from far away, and I got to the area quickly. The students were doing something like CrossFit, and I posted up a little to the side and started warming up my muscles.

My actions didn't go unnoticed, and Nikos called to me across the grounds without coming over.

"You're off today. Or did you chicken out of going to the city because of the rogues?"

That drew laughter from some of the students training, which immediately got three of them an additional 50 reps.

"I wanted your advice!" I shouted as I grabbed a huge hammer and started pummeling the sturdy spring plate.

"One gold per minute! If that suits you, ask away!"

Nikos was in a surprisingly generous mood today.

"I'll give you two for it to be private."

"No — you might ask something intelligent that could benefit everyone."

While I was on my way over here, I'd actually thought Nikos would ignore me, and that he'd shoo me away when I talked to him. But with every sentence, I was sensing... Well, if not kindness, then at least a hint of curiosity and amiability. It seemed like the guard hadn't been exaggerating, and Nikos did actually set me apart from the crowd.

"Then I'll give you three, but each of the others should chip in a silver."

"No... I doubt your questions are worth that much. What the hell are you doing?!" This was directed at a tall guy who'd failed to jump on top of a box. "Ilya! This is your fault! Go and show him how it's done. 100 times!"

Our conversation ended there, and I spent the next hour showing the failing trainees how to do the exercises. Considering that most of them were doing this for the first time, I had to repeat myself over and over.

"All dismissed!" Nikos said when the clock chimed, and as the students stretched on their way to the canteen, he came up to me. "You have five minutes."

*   *   *

The senior investigator at the Department of Rumors cursed the day he first sent his beloved a letter written by his own hand. She'd loved it, and now she categorically refused to communicate through the system.

And the longer it went on, the more this correspondence exhausted Pinter. More often than not, he'd spend three hours pouring his soul out onto 10 sheets of paper, and in response, he'd get a drawing of a heart. Or worse, a cat!

Now he was hammering away at another masterpiece, swearing to himself that this was the last time. He'd tell her later that the Emperor had forbidden sending handwritten letters because... Because of reasons the senior investigator hadn't been able to come up with yet after three days.

"Commander, may I?"

Stilks poked his nose into the office, but this time, the startled Pinter managed to snatch up the sheet of paper, and ink dripped onto the table.

"If it's not important news..." the senior investigator started threateningly.

"Message from Vinus!"

"Stilks, knock next time!"

"Yes sir, commander, sorry!"

"Come in and report, but make it quick."

"The witness in the elf case has been found dead. We double-checked the area where he saw the elf and found residual evidence-destroying magic. Further investigation ongoing."

"Next."

"The monsters that were frightening villagers turned out to be people in disguise sent by the local treasurer. It was all planned so that the treasurer could buy up plots of land on the cheap."

"Is he stupid?" Pinter raised his eyebrows. "Who would he sell the land to later?"

"He was hoping for a clear-out raid from the capital that would make the price go up."

"Okay, so he is stupid. What else?"

"The witness who saw the shapeshifter — "

"Weren't there two?"

"The hobbit ran as soon as he saw it."

"Ah..."

"Vinus thinks the witness is credible, but no

one new has come into the village where the shapeshifter supposedly went. Vinus says she'll take sensor readings for outsiders before she leaves and will stop by another village…"

"So she has nothing to do." The senior investigator smiled. "Alright. The main thing is to see the elf case through to the end. There's something fishy about that…"

"Commander!" The normally stoic dwarf Eustace burst into the office, pushing Stilks out of the way.

"Out with it!"

News of the conflict between the rogues and champions in the main trade city had reached the capital two hours earlier and created a storm of unpleasantness, including in Pinter's department. But Pinter had nothing to blame himself for. He'd heard rumors already that this conflict was possible, but the sources were unreliable and couldn't be verified. Proactive messages had been sent to the rogues anyway, though.

Now his assistant was bringing him analytical data, and his behavior filled the senior investigator with anxiety.

"The Head Thinker found this in the archives!" Eustace pulled out four sheets of paper and placed them on Pinter's desk. "Current events have built a bridge between the primary and secondary sources. They're in constant contact…"

Pinter scanned the papers from the archives and looked at his assistant with renewed worry.

"Have you cross-checked this?"

"All the details match, and there's no overlap in the sources. There's a two-thirds chance that the target is not a champion."

"Who's the target, then?"

The senior investigator's stomach somersaulted with a horrifying foreboding.

"Veterans of the last great war," the dwarf said quietly, his words piercing in the silence.

Pinter's assistants were intelligent and competent. The Head Thinker never forgot a thing and could find connections where no one else could. But Pinter was the senior investigator for a reason. Though the evidence was anecdotal, he was certain it was accurate.

And worst of all, it was unlikely he could report it to the Central Office in time.

"Code black!" he shouted as he rushed out of the office.

Chapter 7

"VERY INTERESTING," NIKOS SAID, pretending to mull over my words, then suddenly thrusting with a training sword. "It's rare to find such ambition in such a young person."

I was already familiar with his way of attacking at the most unexpected times, and I was able to not only parry his blow, but answer with my own as well. Unsuccessfully, of course. I'd just told him my plan, leaving out things like "find a woman and study magic."

"Whatever you have planned to do in the city and outside of it, be sure to do it!" Nikos's sword changed direction sharply and hit me in the shoulder. "The tournament starts in two weeks. You absolutely need to participate. It's good experience and a decent reward."

I'd thought about it already too, but I'd had

second thoughts after Clifford was murdered. I'd have to find out if I could wear a mask or something. But that was a subject for later consideration. Right now, I had to figure out the most important thing.

"What about training?"

"All active guild members have lots of work to do. And when blockheads like you all are hanging all over us, all our free time is taken up, so it's impossible to have additional individual lessons. So — what's that?!"

He shouted, his eyes wide, and indicated behind me.

I started to turn my head a fraction of a second before realizing it was a trick, but I still managed to throw up my sword.

Well, almost. Metal clanged against metal, and pain shot through my shoulder again.

"So," Nikos continued as if nothing had happened, "the only thing I can do for you is let you come to classes for third-rank students. Twice a week. Two hours each. I'll either put you up against one of them or fight you myself."

"Thanks!"

"200 gold per week."

"Ehh... A little expensive for a fight..."

I made a deceptive maneuver and struck a quick blow. It almost landed.

"With third-rank guys?"

"Under my supervision and corrections."

"Still!"

"Alright, 100." He swung.

"50!" I parried.

"90!" He swung again.

"50!" I dodged, by some miracle.

"80!" He made a barely perceptible movement, and the rounded blade hit me in the chest. "Final offer."

"Okay." I raised my hand to tell him I needed a second to catch my breath. "What about knife fighting and archery?"

"That's for fourth-rank students who are so inclined." Nikos decided I'd had enough rest and restarted his offensive. "I'm not entirely sure it's worth it for you. Better to find partners for more conventional training."

"Anything could happen," I countered, backing away from the barrage of quick blows. "You never know, one of them could get attacked by bandits."

"They'd definitely attack you," Nikos said with a grin. "You're very proactive. Alright!"

He put his sword down, and when I stopped, he quickly thrust at my stomach, but was unsuccessful. My sword blocked his attack.

"I won't tell you about knife fighting, but using a bow... There's a guy who can teach you that. Hm..."

Nikos froze, and I prepared myself for another trap. But this time, he was actually thinking. Probably... Good idea to back away further anyway.

"Were you, by any chance, planning to leave the guild tonight?"

"I thought about it."

"Good! In that case, a favor for a favor: deliver

a message and bring back the reply. Then I'll put in a good word for you with a highly skilled archer. I'd go myself, but everyone knows me there, and it's not safe today. I'll give you a good potion to give you a better chance of getting there. You can use it immediately or keep it for later.

Unknown Player! A new quest is available: Deliver a message to Finlay.

Time limit to complete: 12 hours.

Address: ...

Reward: 1 Copper Coin and the gratitude of the quest giver.

Accept/Decline

>>Accept

"Just be careful. Show this to the recipient." Nikos handed me an unremarkable silver ring with a small emerald. "Don't talk to anyone else there. Understood?"

"Yes."

"Well then, if you have no further questions," Nikos said, raising his sword, "I suggest we practice for another 20 minutes. My treat."

Without waiting for confirmation, he rushed towards me. During that very short 20 minutes, the medics were called for me four times. Or rather, after the first time, they just stayed near the training grounds.

After the sparring, Nikos gave me an unexpected gift: he asked one of the mages to relieve my fatigue. The mage grumbled about the waste of mana, but he fulfilled Nikos's request.

Book Two

I was surprised that Nikos was sending me into the city at night, but not entirely. He apparently needed this message delivered, and he treated death (no matter whose) with disdain. He was probably an adherent to the theory that progress is made fastest during moments of fatal danger.

After our meeting, I stopped at the canteen before heading to the main library.

There were still a few hours before nightfall, and what better time was there to finally find out what the "system bible" was?

I was worried there'd be a line, but there wasn't. Everything related to the system automated and operated smoothly. I was pointed to the right door, which led to a circular room about 100 feet across.

A 10-foot tall statue of a slim, beautiful young woman whose race I couldn't determine towered over the center of the room. Probably an elf. There were armchairs along the walls, with a red ball on a pedestal next to each one. I sat in one of the empty chairs and placed my hand on the ball.

Welcome to the system bible.

Your access level: low.

That didn't surprise me. I already knew that you had to be at least level 15 just to have average-level access. Level 30 would get you high-level access, but you could only get full access at level 40.

What would you like to learn about?

Abilities.

Development branches.

Skills.

Magic.

Quests.

Cursed areas.

Monsters and their properties.

Crafting basics.

World history. *Data is updated once every five years. The next update will be in one year, two months, and 19 days.

Well shit, I wanted to learn about everything!

Champing at the bit, I started at the top and began greedily reading everything I could. I was quickly disappointed.

At my access level, the information was extremely limited and was mostly things I already knew. Of course, there were long lists of available abilities and descriptions of the most effective ways to level up. Branches of combat and magic skills. The information about crafting was also interesting, but not useful to me yet. There were also meticulously detailed descriptions of monsters, their mutations, and their specs, but there were tens of thousands of them.

Hm. The only path to knowledge appeared to be the most logical. I had to come here and either learn something specific or something for general development when I had nothing better to do. Like right now.

I ended up sitting in the library almost until closing. And if the staff hadn't said anything, I wouldn't have made it to the canteen in time.

"What, you got ants in your pants?" one of the

guards at the gate said, raising his eyebrows. "Where are you moseying off to at night? We've already gotten reports of five dead guild members and 14 injured."

I'd heard about that at the canteen, as well as about how all those champions had been wearing guild identification and were fourth rank or higher. I looked like just a regular guy. Besides, Nikos had made good on his word and given me an intriguing potion.

Stealth Potion: Increases the stealth ability level by 2. Duration: 30 minutes.

Despite the danger, I would have gone out without the potion and even without Nikos's quest. My morning meeting with Visilius's daughter had terrified me. I was finally able to recognize the distinction between how I perceived myself and what I actually was. I was miles ahead of the average person in this world, but still leagues behind the strongest. And if I were to sit in a cozy little room, even if I did push-ups all day every day, leveling up would take decades. And that was just for one discipline branch. I knew that wasn't the path for me.

Sure, I might have run-ins with thieves. But I'd learned a lot since the last incident. Most importantly, I'd become more confident, and now I could anticipate an attack.

"I'll be careful."

"Have it your way," the guard said, losing interest in me and turning away.

I went through the gate and immediately

turned into one of the dark side streets, where I crouched and prepared for a fight. A few minutes passed. My eyes became accustomed to the darkness, and no one attacked. The coast looked clear. Technically, the most dangerous part was the moment you left the guild, since someone could be watching the gate. I decided to move on and practice stealth.

But if I just sauntered along the dark, empty streets, it would take forever to level up that ability. So, I made things harder for myself.

The address Nikos had sent me to was about 4 miles away from the guild. I could get there through the city center without any real risk, but I took a roundabout way and snuck closely past every group of people I noticed (well, aside from anyone who was obviously looking for trouble).

I'd step closer and closer... And then, when I saw them start to sense my presence, I'd start to carefully go around them without backing off.

More often than not, they noticed me (I hadn't taken the potion yet, after all), and I'd have to cut and run quickly. Naturally, I pulled all these tricks as a hobbit. But it wasn't just stealth I decided to work on that night.

"I hope you're not planning to earn a living like that!" Visilius had said three weeks earlier when I told him I'd finally gotten the first level of the Thievery ability.

"No! I'd rather loot corpses," I'd answered, but the smile I'd expected to spread across his face hadn't come.

Book Two

Grinding that ability in our village had been difficult and fraught with scandal, so we'd practicing in neighboring villages. It had taken almost two weeks just to get to level 1, which wasn't surprising. The first problem had been the lack of targets. Everyone was asleep at night. The second problem was my low stealth level, which made sneaking up on someone unnoticed a challenge. As a result, I'd had to steal a log from a woodpile or a bucket from a well, and none of that crap worked if the owner of the thing wasn't anywhere nearby.

So once I somehow got level 1 in Thievery, we decided not to bother continuing. But I remembered the ability now, and naturally, I decided that grinding two abilities was better than one. I'd return everything I managed to pinch, of course.

My first victim was a drunkard sleeping on a side street.

I crept towards him... Took my time preparing... Then carefully grabbed the bag from under his shoulder. It was empty. Next, I stole his cap and his boots one at a time. Then I gave up and redressed the guy. I likely wouldn't get any real benefit from that.

Instead, I plucked down a vase from a first-floor windowsill and put it on the neighboring window of the same building. Maybe that would help them remember to keep their shutters closed during times like this.

Later, I came across another downcast, very drunk man shuffling along the street. I approached him, pretended to help him along, and started emptying his knapsack.

I'd relieved him of almost the entire contents before he finally caught on. I shoved it all back into his arms and ran.

I hoped the gold I'd added as a little bonus would be enough compensation for the trouble.

It was the fourth incident that spiked my adrenaline the most.

"Your share's six gold," a quiet, but ferocious voice rasped in the darkness.

"And yours?"

"Mine's the rest!"

"But there was 16 gold there!"

"And? Half of 16 is six each!"

"Not seven?"

"Are you stupid?! "Add seven and seven. That's 14!"

"Yeah... Exactly..."

Well, there you go! Go find some other sucker to swindle!"

In one of the nearby dead ends, a robber with better arithmetic skills was deceiving his accomplice, who wasn't as well-versed in exact sciences. While they argued, I crept up behind the bolder one and carefully slipped a hand into his bag.

You've received a set of lockpicks.

I went back in.

You've received a length of rope.

And again.

You've received a level 2 Cleaver.

"Who's there?!"

The robber turned sharply around and was

immediately granted a blow first to the solar plexus, and then to the jaw.

"Where?" the second man shouted before falling to the ground, sputtering (because I'd kicked him in the stomach).

A few more blows left them both unconscious and picked clean. I even took their clothes. Not because I needed them, but just so they didn't get any ideas about coming after me later that night.

The longer I spent in the city at night, the more confident I became, and the more I enjoyed myself. At some point, searching for another hit of adrenaline, I thought I might try stealing from a guard, but I caught myself just in time. Grinding was important, but my health was moreso.

I hadn't heard the bell ring, but I knew I'd gotten some solid experience in stealth and thievery.

* * *

The large house I was headed for was located in a... less than prestigious neighborhood, to put it mildly. I even had to double-check the address, but it was correct.

A few minutes of observation left me no doubt: Nikos had sent me to some kind of seedy hideout. The windows were covered, but through the door that was opening and closing constantly, I could hear loud, not entirely sober voices, laughter, and some kind of odd, sharp sound. But I couldn't see any kind of sign marking it as a tavern or otherwise.

It was apparently a popular spot. I'd already counted six people entering and five leaving. Judging by the ages and makeup of the guests, it was open to all races.

Well, alright then. Time to go in. The longer I stood there waiting, the less time I'd have for grinding or sleep.

I turned back into a human, changed my clothes, and strode confidently to the door. When I opened it, I stopped for a few seconds, stunned.

They said there was something for everyone in the Central City, and I'd even heard of cockfights, but this was the first time I'd seen one.

A wooden counter extended along the far wall of the first floor, lit by torches, where you could order food and drink. In the center were four separate "arenas," where the main action was happening. Surrounding the arenas, people of three races I was familiar with were jumping around, as wildly as the roosters themselves.

There was also a hole cut out of the ceiling, about 15 feet wide, and the space above appeared to be the VIP zone. There were tables up there, where the wealthier spectators could root for their favorites in more comfortable surroundings.

"It's three gold to enter," one of the men at the door said to me.

This agreement with Nikos was going to bankrupt me.

I handed over the required amount and went inside.

I plugged my ears against the shrieks from the

roosters and spectators and hurried towards the counter. It didn't get any easier from there.

"I'm looking for Mr. Finlay!" I shouted to the "bartender."

"One?!" he shouted in reply.

"One what?!"

"You got it!"

The bald and apparently deaf man quickly poured beer into a clay mug and put up two fingers.

God damn! I paid and took a few gulps, then tried again.

"Where's Mr. Finlay?!"

"Another one?!"

Was he stupid?

"No!" I shouted at the top of my lungs, leaning across the counter and shaking my head for good measure. "Finlay! Mr. Finlay!"

"Ahh! Upstairs!" He pointed up at the ceiling.

"Thanks!"

I grabbed the mug of beer that had cost me as much as two all-you-can-eat meals at the canteen and walked towards the stairs.

Upstairs was a little quieter, and I was immediately met by two more bouncer types. Dwarves, oddly enough.

"Reservation?" one of them shouted. He came up so close, I could smell garlic on his breath.

"I have a message for Mr. Finlay!"

"Who from?!"

"Just show him, he'll understand!" I held out the ring to the dwarf.

He took it and walked over to one of the tables. And to my great surprise, after a quick glance in my direction, a hobbit of about 50 (or maybe 100) stood up from the table. He didn't come over to me, but instead headed for the only door, which appeared to lead to an office.

The bouncer dwarf came back and confirmed I should go there, too.

* * *

The door closed and, as I'd guessed, the office was much quieter. The owner hadn't skimped on the soundproofing.

"What do you have?" the hobbit asked in a business-like tone, having already sat behind the wooden desk.

"A letter from Nikos."

I took three steps forward and handed him the sealed envelope.

Finlay's stark face revealed nothing as he read the letter.

Stage 1: Deliver the letter to the recipient. Complete.

Stage 2: Wait.

Finlay took out a piece of paper.

"Sit over there," he said. He indicated a chair, but not the one across from him at the desk. The chair he was pointing to was in a corner of the room, near the door. "You'll have to climb back out through the window."

The hobbit jerked his large thumb over his

shoulder, dipped his pen in the inkwell, and started writing a reply.

I didn't ask why I'd have to use the window. It was obvious: Finlay didn't want anyone to follow me and steal the letter. Maybe I could hint somehow that he should give me a stealth potion. Why not? Every little bit helped.

The hobbit wrote for a long time. I'd already examined every nook and cranny of the office, and was now tinkering around in my inventory.

That might be what saved my life.

Chapter 8

ANOTHER ROUND OF SHOUTS came from behind the office door, then suddenly stopped. Finlay and I both looked at the seemingly strong, sturdy door, which instantly splintered into tiny pieces that scattered throughout the room.

I'd just been looking at the stealth potion in my inventory, and I gulped it down. I also turned into a hobbit on instinct, following some subconscious urge to make myself smaller.

Shocked, Finlay jumped to his feet and leapt spryly back. A second later, a fireball the size of a basketball shot through the doorway and engulfed the armchair where Finlay had just been sitting in flames.

It took a lot of effort me to keep sitting in my chair. I was slightly comforted by the bow in my left hand and the powerful, magic-strengthened arrow in my right.

The hobbit activated a skill and disappeared into the smoke that was rapidly filling the room. Well, he disappeared from my view. Whoever was attacking us saw him perfectly, and a flaming whip split the air and caught its target.

Finlay let out a howl and crashed to the floor 6 feet away from me. His left shoulder, arm, and part of his side were gone. The room smelled like burning meat.

"Clear!" the attacker shouted. "Finishing him off!" He dashed into the office and pointed a stave at the wounded hobbit.

But then he glanced towards the corner of the room, where I was sitting. The bowstring snapped, and the arrow sunk into the left side of his chest.

You've killed a level 33 Human.

Your inventory has increased by 35 pounds.

"Hurry up!" came a shout from near the stairs.

"Everything okay?!" another voice said from below.

Finlay was probably still alive, but I was under no illusion that I could beat at least two more high-level hired killers, and I sprinted for the window.

Greed would at some point be my undoing, but I couldn't ignore the black loot box that had appeared above the man I'd killed or the stave that had fallen from his hand. I also grabbed the unfinished letter to Nikos as I rushed past the desk.

Stage 2: Wait. Completed.

Stage 3: Deliver the message to the quest giver.

I turned around and chucked an incendiary grenade through the doorway, then threw open the window and leapt through.

My feet hit the pavement hard, but thanks to my hobbit body, I was able to roll and get up unharmed. Now it was time to run.

Luckily, the windows in the office were on the opposite side of the building from the entrance, which, coupled with the grenade explosion, gave me some hope for escape.

As I ran, I took out two level 2 bear traps and threw them in the darkest spots I was running past. This trick wouldn't have worked on Earth, but here, the traps activated automatically on contact with a surface.

They probably wouldn't help, but if any pursuers saw my magical trail and were running too fast to pay close attention, then maybe...

"Aaah!" A cry of pain rang out behind me.

That really worked? The system loved me! That would force my pursuers to tread more carefully.

I ran along narrow side streets, trying to head in the direction of the city center when I could. I'd turned back into a human to run. I was used to it, for one, and I'd planned to anyway.

As I turned again, I heard a ringing sound over my ear, and something sparked in the darkness.

Shit! I hadn't even heard the bastard! Or bastards?!

I ran up to another street and immediately veered into it. Another shot whistled past, and I felt a burning on my neck.

The fucker had good aim. I couldn't get away!

I stopped short, turned into a hobbit, and pressed myself against the wall. My pursuer appeared just two seconds later.

"He went through that door!" I shouted, pointing at the nearest house.

The man, who was average height and wearing a black mask, glanced over at me, then at the empty street, and rushed to the door. My bow appeared in my hands. Take this!

The man sensed danger and leapt aside, but the arrow still pierced his back. Not where his heart was, unfortunately.

I shot again and hit him in the stomach, but despite his deep wounds, the bastard returned fire and hit me in the left shoulder. I fell and tried to ignore the blinding pain as I crawled as quickly as possible under the porch for shelter and immediately threw a freezing grenade. My last one. It exploded, and a wave of cold enveloped me, but no "game over" message showed up.

I risked a quick look out from my shelter and quickly hid again. The man was lying in the middle of a frozen circle and looked very much like he was dead... Except that he could easily just be pretending, using a skill or some high-level artifact. It didn't really matter. I had to finish him. I couldn't shoot a bow with an arrow in my shoulder, anyway.

"Vince!"

Shit!

Another masked man darted out from around

the corner. Based on the fact that he was limping badly, he was the one who'd been caught in my bear trap.

I suppressed the urge to throw a knife at him through sheer force of will. Even if it landed, it wouldn't get through his armor. Unlike my arrows, my knives weren't enchanted. The man also didn't seem to have noticed me. Finally, the stealth boost was working! Just as important, I was sitting under the porch, and the light of one of the moons over the street didn't reach me.

But I didn't have anything to kill the men with, and drawing a sword against two killers over level 30 didn't seem like a very good idea...

Oddly enough, I wasn't scared. The only thing I felt aside the pain in my shoulder was an immense urge to waste the fuckers. What if I tried using magic? I couldn't close my eyes this time, though. *Okay,* I told myself. *Feel the warmth in your chest...*

"Vince!"

The second man limped over to his associate, looked around, and squatted down. His back was to me, and I couldn't see what he was doing, but a few seconds later, I saw a white glow. Shortly after, the tenacious scumbag Vince lifted his head and whispered something to the limping man, pointing in my direction.

The crippled man leapt to his feet, and I threw out my hand. My palm exploded with heat, blinding me. I felt like I'd been hit in the stomach with a timber beam and a wave of nausea came over me.

You've killed a level 33 Human.
Your inventory has increased by 35 pounds.
Congratulations! You've reached level 10.
Your regen speed has increased.
You've received one skill point.
You've killed a level 32 Human.
Your inventory has increased by 35 pounds.

The color of the system message adjusted to the flashing glare before my eyes, and I was able to read it.

Blinded and disoriented, I couldn't immediately figure out how to turn around and crawl back to the wall of the house. I found something to hold onto, composed myself a little, and remembered that healing potion helped with blindness. I could see the contents of my inventory even through blindness, so I found what I was looking for easily and drank it right away.

It helped quickly enough, but not completely. I was mostly only able to see darker outlines silhouetted against lighter ones. The potion also lessened the pain from the arrow that was still protruding from my shoulder. I crawled on all fours towards the two men I'd killed.

I could tell I was getting closer from the heat of the cobblestones, and then my hand bumped into something hot and rubbery. Judging by the smell, it was the remains of the limping man.

I put the black box and his sword in my inventory and crawled over to the second body. It was only once I was almost directly next to him that I realized the bright spot in my vision wasn't the residual effect from the spell, but a familiar glowing yellow scroll.

I froze for a moment, stunned, then grabbed the black box and the unexpected loot.

You are now the owner of a(n) [item] that belongs to [unknown group]. There are many people who want it. You have been given the status of Implementer.

Leave the item where it is (no reward) or give it to any interested party.

Reward: A random level 3 elixir.

There are powerful protective runes on the item. When they are triggered, your coordinates will become known to all members of [unknown group].

The protective runes will activate in 0 hours, 29 minutes, and 51 seconds.

Geez! Even shorter than last time. At least I could get rid of this thing at any time... Actually... Maybe I should hide it?

I experimented by throwing the "item" out of my inventory, counting to five, and picking it back up. Damn it. The timer hadn't stopped, so I wouldn't be able to hide it.

Okay then... The important thing was that I could get rid of it, so there were options. Wait, what was I thinking?! Why the hell would I get rid of it? This thing was clearly valuable and should probably be turned over to the authorities. But not to any ordinary guard. I was certain the group would go after them, same as they would me. And

I had no idea where their headquarters was. I needed to go to the Champions' Guild. It was only about 4 miles away. As the crow flies, anyway...

I considered all this as I hurried along the street in the direction of the tower that was sticking out against the dark background of the sky. I was so dizzy and nauseated, and my vision still hadn't completely returned to normal. So it took me a while to realize that something bad was happening in the city.

There were screams all around me, near and far, and I suddenly noticed the glow of fire in several places. We the orcs attacking? That didn't make sense. They were far away. To get here, they'd need to get over the wall, then capture a ton of fortresses and fortified cities. A rebellion? But who was fighting whom? Or maybe the conflict between the champions and rogues had reached a new level. Was the attack on Finlay part of that, too? Somehow, I doubted that.

Well, my task was just to carry this "item." Outside of my inventory, it looked like a glowing scroll with a malachite jewelry box on it.

The protective runes will activate in 0 hours, 14 minutes, and 31 seconds.

I tried to open it out of curiosity, but the system told me I wasn't enough of an "interested party."

The arrow sticking out of my shoulder was making things difficult. Knowing I'd have to run soon, possibly at top speed, I steeled myself, gritted my teeth, and broke the arrow shaft almost down to my shoulder. I didn't have time for anything more complicated, or to treat my injuries.

The protective runes will activate in 0 hours, 05 minutes, and 12 seconds.

My nausea had subsided, but I felt weak. There was no way I'd make it to the guild walking. I took a few deep breaths, gathered my strength, and switched to a light jog. That seemed bearable, but I didn't want to risk going any faster just yet.

Oddly, I hadn't seen a single guard so far. They must have been defending the buildings or people in wealthier neighborhoods. I also hadn't seen any groups of thieves. The only explanation I could come up with was that they just hadn't come out to join in the fun yet.

ATTENTION: The protective runes have been activated. The members of [unknown group] are now aware of your location.

I still had at least a mile to go. Everything depended on where the members of the "unknown group" were right now.

In an attempt to conceal my destination, I decided not to go directly to the gates, but instead went a little to the side and planned to make a sharp turn later.

Three-quarters of a mile left... Half a mile...

My shoulder was throbbing even harder, and my stomach had started to churn again.

A third...

"There he is!"

The shout came from 30 yards behind me, and I quickly turned onto another street and sped up.

A quarter mile to go.

Every time I heard shouts or footsteps behind me, I changed direction. Arrows hit a house next to me a few times, and one even grazed my ear.

500 feet...

I activated a speed boost, and it finally dawned on me to equip a shield in my right hand and at least cover my head, neck, and the top of my spine.

I took a final turn and came out into the square in front of the guild's gates.

"Help!" I shouted to the guards, two arrows promptly striking my shield from behind. "I have an important message for command!"

I improvised that last part. A dozen champions were already running towards me, and more were hurrying through the gate. I was almost in the clear! The important thing now was to not get tripped up right at the end.

"Get down!" someone shouted, and I hit the pavement without a second thought.

A fireball flew past overhead, and the scent of burnt hair filled my nose. Arrows whistled by, mostly fired by the guards. I got to my feet, but stayed low so I could cover as much of myself as possible with the shield, and kept running.

The first three guards had already rushed past me and were making a beeline for my pursuers. Suddenly, something hit my shield. My arm burned, this time from intense cold, and I hit the ground again. I got up again and saw that the guards had closed ranks and were forcing the enemy to retreat. Phew... That was close.

"Are you okay?"

A champion I didn't know came up to me and took my arm.

"I think so..." I gave him a tired smile, and I had a feeling that I would already be dead if it weren't for his help.

"Come on, hero, just a little further!"

"Yeah, coming..."

Stars were swirling in my vision again, and I took 10 steps before realizing that, for some reason, we weren't walking towards the gate, but towards the houses instead.

"Hey, where are we going?"

I looked at my escort in surprise, and my blood ran cold. His face had twisted into a sinister smile, and the light of the moon reflected off the blade of a dagger.

Chapter 9

A DEAFENING SCREAM ECHOED through the night. Shadows flickered, something flashed, and I was suddenly jerked downward.

It was only when I found myself flat on the cobblestones once again that I realized it was my failed murderer dragging me down with him. The fact that he'd failed was obvious. It was hard to kill someone with your head cut off.

"Thanks!" I whispered a second before Viza hid herself back in my inventory, and two seconds before I passed out.

* * *

I opened my eyes to find a glamorous hospital ward. On the oak nightstand next to my bed was a cold mug of beer, and half-naked elf nurses were hurrying around me...

This was how RPG creators described waking from unconsciousness. But their heroes ended up in the homes of rich aristocrats. I'd ended up in the citadel of one side in a war, so I was jolted awake as soon as I was dragged through the guild's gate.

"Why were they chasing you?!" snapped Nikos, whose round face now appeared over me instead of half-naked elves.

It was a good thing there were three medics standing nearby. Their hands were glowing in various colors, and I was feeling better with each passing second. But why was Nikos glowing with some kind of greenish light? Oh! That must be how the parties most interested in the item I'd picked up were indicated.

"Here."

I pulled it out of my inventory with relief and handed him the loot that almost cost me my life. I hadn't delivered the hobbit's letter yet. First of all, there were too many witnesses. And secondly, I had to take a quick peek at it first.

Congratulations! Quest completed!
You've received experience and a Strength Elixir.

The elixir was nice. Of course, level 3 was the lowest, and only improved physical characteristics. But the upgrades were permanent. It was essentially a level up without the skill point.

Nikos's face fell.

"Where did you get this?"

"I passed by this one place today. They have cockfights there, too," I started, distancing myself just in case. "Then some people in masks attacked me. One of them died, and he dropped this thing."

Two of the medics had already finished treating me, but a blue light was still pouring from the hands of the third.

"What's wrong with him?" Nikos said, addressing the medic. "What's taking so long?"

"I'm... not sure." The medic shrugged. "I'm pouring energy into him, but he's still not back to full strength."

"You're always just pulling magic out of your ass!" Nikos straightened up sharply. "Can you walk?"

I sat up and realized that with a little more energy, I'd even be able to fly, but I kept that to myself.

"Yes."

"Go to the canteen. Tell the cook that Nikos decided to set table number five for you. Wait for me there."

He sped off before I could ask him whether he was sure they'd let me into the canteen in the middle of the night.

As soon as the "item" changed hands, the ring of champions who'd been standing nearby lost interest in me and either went back to their posts or followed Nikos.

Well then... I couldn't rest on my laurels for long. I didn't mind, though. The night had, overall, been a definite success. I got a sweet elixir, level

10, and probably reputation at the guild, but most importantly, I'd tried out using magic in combat. And it was really something! If only I could figure out what I did and learn to replicate it whenever I wanted, and without such severe side effects.

The medics had done an amazing job, and I practically skipped to the canteen. It actually turned out to be open. Moreover, it was full of pretty experienced, high-level soldiers, and all of them were shocked to see me. They must have been the day crew relaxing off-duty.

"What are you doing up, kid?" asked a man of about 40 with a magnificent mustache.

"Nikos sent me and said I needed to sit at table number five," I replied firmly and started for the counter.

"He's screwing with you, man," the mustachioed man continued, perplexed.

"Relax, Mitch," said one of the soldiers who'd been at the gate as he came into the canteen after me. "You sleep through everything. The kid brought us valuable information about the attack tonight. He's earned it!"

"What information?" A few champions sprung to their feet.

"Nikos'll be here soon. Maybe he'll tell you," I answered as I got to the counter. "Table number five, please."

The woman who'd been giving me eggs was working tonight, so I got a treat for Viza, too.

"Where'd you get the info? What's happening?" The champions laid into me again, forgetting that

I was just first rank.

"Something dropped from a dead guy. I picked it up." I retold the story as I shoved food into my mouth so I could chew it longer. "I don't know what's going on in the city, though."

I could have let it slip that I'd killed three high-level strangers today, of course. But why would I? Aside from some uncomfortable questions, it wouldn't get me anything, and they'd most likely think I was just blowing hot air.

They left me alone after 10 minutes, and I was able to fully enjoy my food. As an aside, table five was different from the usual fare here in that it had a jug of very good red wine. And to combine business (leveling up my poison resistance) and pleasure (lowering my tension), I took full advantage of it.

*   *   *

Nikos came an hour later as I was idly picking at the remains of my hearty dinner.

He led me to the farthest table and shooed away any soldiers sitting nearby.

"What happened with Finlay?" he asked quietly.

I told him the story, then handed over the letter I'd already read several times.

Hello, my friend!

I can't give you anything useful regarding your question. This whole war between the guilds seems like a front to me. Someone screwed over a rogue, maybe even set him up. Well, you know... The kind of thing that simmers, and then BAM. A champion dies nearby... Who are they thinking of? Themselves. The champions start to simmer, and then BAM again! And a rogue dies.

Many large wars have started this way. But still, I don't think that's the goal. The Emperor won't allow war to break out when the orcs are already at our walls and have completely cut us off from all contact with Zirania... Something about this —

Then the letter cuts off.

"Did you read it?" Nikos asked, lifting his gaze from the letter to me.

"I scanned it," I shrugged.

"Good. Always read documents you receive by chance," Nikos said, surprising me. He ran a palm over his thick neck. "The item you brought me confirms Finlay's suspicions. It's a diversion."

My ears perked up. "By whom and against whom?" I asked.

Before answering, Nikos lifted his head and shouted, "Quiet, everyone!" A deathly silence instantly fell over the canteen, and he continued so everyone could hear. "We've received credible information. Someone orchestrated the conflict between us and the rogues. But the end goal isn't to start a war between our guilds. It's to eliminate specific people."

"Who?" A few champions asked impatiently.

"That isn't clear yet." Nikos grimaced. "But there is speculation that the enemy is killing veterans of the last orc war."

"The orcs have allies here?" I asked, the question coming out unexpectedly loudly in the silence hanging over the canteen.

Nikos paused. "Not just allies, but highly influential and intelligent allies," he muttered.

"Or someone else has decided to attack us," the mustachioed man, Mitch, mumbled.

"Then everything would be fucked!" Nikos stood abruptly. "There will be a meeting for all commanders in an hour. We have already sent a message to the rogues. If they have any sense, we'll be meeting with them in the afternoon."

Once everyone began discussing the news, Nikos turned to me.

"You've been a huge help to us. Come see me tomorrow. I'll update your guild rating. Also…"

Unknown Player! A new quest is available: Find Sylvan and tell him, "Hello from the round one!"

Address: …

Reward: 1 Copper Coin.

Accept/Decline

Accept, of course!

"He's an archer. Find him."

Nikos held out a hand, shook mine firmly, and hurried away.

Once he'd turned his back on me, a wide smile spread across my face. He wasn't really round, of course, but the nickname suited him perfectly.

The Last Portal Jumper

* * *

There was no reason for me to stay in the canteen, so I went back to my room. When I opened the door, I saw a folded sheet of yellow paper on the floor.

Please come see me, no matter what time you get this.

I'm worried!

Griselda

What was wrong? Sure, we hadn't seen each other today, but that was no reason... There were any number of things I could have been occupied with. Although, this whole mess was worrisome...

But as I was walking to the canteen, I'd glanced up at the clock on the tower and saw it was already past 4 AM.

To go or not to go? She had to be sleeping. Alright, I'd just knock quietly. If she was asleep, she was asleep. But if she wasn't, I'd tell her everything was okay and leave.

I walked down the hallway to her door and knocked cautiously. The door flew open almost immediately, and I was pulled inside.

A candle was burning down on the table, and judging by the amount of wax, it wasn't the first.

"Why aren't you asleep?" I asked, looking into her troubled face.

"Where were you?" she asked instead of answering, her eyes locked on mine.

"In the city. I was doing a quest." I waved a

hand and walked past her to sit on the chair. "Am I the reason you're still awake?"

"Yeah... Well, no... Not just that..."

Griselda hung her head and sat on the bed.

"What happened?" I hesitated for a moment, then went over to her and put my arm around her shoulders. "Come on, spit it out."

"Everyone's in a panic here, you disappeared, and my quest got canceled," she mumbled before falling silent again.

"Hey." I turned her towards me and smiled. "There's no panic, it's just people rushing around for work. I turned up. We can talk about your quest, but it seems like you just wanted to get me into your room."

"No!"

She winced and pulled away, but when she saw my face, she finally smiled weakly.

"Come on, then. Concisely and in order. Your quest, I mean. Is it the one you took when we went to the notice board together?"

I remembered how excited she'd been then and in the days following.

"Yeah..." Sadness came over her again. "Basically, I found an announcement on the board, and I knew the quest giver. A distant relative on my father's side. It was just to deliver something somewhere for a little money. So I went right away. I picked up four messages and delivered them to the right people. I made almost 200 gold. I was supposed to deliver a fifth one yesterday, but I was scared to go into the city. And then last night, I got a notification that the quest had been canceled by the system, with some compensation…"

Griselda's breath caught a little, but she gathered herself together and went on.

"That usually happens when there are circumstances outside your control, and it's just not possible to complete the quest anymore. Most often, it happens because the quest giver dies…"

"Well, not necessarily. You never know."

"There's still more…" A sheet of paper appeared in her hands. "Once the quest was canceled, I was able to read the message I was supposed to deliver. Here."

I had my suspicions even before I started reading it.

"Target: Conrade Price. Race: Human. Age: 46. Height: 5 feet, 11 inches…"

After that was a more detailed description of Conrade, right down to his usual routes, which taverns he often visited, and the addresses of his lovers. The message ended succinctly: "Danger level 8. Recommended elimination time: 11:00 PM."

Listen, system, I thought. *Are you sure you haven't launched some exclusive quest for me? How is it that almost everything that happens drags me deeper and deeper into the local conspiracies?!* It's not that I was against it, exactly. I just preferred to play a more open game.

"We have to go to Nikos. This looks like it's related to what happened tonight."

"My relative wasn't a rogue or a champion!"

"It's more complicated than that."

She looked at me, her eyes wide.

"Do you want me to do it? I won't mention you."

"No," she sighed. "I'll do it. We have class with Nikos this morning."

"Maybe not..." I stood up and held out a hand to her. "The sooner we report this, the fewer unpleasant questions there'll be."

*   *   *

Griselda was questioned for about half an hour. They wanted to dismiss me, but I argued that I was a witness and active participant, and in the end, they allowed me to stay with Nikos's approval.

As expected, Conrade Price turned out to be a veteran of the last orc war. Once they'd seen the letter, patrol units were sent to guard Price, as well as Griselda's distant relative, with whom the champions were in especially close contact today.

"Thank you!" Nikos nodded at me and turned to the blanched Griselda. "Your relative was presumably being used and kept in the dark, like you were. And even if he wasn't, that doesn't mean anything about you."

"Did they kill him?" she asked quietly.

"As a rule, people like that are killed to break the chain," Nikos said with a shrug.

"A lot of people have been killed tonight," murmured one of the champions who was part of the interrogation.

On that unpleasant note, we were dismissed.

* * *

"Thanks," Griselda mumbled quietly as we got to her door. "Are you coming in?"

"Not today. I need to recharge before tomorrow. Things could easily get off track."

More importantly, she was the one who needed to rest and gather her strength. I had plenty after the magical treatment I was given.

"Good night, then."

She kissed me on the cheek and went into her room.

* * *

Sunlight was already filtering in through the window, so there was no point in lighting a candle, and I fell into bed without changing. I fed Viza first, of course.

So, what were the facts?

Either accidentally or at the system's behest, I'd undoubtedly touched upon some key events for Shrinanth at least, or the entire continent at most. It was unclear what role Clifford's murder played in all this, or whether my actions had any impact. But the fact remained: things were about to get interesting.

Even the inevitable war with the orcs that was coming was a global upheaval in itself. Until tonight, everyone was certain they'd be stopped at some point, but now...

What about the mysterious, powerful forces weakening the Empire from within? I doubted they'd want to just help the orcs along. More likely, they were playing a more delicate, and probably large-scale, game.

We have to get out!

Viza shrieked above the bed and flopped down on my stomach.

That sounded sensible... Except for the variety of nuances. Firstly, I hadn't leveled up enough, which was much easier to do in the city than in a crowd of refugees or among the hobbits. Secondly, it was highly probable that the system had already started something for me, and if I made a rash move, it might step in and give me some kind of premature exclusive quest. Thirdly, and most importantly, I didn't want to leave!

I was having fun here. I knew that reading about wars in adventure books couldn't compare to experiencing them in reality, at the epicenter. Even so... I had a persistent feeling that everything was going the way it was supposed to, and that my time was just beginning. And that this was exactly where I needed to be.

Which meant I was doing exactly what I needed to be by grinding, studying magic, and diving deeper into this world and figuring out its architecture. As well as my later (or possibly much sooner) participation in key future events.

I'd take that plan of action. Actually...

The vial I'd gotten for the quest appeared in my

hand. It was an extremely expensive level 3 elixir, and it would give me a permanent strength boost. I pulled out the cork drank the contents in one gulp.

Congratulations! Your strength has increased.

On top of that, elixir and quest upgrades went to all my skins at once, though the levels were different for each. I decided to look at my human stats first.

This was my 11th body upgrade, not counting the one that gave me the ability to use magic. I had to go into the archive to refresh my memory on the previous ones.

Congratulations! You've reached level 2.
Your strength has increased.
Congratulations...
Your stamina has increased.
...
Your strength and stamina have increased.
Your internal organs have become more efficient.
Your ligaments have become more elastic.
Your vision has improved.
Your strength and stamina have increased.
Your bones have become stronger.
Your regen speed has increased.

Those were all for leveling up. After killing the scarab, my vision had increased again, and I could tell. Now that I'd drank the elixir, my strength had increased again, too.

Nothing had really changed for my abilities.

Shooting, stealth, quiet steps, and maybe a few others were already at level 3. The ones at level 2 included using weapons that could stab and slash, shield mastery, using two-handed weapons, horseback riding, poison resistance, knife throwing, knife fighting, hand-to-hand combat, swimming, tracking, climbing, the entire group of communication abilities, and a lot more. They'd been at level 2 for a while now, and would probably start leveling up soon.

My list of skills was a delight to read:

Strong Arms (level 1, passive): Strengthens blows by 5%. (Obtained at level 2.)

Tireless (level 1, passive): Increases stamina by 5%. (Obtained at level 3.)

Powerful Blow (level 1, active): Increases the strength of your strikes by 10% for a minute. (Obtained at level 4).

Strong Legs (level 1, passive): Strengthens leg muscles by 5%. (Obtained at level 5).

Good Sleep (level 1, passive): 10% less time required to be fully rested. (Obtained at level 6.)

Strong Arms (level 2, passive): Strengthens blows by 10%. (Obtained at level 7.)

Tireless (level 2, passive): Increases stamina by 10%. (Obtained at level 8.)

Jumping (level 1, passive): Improves jumping efficiency. (Obtained at level 9.)

Speed (level 1, active). (Obtained for Champions' Guild first rank.)

I had one unspent skill point from getting to level 10, and now that the stamina branch had appeared, I had a good amount of options for how to use it.

So far, there were only two skills available, but each of them unlocked a new path.

Strong Composition (passive): Increases the thickness of your skin and strengthens internal organs by 10%.

Magic Defense (passive): Increases your defense against all types of magic by 10%.

Fuck! Why did skill points have to be so hard to get?! I needed all of these! Strong Composition looked awesome and unlocked a branch with a few active defense abilities, but... Magic Defense was even better! The skill itself could be leveled up to 5, to a maximum 50% increase in defense against any kind of magic, including control. It also unlocked even more interesting skills.

Gah! Okay, then... Let's do this!

Magic Defense (level 1, passive): Increases your defense against all types of magic by 10%.

Unlocked:

Elemental Magic Defense (passive): Increases your defense against elemental magic by 15%.

Mental Magic Defense (passive): Increases your defense against mental magic by 15%.

I had to think what to do next. Increase my overall defense, but to a lesser degree, or a specific one by a larger degree? And I had to grind my old skills on top of that. Some combinations would give cool attack skills at level 15, like Battering Ram. Though for that one, the Shield Mastery ability had to be at least level 3.

Although... Better to unlock the tracking branch first. That branch had skills for detecting and investigating all sorts of things that were hidden from the eyes of others... I needed to think hard about this. And about where I could get a fuckton of skill points.

Hm. RPGs were so simple... And it was three times easier for me, since skills were distributed across my appearances.

Well, since I'd already started, I should at least check out the hobbit a little.

Congratulations! Your strength has increased.

That would be the effect of the elixir I'd just drank. Oh! I'd have to try throwing magic as a halfling when I had some free time. Although, it seemed like humans had a greater predisposition for it. But elves were even better than humans! Where were they all hiding?! Where was my goddamned pointy-eared skin?!

Congratulations! You've reached level 2.
Your dexterity has increased.
Congratulations...
Your strength has increased.
...
Your dexterity and strength have increased.
Your luck has increased.
Your ligaments have become more elastic.
Your vision has improved.
Your dexterity and strength have in-

creased.

Your bones have become stronger.

Your regen speed has increased.

Some upgrades were general, and others were more specific. I wondered which ones were for the elf? Shit... That was becoming an obsessive thought.

Alright, well, the hobbit had the same abilities as all the rest. Time to look at skills.

Deft Arms (level 1, passive): Improves knife throwing, lockpicking, and archery accuracy by 5%. (Obtained at level 2.)

Cat Burglar (level 1, passive): Increases your ability to climb vertical surfaces by 5%. (Obtained at level 3.)

Eagle Eye (level 1, active): Increases accuracy on the next knife throw by 50%, critical hit probability 20%. (Obtained at level 4).

Acrobatics (level 1, passive): Gives you 5% greater awareness and control of your body. (Obtained at level 5).

Quick Reflexes (level 1, passive): Reaction time +5%. (Obtained at level 6.)

Deft Legs (level 1, passive): Improves all actions done with your legs by +5%. (Obtained at level 7.)

Deft Arms (level 2, passive): Improves knife throwing, lockpicking, and archery accuracy by 5%. (Obtained at level 8.)

Perfect Balance (level 1, passive): Allows you to keep your balance on both horizontal and vertical surfaces. Indirectly helps with

shooting and dagger throwing. (Obtained at level 9.)

And two free skill points. One I hadn't used yet from getting to level 10, and one for the Champions' Guild rank.

This was the bug Visilius had told me about that would help me.

The skill point went into the general pool, and I could even spend it at the rival guild of rogues.

What else did I have here?

In addition to the existing skill, the same Speed one as the human, I also had:

Soft Landing (passive): Improves landing ability by 10% (including improving ligament flexibility when jumping from a height).

And another intriguing one with a few nuances:

Rain of Arrows (active): One arrow can produce several at once. The efficiency of this skill is influenced by Deft Arms and Perfect Balance, as well as the skill's current level.

Dagger Fan (active): ... This was the same as Rain of Arrows, except with daggers.

All of these were available at level 10 in theory, but not in practice, since there were prerequisites. As I'd read in the System Bible, both required Perfect Balance level 3 and Deft Arms level 2. Such is life... The path to world domination was difficult and rocky.

Additionally, effectively and confidently using these sweet combat skills required them to be at least level 3, but was best at level 5. And those skills would unlock shapeshifting, camouflage, and disguise/incognito. Plus the tracking branch... I'd definitely have to go along that one with one of my skins. It was frustratingly slow, but I had to start somewhere.

Perfect Balance (level 3, passive).

There. Now Rain of Arrows and Dagger Fan were available, except I didn't have the skill points for them.

Well, there was still one pleasant task to do: check out the loot I'd lifted from the three hired killers.

Fire Staff, level 9. Fire spell efficiency: +20%.

Hm... A pretty common item. I already had one, though it was level 7.

Mercenary Sword, level 10. When equipped: Champion skill efficiency +10%; reaction speed +10%; critical hit chance +10%.

Now, that was something! And now I had two of them, meaning I could, in theory, combine them to make a level 11 sword. But that would require a lot of large upgrade stones, which would cost a fortune.

I turned my attention to the black boxes. They hadn't impressed me up to this point, but maybe they'd be useful now? Oh, and I needed to open them as a hobbit. Let's do it!

Mercenary Shield, level 10. When equipped: Champion skill efficiency +20%; magic defense +10%.

Mercenary Boots, level 10. Stamina: +30%.

Powerful fragmentation grenade.

Holy shit! It was all terrific, but not enough! 20 more of these boxes and I could collect a full mercenary set.

There wasn't much to say... I'd had quite a successful outing today!

And the best of all was that clothing barely looked any different from level to level. No one would be able to tell that every piece of clothing I had on cost hundreds of thousands of gold. Maybe even millions!

I exited out of the menu and noticed that Viza had fallen asleep on my stomach. For the first time ever. I couldn't wake her up... Well, I still had at least an hour until classes started. I'd let her sleep. Maybe I'd take a little nap, too. Just as long as I didn't oversleep.

Chapter 10

NIKOS WAS ABSENT from the morning training session, instead replaced by a younger champion. The difference was noticeable. The substitute tried to meet Nikos's standards, but after the work we were used to from the "round one," his lesson wasn't very impressive. And to be frank, he had zero charisma.

Once the clock struck 8:50, we flocked to the canteen.

"I heard there was an attack and battle right in front of the gates last night!" Russel started before we'd even sat down.

"They also say the Earth is round," I replied with a grin as I dug into my breakfast. "And anyway, if that were true, we won."

"Did you see the announcement?" Russel continued, somehow managing to stuff his entire mouth and still speak pretty clearly.

As for the announcement, it was hard to miss it. Or rather, *them,* since they were hanging every- where. Even on the clocktower.

First-rank students: General assembly by the statue at 19:00.

Second-rank students: General assembly by the statue at 20:00.

Third- and fourth-rank students: General as- sembly by the statue at 21:00.

"What do you think that's about?" Russel's nervous gestures almost knocked over his mug of kombucha. "Think they'll cancel classes?"

"Come on, are you stupid?" Brun twirled his finger next to his temple for visual effect. "They're more likely to recruit more ahead of a war."

"Yeah, we need to take care of the rogues. I was looking out my window last night and saw at least 10 big fires in the city, and a bunch of smaller ones."

"You'd be better off sleeping," I added, "or training. They might suddenly decide to start re- cruiting normal people instead of fatties…"

"I have big bones!" Russel pouted and looked at the numerous plates in front of him. "And any- way, I'm probably close to leveling up, so I need a lot of food."

"You've already eaten enough for the next five," Brun guffawed.

"Screw you…"

The Last Portal Jumper

* * *

There wasn't much time after breakfast, so I stopped by the administration building on my lunch break.

The woman working there was the one I'd met when I'd arrived at the guild, who'd told me to punch the wall and lift all my limbs. "What is it?" she barked. She was sitting behind a desk covered in papers and was clearly not in the mood.

"Nikos told me to come in to recalculate my guild rating."

"Ilya?" She looked up at me like she was remembering. "Ah, yes! You also made a very original joke at our last meeting, and unlike many others, you didn't break government property."

"Wait, people actually punch the wall?"

"Happens all the time. It's a good thing there's a medic sitting behind that wall. As soon as he hears the hit, he comes running." She smiled and rummaged around on the table before pulling something out. "Give me your arm."

I extended my arm, and she latched a beige bracelet around my wrist. It was made of a light material that looked a bit like plastic.

"Put your palm on the ball," she said, nodding towards it.

For your accomplishments, you've received a class 5 reputation at the Champions' Guild.
Way to go!

The bracelet flashed and turned green.

"Incredible! Class 5 in such a short amount of time... I don't remember ever seeing that before." She smiled warmly. "If you go into the city in the near future, you should take off the bracelet, just in case."

"What does it do, exactly? How is it different from rank?"

"Your rank is an indicator of your strength level. It can be off the charts, but it doesn't say anything about your commitment to the guild. Your reputation is specifically about the benefits you bring to the guild. It's about your status and reliability. That bracelet opens many doors and gives you the opportunity to get special quests. But keep in mind that, unlike your rank, your reputation level can also decrease if you turn against your own."

"Thanks!"

"No problem."

She stood up and shook my hand. Hm... For some reason, she took off her heavy armor and turned out to be wearing a tight blue blouse. And there was quite a lot to stretch over. Wasn't it uncomfortable sitting there in that shell? Although, what was I saying? It was magic.

"By the way, I'm Abigail. If you need anything, let me know"

"Definitely."

I put on my most charming smile and left the office.

The Last Portal Jumper

* * *

The day passed slowly, especially with all the rumors flying around. Once I heard about how the guild was attacked the previous night (but with the adjustment that the enemies had actually been defeated inside the gates, by the administration building), I stopped listening.

7:00 PM finally came.

The first-rank students gathered in front of the statue of the warrior, and a few minutes later, four champions joined us.

"That's Valya the Ferocious!" Russel breathed. "The head of the guild!"

He was right. The husky, silver-haired man, who looked about 60, introduced himself.

"I'm Valya the Ferocious."

A deathly silence fell over us, broken only by the sound of swords on the training grounds.

"Listen carefully. I will not repeat myself. Firstly, we are not at war with the Rogues' Guild. We were pit against each other through acts of deception. We met with their leaders today and have smoothed everything over. The good news ends there."

Whispers began to swirl, but quickly faded as the head of the guild went on.

"Yesterday, a series of diversions occurred intended to weaken the combat potential of the Empire. There were also some incidents in the capital and elsewhere, but most of them took place here, in the Central City. Several military production facilities were destroyed, and a number of high-level soldiers and well-known military commanders were killed. All of this leads us to believe that the Empire will soon be under attack. As a result..." Valya the Ferocious raised his voice and surveyed the ranks of young champions before him. "Training schedules will be changing at the guild. The best of you will train according to an accelerated and, of course, more difficult program. The second-rank course previously lasted a month. Now, it will be condensed into two weeks. There will be less theory and more practice, and there will be only one day to enter the dungeon. The list of those who have been selected this special program will be read now. This list is not final. If you believe you are strong enough, you may submit an application and take the compliance test. If, on the other hand, you don't think you can handle it or simply don't want to, you may decline. This is all about self-assessment first and foremost. You must choose between drinking and fooling around and intensive study. Questions?"

Naturally, no one dared to ask anything.

"Good!"

Valya the Ferocious nodded to his assistant and marched off.

Another champion took his place. His eyes glazed over, and he started reading the list in the system.

"Ilya! Instructor Nikos."

Well, I knew I'd be put in the special group, but

The Last Portal Jumper

I still hadn't expected to hear my name first.

* * *

The evening we learned about the schedule change would become a turning point for my life in the Central City. Or, to be more precise, I would have to practically forget all about the city for some time.

The schedule for the special group had been created by a madman. I wouldn't have been surprised if Nikos himself had drawn it up. There were 30 of us in the group on average. Why "on average"? Because every day, three or four people dropped out. But they were replaced by others who wanted to test their strength.

The schedule was laid out like this:
07:00–09:00: Warm-up
09:00–10:00: Breakfast and rest
10:00–10:50: Theory
11:00–15:00: Combat training
15:00–17:00: Lunch and rest
17:00–21:00: Combat training
21:00–22:00: Dinner
22:00–23:00: Theory

Of course, the "warm-up" wasn't anything close to a warm-up. It was two hours of rigorous training to the point of exhaustion. We did get a regen buff from the mages afterwards, but you really only started feeling the effects by the time combat training started.

The combat training went in intervals. While

we were still fresh, we practiced archery and fighting with various kinds of weapons. Towards the end of that, it switched again to combat scenarios like putting on armor that weighed 100 pounds to huff and puff through the obstacle course, and running like that until lunch or until you dropped dead. Then we'd get another regen buff.

We'd arrive at lunch at the canteen (where, by the way, food was temporarily free) hungry as a herd of elephants, devour our dishes in silence, then disperse to our rooms to spend at least a little while in bed, ideally sleeping.

The second four-hour block of combat training wasn't much different from the first, except perhaps in the amount of fatigue we accumulated.

None of my friends had gotten into the special group. These were the best of the best, and I liked it. The sword battles I was used to now looked completely different. We were constantly being shuffled around, and the regular fights with challenging opponents caused my combat ability to increase much more rapidly. By the third day, I'd already gotten to level 3.

And then, suddenly, Nikos appeared next to me.

"Well."

He dismissed my sparring partner, took his sword, and lunged at me. I started to fight back, and handled it well. I knew Nikos wasn't using his full strength, but I was now able to block some of the blows that had previously gotten past me.

"Let's go!"

He took me aside.

"Did you get level 3?"

"Yes."

There was no reason to play dumb when he'd figured it all out within seconds.

"Today, you'll only be fighting me. Tomorrow, you'll practice sword fighting with the special group of third rank students. Just try not to stand out too much... And don't kill anyone by accident."

"Sir," I started, deciding to take advantage of the opportunity that had presented itself, "I need to go into the city at night once a week."

"Okay. Go, then."

"Theory classes end late, but they don't let anyone out after them, and I don't want to miss them."

"Right. I'll make arrangements..."

"And I'd like a regen buff on those days after our evening training. So I don't have to sleep that night."

"Oh, is that all?!" Nikos said, flabbergasted by my boldness. "Maybe you'd like me to go to the brothel with you and help you pick a girl, too?"

"I'm not going to a brothel, I'm going to training."

I wasn't going to tell him it was magic training, of course.

"Hm..." Nikos scrutinized me, then apparently decided I was telling the truth. "If only everyone worked as hard as you do... Okay. I'll make arrangements."

But before I went to Linda's, I'd go to the guild dungeon with my friends.

* * *

"Russel's out!" I pointed at him, made a disapproving face, and added, "Don't even take your bow with you. Since you're such a terrible shot, you can mine ore."

"The wind just took my arrow," he said, sulking and getting out of the line.

"Griselda, Brun, five steps back."

"Ready!" Brun shouted.

"Ready!" Griselda echoed.

They stood on their marks and got ready to shoot.

"Fire!" I shouted as I pulled the lever that made the target move.

My friends took five shots with nearly identical, good results.

"Five more steps back!"

Both of them turned out to be decent shots, but Griselda handled the bow a little better. So she became the archer of our group.

Confirm party composition.

>>Confirm

Do you want to enter the first level of the Champions' Guild dungeon?

>>Yes

Select the area you want to transport to. Near/middle/far.

>>Far

ATTENTION: A new exclusive group quest is available: Destroy the spider nest.

Reward: A free body upgrade for each participant.

This offer will be active for one minute.

Accept/Decline

I glanced quickly around at my friends, and could see by their surprised faces that they were also seeing the message.

"Well, maybe we — " Russel started.

>>Accept

Quest accepted.

Stage 1: Find the entrance to the spider nest.

Defense duration has ended.

"Just because I accepted it, that doesn't mean we have to do it," I reassured them immediately as I cut the head off of a fighter ant that was lunging at me.

"But why did we get it in the first place?" Griselda stuttered, turning over a beetle with Brun. "It seems like our average level should be higher for that…"

"Maybe because I did an exclusive quest last time," I said. "Or maybe we just got lucky. Don't worry about it too much."

"Lucky…" Russel dodged an attack from a worker ant and slashed at it from behind. "You're always getting 'lucky.'"

"What are you bitching about? I said we don't have to do it."

"I'm down," Brun said. "There's gotta be tons

of money in it."

"Me too," Griselda followed suit.

"I guess I don't mind," Russel backtracked.

"Then quit chatting and go look at the walls."

The quest meant we had to make some adjustments to our original plan. We'd initially planned to work on every vein of ore and metal we came across, but now, to save our strength, we decided to focus only on the most valuable.

The work went slowly. We'd go into a cave, fire a barrage of arrows at the bats hanging from the ceiling, if there were any, then deal with the rest of the enemies. Brun and I would dissect the bodies wile Russel and Griselda collected moss from the walls.

Once my friends got the rhythm down and felt more confident, I left them more enemies. Eventually, I took a page from Visilius's book and had them finish off enemies I'd wounded.

"What level are you anyway?" Russel asked, surprised at my generosity.

"Curiosity made the cat collect only moss and ore for the rest of its life..."

"Is that zulinium over there?!" Griselda sprinted wide-eyed over to a corner of the cave, then happy added, "It is!"

Zulinium was a type of metal with a bluish tint. It was used to craft some magical items, and was considered extremely rare. There wasn't even much of it in the mountains of the dwarves, and was mainly found in the first level of the Champions' Guild dungeon.

"Nice find!" Russel rubbed his hands together and pulled out his pickaxe.

"Wait!" I raised my arm. "Let's clear out the caves next to this one first, otherwise the sound could attract a ton of monsters."

They agreed, and we went into the two neighboring caves before starting to mine our loot.

"Come on!" I nodded at Russel once we'd finished clearing the caves.

He smiled and slammed his pickaxe into the vein of zulinium as hard as he could.

The sound echoed through the entire dungeon, and after a slight delay, hordes of the local inhabitants began rushing towards us. Of course, I forgot about my generosity at this point and bounced around like a grasshopper, slicing the heads off of countless ants, flipping over beetles, or shooting at bats and the occasional spider.

At first, Russel was fighting shoulder-to-shoulder with the rest of us, but once we'd killed enough of the monsters, he exchanged his sword for a pickaxe and went back to chiseling away at the stones.

"Look at you!" Brun shouted, decapitating yet another ant. "I've never seen our ginger friend so full of pep. That's what 150 gold per pound will do!"

"170 with the copper!" Russel shouted back, then lowered his pickaxe again. "And in the run up to a war, the price will only go up!"

"You should have gone to the Artisans' Guild," I said.

"I wanted to... My dad wouldn't let me."

To keep our chubby friend from getting exhausted too soon, after we finished off the monsters, we started taking turns mining the metal. While one of us worked, the rest would get the valuable loot from the hundreds of mutilated monster bodies.

In total, it took about two hours to finish everything. Once we were finished, we sat, tired but happy, for lunch.

"Say what you want," Russel mumbled through a mouthful of food, "but I can see my progress. 20 days ago, I would never have been able to swing a sword and pickaxe for that long."

"That's for sure," I nodded. "But all the same, fatigue will accumulate over time, so we need to start with the spider nest, and then we can keep mining ore."

"If we come across another vein of zulinium, we can't just leave it," Brun objected. "Especially since someone else could find it while we're working on the quest."

"True," I agreed, since I couldn't rule out that possibility.

Twice that day, we'd stumbled upon intact monster remains, which meant that someone had been there within the last few days.

As an aside, we'd managed to extract 15 pounds of zulinium, which would get each of us at least 550 gold. That wasn't a ton of money to me, but my friends were glowing with happiness.

* * *

Once we'd rested, we continued on our way, and about an hour and four more caves cleared, we finally found the right one.

Stage 1: Find the spider nest. Complete.
Stage 2: Destroy the spider nest.
Do you want to enter?
Yes/No

"Okay, listen closely." I turned to my friends and indicated the portal that was opening in the wall. "Once we go in, the entrance will close behind us until the last spider is dead or we are. It's a group quest, so we have to work together. Whatever happens, no matter how scary it is, you can't run and leave your allies behind. No wound, except a fatal one, is critical. We help each other, and we'll manage just fine."

"What're you looking at me for?" Russel said, bristling.

"Now's your last chance to change your mind."

"No way." He frowned. "My goal is to get out of here with at least enough to get us half a thousand gold!"

"If you listen to me, you'll leave with three. Are the rest of you ready?"

Brun and Griselda nodded in unison.

"Then let's quickly go over what we know about spiders, get some fire ammo ready, check the Quick Access menu, and go in."

Book Two

*   *   *

What I was most worried about was that "nest" meant there would be a spider four times as strong as the scarab I'd previously dealt with. I wasn't so much worried for myself as I was for my somewhat weaker companions. I couldn't rule it out, but everything started pretty smoothly.

We found ourselves in a large cave with one exit, out of which spiders the size of wolves immediately charged towards us. The walls were covered in the familiar glowing bluish moss, which provided enough light that we could start fighting right away without having to light torches.

This species of arachnid didn't shoot spiderweb, and we'd prepared our weapons with grease to give them additional fire damage, so we took care of the first batch of eight-legged enemies quickly.

"15 spiders in two minutes. Easy peasy!" Russel chuckled, but his smile faded when he saw the looks on the rest of our faces. "What?"

"Nothing. Light a torch, let's move on."

I indicated the dark tunnel now covered in dead spiders.

"Why me?"

"Losing you wouldn't have much effect on the tactical effectiveness of the squad."

"Very funny..."

"Who said I was joking?"

Russel shook his head, but he took out a torch

and lit it. He equipped a shield to his other hand.

"Try lighting the spiderweb on fire," Griselda suggested as we approached the dark passageway.

"Won't we choke on the smoke?" Russel asked doubtfully.

"Look at the flame," I said. "See how it's pointing ahead, into the tunnel? The smoke will blow that way."

"You're the boss," Russel said with a shrug, then prodded the spiderweb with his torch.

A small area ignited with a bright flash, then instantly went out.

"Try the one by the entrance!" Brun sighed, taking the torch. He walked up to the tunnel and lit the largest cluster of spiderweb.

"Holy shit!"

I stumbled back from the heat that nearly burnt my eyebrows off.

The fire crackled as it quickly worked its way further into the passageway, followed by the shrieks of many voices.

"Pull back!" I shouted, retreating to the middle of the cave.

The others followed my lead. Just in time. Pushing and shoving each other, dozens of charred, enraged monsters poured from the opening.

For the next five minutes, the men in our group melee attacked the attacking enemies, while Griselda stood behind us shooting fire arrows (five gold apiece!) at the occasional web-throwing monsters.

Book Two

We were pushed back almost to the wall where the portal had appeared, but finally, the stream of spiders ebbed.

"It goes faster like this!" I smiled in relief, and sliced one of the last enemies in half with a heavy blow.

I reflected briefly on the fact that not too long ago, I hadn't been able to cut off a small grunt's head with one blow, and now I could get through a tough battle with no problem. I could feel the fatigue in my arms, even though I occasionally switched my sword and shield to the opposite hands.

"We should rest!" Brun shouted as he plunged his spear into the abdomen of the last spider. "The weapon buffs will refresh anyway."

"Sounds good," I nodded. "The quest didn't take that into account. By the way, Griselda, you should be less tired, so go poke around the bodies."

"Okay!"

She equipped a spear to her left hand and started methodically jabbing at the spider bodies. Russel couldn't sit still either, so he cut open the nearest corpse.

"Nothing we could sell," he said sadly.

"Cheer up," Brun said with a grin. "That means we don't have to spend hours dissecting them. But if your profiteering little soul needs loot, go cut open the ones that were shooting web."

"Oh yeah!"

Russel ignored the snark and hurried over to

one of the ranged attackers.

"What are you so chipper for?" Brun said, picking on his friend a little more. "Did you kill them? Or were you hiding behind me?"

"He did it! He definitely killed at least three!" Griselda laughed.

"Hey!" Russel turned towards her sharply. "They'll believe that!"

"Well, okay, four then."

"Brun," I said, turning to him, "we still have to cut down the bulk of them. I suggest we focus for half an hour."

He nodded. "Agreed. Russel, let's go half an hour without the jabs."

40 minutes later, we were ready to fight again, and we went into the dark tunnel with renewed confidence.

That confidence was shaken when we saw the large den the tunnel led into.

Chapter 11

"WELL, AT LEAST IT'S NOT the big boss," Brun said in a barely audible whisper.

We did dodge that bullet. That was exactly what we were most afraid of as we made our way here. Though the mini-bosses that were currently guarding a massive clutch of eggs were next on the list of dangers.

There were four different spiders working seamlessly together as a group.

I gave my squad the signal, and we retreated into the dark tunnel.

"Does everyone remember what each of them does?"

"I forget what fat black one with the red cross on its belly does," Russel mumbled.

"It doesn't do shit," I said, grinning. "It just has the strongest armor and the sharpest fangs and claws. The gray one with the big ass shoots spiderweb from far away, then pulls it back. The smaller yellowish one is fast and can jump well. And the green one spits acid from 15 feet. They're all dangerous in melee battle."

"Should we start with the smaller one?" Brun asked.

"Yes, that one's the most dangerous. Then we'll retreat here and lead the black one into the passageway. Hopefully, it won't get stuck in here, otherwise it'll take a long time to get out. Then we'll attack the acid spitter, and finally the shooter. Don't be precious with the fire arrows! They'll pay off with interest. Everyone ready?

They all nodded, but only Brun did so confidently and with a smile. Russel and Griselda were noticeably anxious.

We walked back to the entrance to the den. The closest enemy to us was the black spider, about 40 feet away. 10 feet further was the runner spider we wanted to start with, and a lot depended on how the first volley went.

We'd decided that Russel wouldn't even try to hit the small one, but just start burning the big one right away.

I stood in front and raised my bow as an example.

"One," Brun whispered behind me, "two... three!"

Four streaks of fire flew through the cave, and a deafening shriek followed one. They'd all hit their targets, but I couldn't evaluate the effectiveness yet, since I was already loading a second arrow.

The one with the cross on its belly was the first to charge in our direction, but I was aiming for the fast runner hobbling behind it.

I released the bowstring, and the fire arrow plunged directly into the most dangerous beast.

Perfect! Now it was time to get out.

After the first shot, my friends had retreated to the tunnel, and they were now standing at the ready 30 feet from the entrance to the cave. I squeezed between them and raised my bow again.

Suddenly, the tunnel was plunged into darkness. The black spider had charged into the tunnel and was blocking almost the entire thing.

"Fire!" I shouted.

Three arrows sped forward and hit the spider in the head almost immediately, igniting its long hair. The fire didn't provide much light, but it was enough for me to see my arrow strike one of the monster's two biggest eyes.

There was hardly enough room in the tunnel for the four of us, and the spider's booming shriek lashed at my eardrums. But working together, we were able to retreat 60 feet without tripping once. The wounded spider's clawed feet rasped loudly on the stone as it scrambled after us, but the tunnel was too narrow, and it couldn't move fast.

"Ready!" I shouted and took out my bow again.

The arrows sticking out of its head were still smoldering, so we could see it getting closer.

"Hold... Hold... Fire!"

This time, we all fired at once, then retreated

quickly. The circle of the entrance to the second cave appeared, and we flew towards it.

Your group has killed a Runner Spider (mini-boss).

Oh! The first one we'd shot had succumbed to its injuries. Good! And even better, I didn't have to do the whole song and dance of leaving monsters for the others; the experience from killing bosses and mini-bosses would be split among all members of the group.

"Fan out! Russel, shoot regular arrows at its eyes. The rest of you, use your best judgement."

Luckily, the black spider hadn't died in the tunnel or turned around. Still shrieking and scraping, albeit more quietly now, it jumped out at us.

"Fire!"

Four more arrows pierced its head. It had started with at least 20 eyes of varying sizes. Now the ones we hadn't destroyed were either burning or pouring blood. The spider was wobbling badly, but continued to push forward towards Griselda.

"Bait it!" I shouted to her, then ran around the monster in a wide arc.

Okay... The best thing would be to jump onto it. It was a shame I couldn't turn into a hobbit. Deft legs would have been really helpful.

I put my shield away for the sake of convenience and charged forward. I jumped and pushed off of the protruding joint of one of the spider's feet. Yes! Our daily trainings on the obstacle course had paid off after all.

The spider felt my weight on its back and tried to shake me off, but it was too late. I swung and sunk my spear, which I'd augmented with fire damage, straight into its vulnerable spot: the area that joined its head to its abdomen. My weapon cut through like a knife through butter. The spider reared up on its back legs and threw me off... But that was the last thing it did. Almost instantly, its legs gave way and it fell to its belly.

Your group has killed a Cross Spider (mini-boss).

"Behind you!" Griselda shouted.

I leapt aside without turning around and rolled.

That precaution turned out to be unnecessary. The acid spider that had just crawled out of the tunnel hadn't gotten within spitting distance.

"Reload! Fire when ready!"

The third monster's low speed and the large area of the cave were helpful for this battle. We ran around it shooting, and after a few volleys with fire arrows, we switched to regular ones.

I was also reminded again that I couldn't, under any circumstances, skip monsterology, which had been added to the new course schedule and was taught in the evenings. That class was the reason I knew the specifics of how this type of monster used acid.

It took a couple of seconds for them to get ready to spit. The acid was potent and plentiful, but it was enough time to retreat a safe distance away. Moreover, if you forced the spider to attack a lot, its reservoir depleted quickly, and it would need more time between spit attacks.

That was what I was doing now: getting within 15 feet to draw an attack, then pulling back. After a few minutes, the tactic started to pay off, and the pauses between attacks got longer.

"Brun!" I yelled to my friend, who was standing on the other side of the monster. "Provoke its next attack!"

"Got it!"

Brun moved closer to the spider and sunk an arrow into it. The spider turned around and started to get acid ready as expected.

The second it spat, I rushed forward and leapt onto its back with the same strategy I'd used on the black spider. The rest was simple. I equipped my spear and plunged it between the head and abdomen. And again.

Your group has killed an Acid Spider (mini-boss).

The last enemy didn't present much of a threat on its own. It was too slow, and its main function was to immobilize prey. It shot spiderweb out of its large, round ass, which prevented it from squeezing through the tunnel and helping its peers. Instead, we made our way to the spider and started running around circles, slashing at and stomping on the hundreds of large spider eggs in the cave.

We decided not to use any more fire arrows, instead shooting at the slow monster's eyes with regular ones. We knew that at this rate, we could blind it eventually, but we'd have to do more to kill it. We had another plan for that.

The spider shot large clusters of spiderweb that weren't too hard to dodge and dried up after 30 seconds. We systematically collected those large dried wisps of white thread threw them into one pile. After 10 minutes, the pile was about the size of the spider itself.

"Now!" I shouted.

That was the signal. Griselda and Russel retreated into the tunnel, while Brun ran over to me and lit a torch.

The pile of spiderweb sat between us and the spider, and we started to pull back to lure it over. Then, when the monster came running, Brun threw the torch.

The roar of the flames drowned out the scream of pain. Just in case, we dispersed and continued shooting at it, and that was where the spider, frenzied by the flames that engulfed it, made a mistake. If such a thing could be said of a non-sentient creature, anyway. It tried to shoot spiderweb again, but as soon as the web touched the flames, it ignited, allowing the fire to spread into the spider's body itself.

I even felt a little sorry for it. As soon as the flames died down, I went up to the beast, which was writhing around on the stone floor, and finished it off with my spear.

Your group has killed a Shooter Spider (mini-boss).

We didn't get a message that we'd completed the quest, so we spent the next few minutes scampering around the cave destroying the remains of the egg clutch.

Congratulations! You've destroyed the spider nest.

Quest completed!

Your stamina has increased.

Fantastic! And pleasant. Even if it was a minor improvement, I could feel it in my body. The fatigue subsided a little, and my muscles felt like they'd been worked on by a good massage therapist.

"Woohoo!!" Griselda shouted, and pulled me into a hug.

I didn't stop her, of course, but I didn't understand her exuberance at first. It took me a few seconds to realize that I was already level 10, and I'd already gotten several free body upgrades. For the rest of them, it was, without exaggeration, an extraordinary event. And it turned out that wasn't the only thing they'd gotten.

"I just got level 4!" she announced happily. "Thank you!"

"I didn't do anything..."

"Without you, we never would have come here!" Brun came up and clapped me on the shoulder. "I got level 5! Thanks!"

"And I got level 4," Russel said, smiling widely. "Thanks, my friend!"

Hm. It was a good thing I was an outsider and had some bonuses. And I was lucky to have met Visilius.

"Ilya," Brun said, "I just got level 4 the last time

I came here. Now I've leveled up to 5, which means we got a ton of experience today... The others were a little lower, and they were already on their way to the next level before we came. Maybe you and I can try to help them level up again now instead of killing the monsters?"

It was possible in theory, even without an outsider bonus, since they'd done a great job killing the four mini-bosses. And we'd also killed a bunch of smaller enemies.

"Of course, let's do it!"

"Guys..." Griselda pulled away and looked at me fearfully. "You need it, too..."

"I wouldn't say no!" Russel said.

"Well, since you're okay with it, go eviscerate some spiders!" I grinned and pushed the backpack with containers in it into his arms.

* * *

It took at least an hour to gut all the spiders. We also found two areas with a rare species of moss and spent about 20 minutes scraping that.

"Hey, am I imagining things, or do you have an upgraded inventory?" Russel asked when I threw another backpack of loot into my storage.

Shit... Well, at least I already had a story prepared for this. What better time was there to test it out?

"Yeah, a little."

"Did you kill someone from another race?!" Griselda cried.

"Yeah," I raised my head proudly. "Six months ago, my grandfather and I were attacked. By hobbits, four of them! I killed one myself, and my grandfather crippled the others and let me finish them off. They were all level 6!"

"Wow! Lucky you," Russel sighed with envy. "30 pounds extra in the same amount of space."

Ah, I thought. *If only you knew my inventory could hold over 200. But the less you know, the better you'll sleep.*

* * *

We left the spider nest and starting working to level up Griselda and Russel. We were all so excited about the idea of getting everyone up to level 5 that we threw out our initial strategy of working on metal and ore veins. Now we were only collecting certain kinds of moss, and only killing spiders.

About four hours later, when our zeal had just about run out, Griselda suddenly let out a loud squeal and threw her arms around my neck again.

"I got it! I got it!"

"Hey, thank Brun, too," I said smiling, and pecked her on the cheek.

"Thank you!" She hugged Brun, though with a bit less enthusiasm.

"Congrats! Maybe we can get me there another time..." Russel dropped exhausted to the stone floor. "I can't even move my arms anymore. And I'm hungry..."

"Like hell!" Griselda turned sharply to face

him. "Come on, let's focus for an hour. Now you can get all the experience, so we can get you to level 5 quickly."

* * *

She turned out to be right. When the three of us left Russel the monsters we'd crippled, everything went much faster. It only took half an hour longer for him to level up.

"Level 5!" the dumbfounded Russel started. "I could never have imagined. And another free body upgrade! All in one day! Working in a team is awesome!"

"Depends on the people," I said, grinning.

"Well, yeah... You didn't get anything..."

"Don't sweat it! I'll get mine."

I didn't bother to clarify that for the gap between levels 10 and 11, these ants were a drop in the ocean, even with the 100% buff. But I was genuinely happy for my friends.

* * *

Tired but happy, we went to the warehouse and handed over the loot.

"You three are freeloaders!" the bald inspector said, pointing at each of my companions. "Ilya taught you the first rule: take everything from monsters. So now you should hear the second from me!"

My friends glanced at each other, bewildered.

"Accept all exclusive quests?" Griselda suggested.

"No!"

"Study monsterology?" Russel tried.

"Ah! If you have a quest based on logic, don't let this one answer," the inspector chuckled. "Any other guesses?"

Brun grinned. "Stick with Ilya?"

"That's it!" the bald man noddled contentedly. "Almost — the most important thing is the makeup of your party. You know you should have a tank and an archer. Preferably a mage. But above all else, you need someone shrewd and courageous to lead the group. Someone who will take responsibility, not recklessly, but with an understanding of the circumstances. Alright, now line up and place your hands on the ball. It'll recalculate your reputation."

My friends didn't have enough to get to the next reputation class, and I only got enough for one more. But we got 3,110 gold coins.

"Holy shit!!" Russel shouted.

Brun chuckled and gave me a thumbs up, and Griselda once again threw her arms around my neck with a squeal.

"Head to the canteen before it closes," the inspector said, laughing, then handed me a box. "If anyone finds out, your reputation will dramatically decrease…"

The box contained a small bottle of krinch, the local equivalent of vodka. Interesting… Apparently, there was more to this man than it seemed.

He was present for highly emotional times in the lives of young champions, hammering rules into them while simultaneously providing positive reinforcement with unexpected little perks like this. A sensible arrangement.

"Thanks!"

I shook his large hand and left the warehouse first.

"What's in the box?" Russel ran up to me as soon as we stepped outside.

"What you'll be drinking tonight to celebrate leveling up." I grinned and handed the box to Griselda.

"What about you?" she asked, furrowing her brows.

"I have some business in the city."

"Oh..." She drew out the word and hung her head.

"Aw, come on!" I hugged her. "Nikos gave me a pass, and the medics will even give me buffs and remove my fatigue. It's important business!"

I was bending the truth a little, of course, but it would at least keep her from imagining all sorts of nonsense. And there'd be no doubt that I was interested in her.

"Oh!" Griselda's face broke into a smile, and her blue eyes sparkled. "In that case, we won't celebrate tonight either. We'll do it another time so you can join!"

"Um..." Russel raised a finger, but she shoved an elbow into his ribs.

"Without Ilya, all we would have done today is

kill 20 ants! We can't celebrate without him."

"Agreed!" Brun said, clapping Russel on the back. "Let's just have kombucha tonight."

I wasn't against kombucha myself, nor a hearty dinner. In all likelihood, I'd burned a ton of calories during the day, and I wasn't sure that Linda would feed me.

* * *

At 10:30, I went to see the medic on duty, who, after checking the list with some surprised, cast a whole horde of spells on me. I left through the guild's gates, nearly bouncing from my overflowing energy.

I was on my way to my first real magic lesson. Assuming, of course, that Visilius's daughter was home, and hadn't gotten some unexpected idea in her head.

Chapter 12

"I CAN SEE YOU'RE NOT too interested in a career as a mage," Linda said in place of a greeting.

She was standing at the doors of her flower shop with a sour look on her face. I had to consciously fix my stare on her face, because I was afraid to drop my gaze. Aside from soft, white slippers and a short, semi-transparent nightgown, she wasn't wearing anything.

I wondered how old she was. She didn't look any older than 30, but Visilius had looked much younger than his 80 years. Or however old he really was.

"Come in!"

Linda pushed back a lock of hair that had fallen in her face and turned into the house.

Holy shit! How could I not look at those supple, barely-covered thighs that swayed as she walked?!

Stop it, Ilya! First of all, she was Visilius's daughter, for God's sake. Secondly, she could be 50, maybe even 60! And thirdly, I was here to learn! Of course, she could have gotten dressed. All she had to do was tap a few buttons in her inventory.

We didn't head to the office, as I'd expected, but to the cellar.

"There's magical containment down here," Linda said. "If anything happens, you won't light anything on fire."

The cellar turned out to be a room with five doors leading out of it. Four of them were closed, and we went through the fifth. The rectangular room was about 15x30 feet. It had a dirt floor and brick walls, but I couldn't tell what the ceiling was made of. There was a single armchair in the corner, and three torches burned on the walls.

"Have you practiced?"

"I had to one time..."

"Had to?" Her eyebrows lifted.

"The night of all the fires, I got into trouble. I fought back."

"Meaning you used magic in battle?!"

"Well, I'd learned a spell, so I used it."

"Right. You learned. A spell. And used it. A champion. With a fireball." She sat in the armchair. "Use it again. Throw one at that wall."

I looked away from her with relief. How was I going to do this? Eyes open. Concentrate. Feel the energy inside... I didn't need much. I didn't need to waste all my energy and go blind again. Okay.

Now put out your hand... and throw!

A bright flash lit up the room. A flame the size of an orange shot from my palm. A few seconds later, it hit the wall and burned up.

"Fucking hell..." Linda whispered.

Meanwhile, I was tuning in to my senses. Nothing bad. Moreover, despite the lack of practice, this time was much easier than the last.

"Last time, you likely used all your mana," Linda said, hearing my thoughts. "That broadened the channels. That's what you needed to do, but better not to do so in battle. You could lose consciousness, and then they'd just kill you. I'll tell you right now, we're going to end every lesson with a blow at full strength. But it's better to save your strength before then. That's where we'll start with this."

Linda finally thought to change into a long, black robe that was more suitable for the occasion. She spent the next half hour telling me what I needed to do in order to increase and decrease the flow of energy used for spells.

Then I started throwing fireballs again, changing their shape and strength.

"What's wrong with you?!"

After what I thought was a great attempt, Linda shot up from the armchair.

"With who?"

I looked at her in surprise.

"With men!"

"What is it that's wrong?"

Instead of answering, she waved her hand. I

felt a chill, and a five-foot square block of ice appeared in the middle of the room.

Melt it. Just don't lose consciousness."

Piece of cake! I concentrated, conjured up a fireball the size of a volleyball, and threw it at the target. And what a fireball... The only indication that anything had happened at all was a small indentation in the ice.

"Okay, now watch!"

Linda rubbed her fingers together, and a fireball no bigger than a ping pong ball shot out. Not only did it fly much faster than mine, but it also tore right through the ice.

"Understand?"

Well, considering her remark about men...

"Size doesn't matter?"

"In magic it does! If you need to destroy a whole house, you can make a large ball. But if you need a precise shot, it's better to use a small but dense one. Try it."

I tried, and made out a little better.

"By the way," I started, remembering something, "is there any reason to use a stave?"

"For you, not yet. A stave works like an amplifier. Typically, it just increases the power of the spell. But when your opponent sees one in your hand, he starts to get nervous and be more cautious. So it's better to be inconspicuous about it and cast the spell from your hand."

"Makes sense."

I threw fireballs for the next few hours, and the more I practiced, the better I got. A few times,

Linda gave me some of her own mana supply.

"What about elements?" I asked during one pause.

"Meaning?"

"Well, you use fire, water, and control. I read in the system bible that there are different specialties."

"Anyone can cast the basic spells. For more complex ones, yes — you need to get skills along a specific branch. Otherwise, it's not possible to..." She trailed off and looked at me. "Although, what you're doing now is also impossible without those skills... Let's try something."

For the rest of the night, she taught me how to better fine-tune and redirect energy. We continued working with fire magic. By the time morning came around, I was able to create a very simple fire shield.

"Fuck!" I shouted when an icicle Linda had thrown pierced my shoulder.

"Sorry!" She conjured a blue light in her palm, and the pain immediately dissipated. "It's just that typically, a mage has to be at least level 20 to produce that shield... And they're more powerful. I forgot."

"So, it's of no use to me?" I asked, disappointed.

"Not in battle, for now. But given your progress, it won't be long. And actually, this shield itself can speed up your progress."

"What does that mean?"

"You can't practice with fireballs at the guild.

But putting up a shield is easy. If you practice for at least an hour before bed every day, you'll improve your magical channels quickly, and your magic supply will increase a little. Or a lot... I can't be sure with you."

"Doesn't the supply increase when leveling up?"

"Leveling up affects the base quantity. The real supply depends on frequency of use. The more often you use magic, the larger the supply. And experience, of course." She looked at me, her blue eyes glistening. "You'll only be able to control the power of your spells and use them quickly through regular practice."

"Are you not going to teach me other spells? Like finding hidden things or defense from magical control, for example..."

"Haha!"

Linda burst out laughing, but stopped when she saw I was still waiting for an answer.

"What rock were you living under?!"

"White Water."

"Shite Water!" She took a step towards me, her turned up nose ending up just centimeters from mine. "You're not a mage, and you'll have a mana problem. If you want to be a genuine, powerful spellcaster, you'll have to find a few more of those vials my father gave you. But while you're looking for them, you'll have to burn out your reserve once a week with a single spell. You'll have to come here to do that and practice."

"Okay."

Neither of us moved.

"You have the look of a grown man," she said, suddenly changing her tone. "A predator."

"It's just dark in here." I smiled, finding myself thinking about how much I wanted to kiss her. Well, not exactly... More like pounce on her, press my lips into hers, throw off her clothes, and... "So, what's with the reserve burnout?"

I heard a bell ring in my head. What was that? I looked away, confused, and tuned into my sensations.

"The bell?"

"How'd you know?"

"I've been trying to get you there all night!" Linda smiled contentedly. "I don't like to associate with people who have weak mental defenses. They could be made to betray you at any time."

"Especially young guys with amnesia?"

"Since the last time you were here, you got level 10," she observed, though I hadn't told her that. "And you improved your magic defense. That's good. But 10% isn't much... Luckily, there's also an ability for defense against mental influence. You work on it by talking, as a rule, to people of the opposite sex who are trying to manipulate you. Or mind control mages. You already had level 1 of that ability, which isn't surprising, knowing my father. Today, I spent all night giving you small doses of... seduction. You resisted them and got experience for the ability. So, I cranked up the heat, and you were able to level it up. Well done! Your mental defense is now level 2. It's not much, but it's better than 90% of men. Without skills, men are terrible at improving it."

She was conducting a fucking experiment! Her sexist remarks were provocative, but... also pretty spot on. I had no reason not to believe her. In which case...

"Thanks!" I said with a smile.

"Like I said: I don't like to work with people who have weak defenses. They can fail you at any moment. But it seems you could be useful to me."

Of course I could.

"Okay," she continued. "Make the most powerful fireball you can. Quick!"

For added incentive, she conjured up another ice wall, which she then threw at me.

I threw out my hand and summoned a fireball.

There was a flash, then darkness.

* * *

I went a little overboard. It took Linda half an hour to bring me, more or less, back to normal, but I still wasn't feeling quite right as I walked through the gates to the guild. And I only got to our warm-up a minute before it started.

Nikos could probably tell I wasn't at my best, but he made no concessions. On the contrary, he drove me even harder than usual. Given how the global situation was developing, though, it made sense. The best results come when your body is pushed to its limits.

I ate breakfast in a hurry, then asked my

friends to keep an eye out for me and fell asleep right there in the canteen with my head on my arm. I grabbed another half hour of sleep during the theory lesson. Thankfully, I already knew what was being taught.

By the time combat training came around, I felt almost normal again. And it wasn't just my especially resilient body. The thing that helped the most was an artifact Linda had given me when I left. It looked like a nondescript ring containing a piece of amber, but it actually allowed me to recover much faster after using magic.

"Ilya, a word!" Nikos shouted when the clock hit 2:50. When I went over to him, he asked, "Did you go to see Sylvan last night?"

"No," I said, shaking my head.

"Are you going to?"

"Of course, but not today..."

"Yes, I can see you're half dead." Nikos shot me a skeptical look. "Okay. Tomorrow, after you get your last regen buff from combat training, skip dinner and go see him. You'll need to for the tournament if you want to stand out at all, and also to give him something."

Find Sylvan and give him a package.
Address: ...
Reward: 1 Copper Coin.
Accept/Decline

Ah, so that was the real motive for his attentiveness... Well, fine. He was right about the tournament.

>>Accept

"Dismissed."

* * *

"What'd Nikos want?" Russel asked as I placed my tray on the table and sat.

"He asked if I was ready to participate in the tournament."

"You have every chance!" Griselda said, smiling. "And in multiple disciplines, too."

I thought so too, and had high hopes for the tournament.

It was a yearly tournament organized by the system that had recently been started. Only those who'd connected to the system within the last year could join. In other words, no one over 19. And the rewards were so good that it made me think the guild higher-ups had arranged things specifically so that our accelerated class would take our exams just a day before the tournament, which would last for two days.

As for the disciplines, they included fighting using cold weapons, archery, horseback riding, knife throwing, and hand-to-hand combat.

There was a magic section too, but for obvious reasons, I wasn't going to participate.

Each participant could choose two disciplines. The winner would get a level 1 elixir. Second place would get a level 2 elixir, and third and fourth places would get a level 3.

There was also an overall winner, which was the person who took the highest place in their nominations. The reward for that was a skill point.

When I found out about the rewards, I was shocked at first (to put it mildly) and considered them excessive. But my friends explained to me that this was how the system incentivized people, by showing them that the best performing would get real perks. There were similar tournaments for other ages, and the rewards were even better. Of course, the competition was tougher, too.

"How many people do you think there'll be?" Brun asked as he devoured his mushroom soup.

"A fuckton!" Russel said. "The whole Empire will show up. At least a thousand people."

"Where will they all stay, by the way?" I asked.

"There's an alternate reality for the tournament," Brun said, raising his brows. "You didn't know that?"

The last time we'd talked about it, I was more interested in the disciplines and rewards.

"Don't pick on him!" Griselda hissed. "The competition happens in a magical reality that the system creates just for that purpose. There's tons of space."

Holy shit. That meant...

"What are the battle conditions?"

"Fight to the death," Brun said, confirming my suspicions. "That's the whole point. Grinding goes really quickly in tournaments, because even if you're resurrected later, the feeling of having your head chopped off, I've heard, is not very pleasant."

"Not fun..." I said, turning the information over in my head as I chewed my food.

"Are you going to join the archery battles?" Griselda asked.

"Since I'm only level 3 with stabbing and slashing weapons, I don't really have a choice... I'd also be interested in knife throwing and riding a horse through an obstacle course, but you can only pick two."

"You can always do it outside of the tournament," she said, finishing off her third plate. "I'm going to try everything... In a setting where heads don't get cut off."

"You have to participate in battles if you want to level up," Brun noted.

"No... There'll only be level 2's in the battles, or 3's like Ilya. I'm better at other things."

Frankly, I agreed with her. Especially since there was a chance we'd be put up against each other, and I didn't want to even pretend to kill my friend.

We talked some more about the tournament, but once all my plates were empty, I left my friends and went back to my room. My body needed rest, and I had a little over an hour to sleep.

* * *

The daily routine began again, and went through the evening of the next day. Following my agreement with Nikos, I got regen and energy buffs right after combat training and went out into the city.

I ate on my way to save time. I'd fortunately had the forethought to stock up on provisions at the canteen earlier.

Sylvan lived about 3 miles away, right at the outskirts of the city. Luckily, it was in the opposite direction of the river, so I got there without incident. But getting inside was a completely different story.

First, I knocked on the door of the unremarkable two-story house. It opened immediately. I went in. The door slammed shut behind me, and I clearly heard the sound of a lock turning. A silhouette suddenly appeared in front of me and froze, forcing me to step back. It was a dog was the size of a calf.

Something rustled overhead. Looking up, I saw a gigantic owl sitting on a perch 10 feet above me.

Neither animal made a sound. I looked around, suppressing the first twinge of panic.

Woah!

Apparently, Sylvan had rented four identical neighboring houses and bribed someone so they'd agree to combine them into one long building. Now it was a large shooting gallery. It was also furnished curiously.

The owner was clearly trying to simulate all possible scenarios you would need to shoot in. Three torches lit up numerous platforms, ledges, and obstacles. Ropes hung from the ceiling, along with something like a swing on heavy chains. And scattered or set up all around were dozens of devices for unknown purposes.

"Hello from the round one!" I said, even though

I couldn't see anyone.

Quest: Find Sylvan. Complete.
You've received one Copper Coin.

Wow, good thing I came! Now I had to hand over the package, and I'd get another one. I could go back with a sense of accomplishment.

Sneering to myself, I looked from the dog to the owl and back, and waited. Finally, he deigned to appear.

The nearest torch was somewhat far away from me, and at first, all I could see was a figure of average height. But the characteristic gait told me the man wasn't sober. Apparently, very far from it.

"Are you the talented kid who can't shoot?" he asked, choosing to remain in the shadows.

"I'm actually at level 3 in that ability..."

"Ah, my apologies, then! I couldn't see what an outstanding individual you were in the darkness."

"He also sent this." I held out the massive package, realizing I'd embarrassed myself.

Quest: Give Sylvan a package. Complete.
You've received one Copper Coin.

"Now that's something else!"

He took a few steps forward, grabbed the package, and started to unwrap it.

I stood frozen with my arm extended, finally able to see his face. It was the completely ordinary face of a man about 50 years old... Except that where his eyes should have been, there were just two gaping black holes.

Chapter 18

THE PACKAGE TURNED OUT to contain a letter and a pot-bellied green bottle. I heard a noise above me. The owl flew off its perch and swooped down to sit on its owner's shoulder. Meanwhile, Sylvan turned the letter over and started to... read?

"What? You've never seen a blind man read?"

"Ah... It's a system message."

I realized belatedly that the technology was different in this world.

"The letter?" He waved the paper in front of me. "No, it's a regular one. What the Round One put in here can't be sent through the system. It's safer to do it the old-fashioned way, put it in code and scrape it together with a pen."

His speech was slow and syrupy, and I was even more certain that he was three sheets to the wind, but that was the least of my worries.

"Hm. The Round One seems to have overesti-mated you. You're too emotional. Well, alright. If it makes it easier for you..."

A black ribbon appeared in Sylvan's hand, and he fastened it around his head to cover his eye sockets. Then he turned around and headed into the depths of the building, confidently avoiding the devices as he walked.

Of course. That made it so much easier. All my questions disappeared in an instant.

"What're you waiting for?" Sylvan said without turning around. "Let's get to know each other."

I sighed. I shook all thoughts out of my head and followed him, trying not to look at the dog, which was still as a statue.

We walked to a corner of the gallery and sat down on the simple wooden chairs next to a large crate made of planks and covered with a table-cloth. "Getting to know each other" turned out to mean drinking together.

"I'm level 2 in poison resistance," I warned him.

"Are you bragging about that like you did with your level 3 in shooting?" Sylvan grinned.

He took out two glasses and the bottle I'd brought from Nikos and poured. I even leaned for-ward to check. Both glasses were exactly half full. To the fucking millimeter. I had the strong urge to wave my hands in front of his face, but I pushed it down with all my willpower.

"No, I meant I have classes tomorrow."

"Remember, kid: the ability to fight hungover

is one of the most important life skills. You won't live long without it." With that, he raised his glass. "Sylvan."

"Ilya."

I raised mine. We clinked mugs and drank.

The lack of food, decent portion, and the pleasant smell of the drink misled me. For some reason, I thought it wasn't very strong. I was wrong. My throat burned, and tears welled in my eyes. I grabbed the first pie I could find in my inventory and started chewing it frantically.

"The problem with the world, eh?" my host asked with a grin, "looking" at me.

"Everyone's a few drinks behind?"

"You get it!"

Damn it, system! Did Humphrey Bogart exist in Shrinanth, too? Whatever, didn't matter.

"Why am I..." I started, but Sylvan just shook his head and handed me the same half-full glass. Maybe it was magical and never needed to be refilled?

This time, I was ready, and things went much better.

"Liquor before beer..." I said, starting the saying this time.

"Never fear!" Sylvan said, confirming that our sayings were overall pretty similar.

"So, about shooting?"

The strong alcohol was quickly lowering the communication barriers.

"You need one more... to relax your muscles. Not to mention that you ate, which reduces the effectiveness."

"How do you know all this? You're blind!"

"I'm not deaf... You chew loudly. And I can smell. The first pie had potatoes, and the second was squab."

"Hm... It was from the guild canteen. It should've been chicken..."

"Well, could be," he said, and refilled the glass again. "Go on, drink, and then we'll get into position."

* * *

My feet felt like lead as I walked over to the spot, which was located in the exact center of the long hall.

Sylvan was standing against the wall in a specialized booth. There was also a barely noticeable, flickering field separating us. Magical, by the look of it. Made sense, considering he got his students drunk.

The dog and owl were also behind the barrier, as well as a large rat that went scurrying past. At first, I thought it just lived there, but a few seconds later, it appeared on Sylvan's shoulder opposite the owl.

Interesting. If the first two animals could somehow be explained as trained working animals, the last one was almost certainly a pet, like Viza. Which meant the other two probably were as well.

"Listen carefully!" Sylvan shouted, cutting off my train of thought. "I'm going to set up the targets and tell you what to do. It could be a regular shot, a shot to a particular area, or a double shot. Or maybe an instruction not to shoot at all. On my command, you'll run to the place I tell you to. Jump, get down, and so on. Understood?"

"Yes!"

Something clicked, and the floor underneath me began to shake, while white targets of varying sizes appeared on the walls simultaneously.

"Fire!"

What happened next was hard to explain. I ran throughout the shooting range. I climbed the walls and jumped onto the swinging platforms. I shot while running, jumping, hanging upside down on a rope, and standing on one leg, as well as backwards.

Sylvan put emphasis on shooting speed, and soon enough, I stopped aiming and just launched one arrow after another. Curiously, I often hit my target.

"Stop!" Sylvan finally shouted. Breathing heavily, I went over to the chair and sank down into it. "Have you sobered up?"

"Completely."

"Then take this!"

I hadn't even noticed him filling the glasses.

"But why?"

"Shooting in a real fight is all about reflexes. Alcohol turns off your brain so we can train your reflexes directly."

Well then... Nikos clearly knew where he was sending me. I drank and had a snack.

Once I was intoxicated, the barriers came down again.

"How do you get around so well? I mean, you walk so confidently. You're familiar with the surroundings here... But you comment on what I'm doing, too."

"When you run, you huff an puff like an elephant, you wave your arms around... You're sweating again."

"Okay... So, your range is limited to your other senses?"

"You'd be surprised to find out what that range is," Sylvan said with a grin.

Just then, the owl, which had been sitting on one of the many ledges, swooped down to sit on Sylvan's shoulder again. The rat appeared on his other side, and something brushed past my foot. I looked down to see the dog.

"Hm..." Sylvan suddenly turned serious. "They're telling me you have a pet."

What the... This magical world and its magical creatures... Wherever you went, someone who could see your hidden secrets was always within spitting distance. Visilius had been right. It looked like I wouldn't be able to wander around incognito here for long.

"I do."

"Show me."

"Yours won't attack?"

"Please," Sylvan laughed. "They want to meet it. They're bored with me, but other animals... They're just animals."

Don't wowwy, he's telling the truth.

A weight appeared on my shoulder, and I felt a membranous wing touch the back of my head.

"Woah, what a beauty!" Sylvan smiled widely. "What does it eat?"

"Only eggs." I grinned and pet Viza's head.

And bwud!

"And human blood, but I don't give her that."

"Too bad. Sometimes it's good to spoil them. That's how you can reveal hidden abilities. Well, and grinding goes faster, too."

Sylvan filled our glasses again, and Viza flew 15 feet away to sit on one of the platforms. All three of Sylvan's pets immediately headed over to her. Soon the dog, owl, rat, and bat formed a small rectangle. And still, none of them made a sound. It was a somewhat eerie sight, to be honest.

"Are they communicating?" I asked.

"Of course!"

Don't wowwy, I won't say anything stupid, Viza said, seemingly reading my mind. *It's taboo for us to tell each other anything that could harm our companion.*

"Have you had her long?" Sylvan asked.

"About two weeks."

"Aww. She's so young!" He seemed touched. What a strange man. "Heh... I'm even a little jealous. You still have so much to learn about each other. So much to go through together..."

"Can you tell me about it?" I decided to take advantage of the opportunity, since I knew so little about pets, and I still couldn't access the section of the system bible about them.

"What's there to say? You have to experience it. What I can tell you is that you're very lucky. She probably can't do much yet, but with time, she can become a loyal, powerful ally, helper, and..."

It finally dawned on me. "Eyes?"

"And not just that!" Sylvan laughed and decided to be open. "My injuries are actually the result of a good deed. I gave them to Martisha. That's the owl. It helped her evolve, and it improved my other senses a hundredfold."

See how you have to love your pets?! Your eyes are pretty neat, too...

"But you were an archer," I said, taken aback.

"What do you mean 'were'?"

Sylvan abruptly stood and turned around. A bow appeared in his hands. There was a bright flash, and 10 streaks of fire flew towards the classic dart boards hanging on the wall. That must have been the Rain of Arrows skill. Which meant that my suspicions were correct: my instructor was a rogue.

"Go and see."

I walked over to the wall. All five dart boards had been struck in the exact center.

"Holy fuck..." I whispered without thinking.

"Now, get in position!"

What I'd seen left an unforgettable impression on me that caused my new acquaintance's already high status to take off, crash through the roof, and shoot into the sky. If I were ever able to do something like it, it would be worth every effort.

The night continued in that vein. An hour of intense archery work with increasingly difficult tasks, followed by five minutes of drinking, during which Sylvan talked about his pets, their combat abilities, and their difficult dispositions.

I especially enjoyed the story of his rat, Shrila. She was extremely headstrong, and it took her a long time to be comfortable with her owner. But when he was taken prisoner by some rebel count, and his dog and owl could offer no help, Shrila single-handedly tore out 40 throats in one night, found a secret passageway, and brought her owner — her partner — the keys.

* * *

When I left in the morning, Sylvan understood the situation and not only me some kind of miraculous tincture to drink, but also sent me off with several more vials of it.

Feeling better with every passing minute, I walked through the slowly awakening city, turned my face to the rising sun, and smiled.

I'd learned so many new things about pets, worked on my poison resistance, and, most importantly, made significant progress in archery, giving me better chances for the tournament. On top of that, Sylvan had shown me a few different shooting techniques that I could refine at the guild in the coming days, and we'd agreed to meet again the day before the competition.

The Last Portal Jumper

* * *

The following week was intense and strenuous.

A full schedule and difficult training with the third-rank students and Nikos himself. Hours spent with my bow at Sylvan's shooting gallery. And constant practice producing a fire shield.

The last part I always practiced alone in my room while cleaning up and getting ready for warm-ups, stopping in my room after lunch and talking to Viza, and before bed. It was hard at first, and the only thing that saved me was the ring Linda had given me. But the more I worked at it, the faster I was able to create the shield, and the less energy it took. After a few days, I'd learned to raise the shield practically on instinct and without needing to take my focus away from other things.

* * *

Finally, the two weeks allocated to our advanced group passed, and the day of the test arrived. By that point, there were 22 students remaining.

This time, the challenge consisted of three steps.

We completed the theoretical portion by the statue again. I answered 44 questions out of 50 correct.

Not good enough, of course, but considering that the mistakes were minor and not on the most important subjects, it was acceptable. It would

188

have been freakish for me to have remembered every single thing we'd been taught when I was constantly exhausted.

The second step of the test took place at the obstacle course. The most difficult one. And it had been modified just for us, too. Now there were high-level champions standing with training swords every 50 feet who would clobber everyone running past.

In principle, it was impossible to screw up on this part, since if you got hurt, the medics would run over, treat you and restore your strength, and you'd just start over from the beginning.

The idea was probably to grind some abilities and perseverance.

I almost made it on the first try, but on the second-to-last obstacle, one of the champions caught me on the ninth lap, and a very unlucky fall broke my leg.

"Fuck!" I spat in the dirt, writhing in pain as I waited for the medic.

"Sorry, buddy!" shouted the champion who'd hit me.

I looked at him and recognized Dromdir. The one who'd escorted me to Linda's shop the first time.

"No biggie," I said, waving it off. "It's my fault anyway. I should've cut you down."

"Good attitude!" He laughed rushed towards another student.

The medic needed high-level magic to treat the break, and it took him 15 minutes to heal me. But that gave me time to analyze my first attempt and watch the others.

As a result, I completed the obstacle course on the second try. One of three students to do so.

The third step involved going to the guild dungeon. Of course, I was already familiar with it, but there was a surprise waiting for us.

"This," Nikos said, raising a glowing purple belt that we were all now wearing, "is a return belt! Exactly two hours after you go into the dungeon, it will pull you back out."

A wave of discontent passed through the crowd of students. Understandably. We all wanted to earn some cash, and now we were frustrated.

"The belt also contains a calculator for the experience you earn. It will record how many monsters you kill. Your task is to kill at least 60."

That wasn't too bad... Of course, it was nothing for me, but it might not be so easy for the others.

"Those who don't manage to do so will return to their regular groups and will take the standard exam with them in two weeks," Nikos continued. "As compensation for money forgone during this exercise, every student who passes will receive a thousand gold."

That made everyone smile. Everyone except me, anyway. I thought I could probably earn a little more.

"Additionally," Nikos said, raising his hand, "if anyone receives an exclusive quest, you can take the belt off before going into the cave. Just don't forget to put it back on. Completing the quest will amount to passing the exam early."

The funny thing was that, as he said all this, Nikos never took his eyes off of me.

* * *

Do you want to enter the first level of the Champions' Guild dungeon?
>>Yes
Select the area you want to transport to. Near/middle/far.
>>Far

ATTENTION: A new exclusive quest is available: Mine a vein of enriched crynite.
Reward: A free body upgrade.
This offer will be active for one minute.
Accept/Decline

Ah.

And that would count as passing the exam? Although, what was I saying? While I mined the ore, I could kill 60 common monsters anyway. Besides, there was nothing stopping me from doing that first.

>>Accept

The defensive field encircled me, and I still had time to look around.

Nothing new. The same caves as always, five ants, and three beetles wandering around lazily, completely unsuspecting of their impending death.

Mercenary Sword, level 10. When equipped:
Champion skill efficiency +10%;
Reaction speed: +10%;
Critical hit chance: +10%.

Mercenary Shield, level 10. When equipped:
Champion skill efficiency +20%;
Magic defense: +10%.

Mercenary Boots, level 10. Stamina: +30%.

And I was level 10 myself with a bunch of up-graded abilities.

I stood still, smiled, and felt like a cheater.

Defense duration has ended.

Now the monsters had nothing protecting them from me.

I raised my sword. Charging towards the nearest ant, my mind clear, I severed its head with a single, powerful blow.

Stage 1: Find a cave with a vein of enriched crynite. Complete.
Stage 2: Mine the vein.
Do you want to enter?
Yes/No

I'd killed over 60 monsters on my way here, so I'd already fulfilled the requirements to pass the exam. But now I had to take the belt off so it didn't pull me out early if mining took a long time (which it definitely would).

>>Yes

Book Two

It was impossible to mistake the crynite vein for anything else. It cut through one wall of the giant cave I'd ended up in when I entered the portal. On the rest of the walls were numerous holes about three feet in diameter.

I knew what awaited me from the theory classes, and I grinned in anticipation.

Not even because completing this quest would get me at least 5,000 gold and a free body upgrade, but because now I had some extremely intense, useful, real-life combat training ahead of me.

I walked leisurely over to the vein and checked my Quick Access menu.

Let's do this!

My pickaxe whistled through the air, and...

CLINK!

Sparks flew in all directions. But the echo that was gradually receding was cut off by an entirely different sound.

I turned my back to the vein and equipped a weapon. From the many dark hollows, hundreds of yellow eyes glowed.

Chapter 14

THERE WERE A LOT of different kinds of monsters I could have encountered. And I got lucky. They turned out to be three-foot-long woodlice. Lots of legs and antennae, and small fangs. The only way they could kill a victim was to knock them off their feet. And then, given how many of them there were, they would tear the victim apart quickly. But as it stood, the would-be massacre just became an endurance marathon, and thanks to my high level and artifacts, I had stamina in droves.

I ran in unhurried circles, periodically stopping to cut down monsters who were charging forward. These enemies didn't seem to have brains, and they made no attempt to split up, surround me, or block my path.

Once I'd fully settled in and understood their (lack of) tactics, I threw my first fireball. Well, "fireball" was a little generous... More like a fire ping pong. An inch in diameter. The idea had been to hit several monsters at once, but that didn't happen. Then I tried another way: I decreased the power of the fireball, but increased its size to three feet. Hey! That was much better.

Two woodlice immediately doubled over and died. Three others started squealing, having received varying degrees of burns.

After a few more experiments, I settled on keeping the size of the fireball to a bit less than five feet. I probably could have killed the enemies with a sword faster, but where else would I find a training ground like this to use my only attack spell?

The battle took over half an hour and left about 200 twisted, charred, or chopped up bodies, all level 5. And purely because I was a portal jumper and had the bonuses that came with that, my invisible experience bar had probably increased tremendously. But the tournament was tomorrow already, and I definitely wouldn't get to level 11 before then. Although... I get experience for winning against opponents there? Not likely. They wouldn't actually be dying. But I could definitely grind my abilities.

As I mulled all this over, I swung my pickaxe methodically, chipping away pieces of enriched crynite.

I collected 40 pounds in total.

Congratulations! Exclusive quest: Mine a vein of enriched crynite. Complete.

Your strength has increased.

Strength was always a good thing to improve, even more so when it was free. The guild's dungeon had unexpectedly become somewhere I could seriously advance. Here, I outperformed the average champion. The system saw this and gave me exclusive quests. I couldn't get that otherwise. But maybe that was for the best.

It was a shame this would be my last visit to this level of the dungeon. After I got the next rank, I would only be able to go to the next level. And I might not be a big fish in a little pond anymore, or I'd get quests of a completely different complexity. Well, I'd have to wait and see. In any case, I still had the Rogues' Guild to get to, and they had their own dungeon, too. Though I'd heard it was vastly different.

I didn't bother rummaging around in the bodies of the woodlice. The hours I'd waste on that could be spent more productively, and it could also raise unwanted questions, since we'd only been given two hours.

Remembering that part, I put the belt back on... and immediately found myself on the guild's campus, where, following instructions, I headed straight to the warehouse.

*　*　*

"You're the last," the bald assistant said, smiling. "But something tells me there's a reason for that."

"Yeah."

I handed him my belt, then dumped the enriched crynite onto the table.

"Whew, lucky you! And I still owe you a thousand for the time limitation!" He laughed and weighed the loot. "6,900 gold total. Listen, don't go hiding your coin purse under your pillow. It'll get stolen in no time! Hand on the ball!"

Congratulations! You've received Second Rank in the Champions' Guild.

You've received a skill point.

"Well done!" He shook my hand firmly, but decided that wasn't enough and clapped me on the shoulder with his free hand. "A little more and you'll get the next reputation class."

"Not much use in that," I complained.

"Ha! That's what you think. People already know about you and treat you accordingly, but if you get a blue bracelet in your first two months... And you will. Trust me, they'll take notice."

Ilya! came the displeased voice of Visilius in my head. *Is this what you call not standing out?!*

Well, what was I supposed to do if things just shook out this way?!

"See you!" I waved at the assistant and left the warehouse.

*   *   *

2:15.

The tournament was starting the next morning, and since I'd been able to finish early today, it'd be a good idea to go see Sylvan and practice the abilities I'd learned in the past week. Well, and celebrate getting second rank, too. He wouldn't let me practice dry anyway. Luckily, his elixir would sober me up on my way back.

And of course, I'd have to go see Linda. I'd made good progress, and I was ready to learn new spells. Like Healing, for example. That was also a basic spell and could be incredibly useful at some point. Or even better, Strength Regen. Ah, dreams...

So, I'd go to see Linda as soon as I could, but for now, I had to focus on the tournament. The rewards were so good. And even though I had a lot of competition, I had to do everything possible to get into the top four in each of my two choices. Or even better, the top two. Although, what was I saying? I was an outsider! I had to blow them all out of the water!

I ate again as I walked, and desperately hoped Sylvan was home.

He was, and was already in his usual stupor, which somehow had no impact on his competence.

Understanding the severity of the task at hand, he didn't bother with idle conversation today. But the workout almost killed me. After a few hours, even muscles I didn't know I had were sore. After Visilius and Nikos, I hadn't thought that was possible. And we were only halfway through the day's session!

"Quit your whining," Sylvan said as he filled our glasses again. "No healing or regen for now. Your body should feel like it's on fire and you can't walk."

"Will I definitely be in shape by tomorrow morning?"

I could hardly even raise my arm to drink my "stimulant."

"You insult me!"

Well, this was a magical world, after all. This was where spells that aided metabolism came in. If magic had existed on Earth, its main application probably wouldn't have been war, but cosmetology.

Sylvan hadn't been lying. And when both my legs were cramping another few hours later and I fell off a platform like a sack of flour, launching an arrow into the ceiling, he ran over and first gave me a disgusting liquid that smelled like a swamp, then rubbed ointment onto my aching muscles.

"Take the rest with you and use it again before bed," he said, handing me two vials.

"How much do you have to grind to get to level 4 in archery?" I sighed with relief as I felt the pain start to recede.

"Depends on the person. As well as your other abilities and stats. On average, it takes a couple months of intense training. But you've already made a lot of progress, and your potential is clearly higher than average. So, I think you'll probably need less time."

And I was an outsider, so even that time should be cut in half. Shame I couldn't do it today! Thought I was now definitely well ahead of the competitors who'd only just gotten the ability to level 3. I had another advantage in that only feudal lords could afford to grind hard in the first year after initiation, and they used swords more than a bow. It also wasn't likely there were wackjobs like me among them, either. They didn't have the incentive.

* * *

I got back to the guild around 9:45 that night. I hurried to the canteen, but it turned out there was no need for the rush. Its hours had been extended to 11 in celebration of the first accelerated course passing the exam.

"Finally!" Russel shouted as soon as I entered the canteen.

I waved to my friends and headed for the counter. Their impatience was understandable — we'd only seen each other for brief moments recently. And then there was the exam and the upcoming tournament.

There were only two young champions in line, and they let me go ahead of them. Not because they knew me, but because of the red bandages on my arm, which told them I was in the supergroup. And we had priority.

"Did you pass?!" Russel asked impatiently when I walked up to the table.

"What a dumb question," I said with a grin as I sat next to Griselda.

"Then here!" He handed me something that smelled like kombucha. "We wouldn't start without you!"

"That's because I have the bottle," Griselda

pointed out.

Ha... I sometimes got the feeling that my poison resistance was increasing faster than anything else and I'd get level 3 very soon. Well, good! I had concoctions that removed all the negative effects and side effects of alcohol.

I didn't mention that I'd gotten another exclusive quest or gone for extra training in magic and archery, but I explained everything else in detail to my enrapt friends.

"Cool!" Russel said, nodding. "Use the skill point for Strong Arms. It'll help you tomorrow!"

The redhead had touched on an important and complicated topic. It wasn't as simple as he thought, since, being higher level, my choice was much more difficult. On top of that, the description for the Strong Arms skill didn't say whether it was helpful for archery, though I'd heard that was the case. And logically it should have been, but... the system condensed it all down to "strengthens blows."

So, on the one hand, that skill would actually be the most helpful for the tournament. But considering my skill levels as a whole, it would make way more sense to improve magic resistance, or just save the skill point until stronger skills unlocked.

I really did have every chance of being a prizewinner, so it made sense to bet on that. Okay, then!

Strong Arms (level 3, passive).
+15% of the base value. Not bad!

"Were you in the city today?" Brun asked me.

"Yeah."

"Were people coming in?"

"Yes. There were a ton of young people outside," I nodded.

"Shit..."

We sat there until the canteen closed, but we couldn't keep hanging out afterwards on the night before such an important event, so we said goodbye and went to our separate rooms.

It was the first night in a long time that I skipped practicing with the magic shield, instead acting like any other kid: I fed Viza, applied the restorative ointment from head to toe, and drank the hangover cure and swamp water Sylvan had given me. Then I laid down and passed out immediately.

* * *

The entrance to the challenge was about three miles outside the Central City's borders. It was a 65-foot-tall sparkling blue tower. And it had appeared exactly at midnight.

We got there at 8:00, an hour before the tournament started.

"Just touch it," Griselda reminded me once we'd gotten within 15 feet of the tower.

I liked when things were simple like that.

The sparkling surface was vibrating, humming, and giving off warmth. I put out my hand.

Unknown Player!

You are invited to participate in a tourna-

ment for new initiates.

Prizes:

First place in one discipline: A level 1 elixir of your choice.

Second place in one discipline: A level 2 elixir of your choice.

Third and fourth place in one discipline: A level 3 elixir of your choice.

Grand Prize:

1 skill point will be awarded to the partici-pant whose cumulative prize place (in their two selected disciplines) is highest.

Enter a nickname to participate.

Ilya? Or should I wear a mask and go incognito?

No... A mask would be uncomfortable, and there won't be anyone over 19 there, so I didn't have to worry about the Count's men, or Mr. Phillips' men, seeing me.

Maybe "Ilya the Dominator"?

No, too soon for that.

Just Ilya then! It was a unique name in this world, so it wasn't likely to be taken.

Although, once I became a legend, people would name their kids after me! Or would be scared of my name...

Select two disciplines you would like to participate in.

Fighting with cold weapons.

Archery.

Horseback riding.

Knife throwing.

Hand-to-hand combat.

...

The first two!

Your selection has been accepted. Registration will close in one hour and the tournament bracket will be formulated.

Further information can be found on the information board on the tournament grounds.

Good luck!

The world flickered, then quickly reappeared.

Just magic being magic! Or maybe it wasn't magic, but advanced technology...?

Whatever the case, I was no longer standing on the outskirts of the Central City. I didn't know if I was even on the same planet at all.

The tournament ground were enormous with varying sizes of tents, houses, and arenas for different purposes.

"There's a map over there," Griselda said, appearing next to me and continuing to look out for me.

A new line had appeared in the menu, too. It said:

Tournament grounds.

Your location is marked with a green pin. The locations where you'll be competing will be marked with red pins. The start times will also be displayed. You can add others as friends (up to 10), who will be marked with blue pins.

"Let's add each other as friends," I said, "and go look for somewhere to meet up when we have free time."

There were tons of places to choose from. In general, all the buildings could be split up into two types. The first were places where you could practice your abilities in any of the available disciplines. The second were places to eat and sleep.

"That looks like a good spot," I said, pointing to a tavern curiously named The Saber-Toothed Squash.

The sign, accordingly, showed an evil-looking vegetable with its toothy mouth wide open and pouring green juice.

"Doesn't look very appetizing," Griselda said doubtfully.

"Well, then let's go there." I pointed to the tavern opposite.

This one was called Dead Man's Smile, with a corresponding image.

She grimaced. "There used to be something with a pony..."

"The Pony Kebab," Brun said with a smile.

"Alright," Griselda sighed. "Let's go with the squash."

We noted the spot on the map and went inside. It was fairly cozy, with wooden furnishings, pictures of aggressive vegetables hanging on the walls, and plants wrapped around furniture legs, the bar counter, and the ceiling supports. They even seemed to be moving. What ambience!

Most people were still wandering around outside, so aside from us, there were only a couple of hobbits, who didn't pay us any attention.

"Well, should we have some food and beer?" Russel suggested.

Griselda turned her maternal tone on again. "You can get tanked since you have no shot, but none for the rest of us!"

"I've heard that a little bit is even necessary," I said. "I suggest we get two mugs for the four of us."

The others agreed. We spent the remaining time before the tournament started nursing beer and chatting with the tavern keeper about all kinds of things. He turned out to be an ordinary resident of the Central City. Like many others, he'd specifically looked out for a quest on the notice board to work here. These events happened regularly, and the old-timers knew in advance when they had to be a Johnny-on-the-spot.

Meanwhile, the prices at the tavern a pleasant surprise. It only cost five silver for a mug of beer... But they could have made it free for participants.

Attention participants!

The location of your next challenge will be marked in red. Three routes to get there will also be shown. Green means the route is clear, yellow means traffic is heavy, and blue means the route is full of people. Choose the optimal routes and avoid creating unnecessary congestion.

Remember: Fighting is prohibited on tournament grounds. Violators will be removed from the tournament.

While here, your inventory will be locked

and artifacts will lose their properties. All necessary equipment will be given to you at the start of the challenge.

Due to the immense interest in battles with cold weapons, a portion of the weakest participants (based on a set of parameters) were withdrawn from the competition. These participants will be able to select another discipline.

Good luck!

"Damn it!" Russel slammed his palm on the table. "They withdrew me!"

"Wow, I didn't think you'd choose that," Brun said, looking at him with surprised.

"I didn't either, but I made a game-time decision."

"Ilya's been a bad influence. You've gotten brave."

"Screw you."

Only half listening to my friends, I looked over the new information in the menu.

Battle with cold weapons. 128 participants.

Please proceed to Pavilion 18, Arena 3.

Time until battle begins: 14 minutes, 53 seconds.

Archery. Recruiting participants.

Hm. 128 participants. And there were at least 2,000 people here. The organizers had cut quite a few... Well, so much the better. In order to win overall, I'd have to win all eight battles.

In theory, if this tournament was anything like those on Earth — say, a tennis tournament — the system would put stronger participants against weaker ones first, so that the strongest would have a chance to meet in the finals. If it was considering participant level and number of skills, I was definitely the first seed.

"See you later!" I waved to my friends and left the tavern.

* * *

The pin was at a large tent, the interior of which was split into four squares with 20-foot sides. A number shimmered over each of them.

Waiting for me under number three was a young dwarf, whose ginger beard was still fairly short.

Hm... Unsurprising, and not very pleasant. Some of the champions had beards, of course, and we'd practiced techniques against enemies opponents equipped with spears, axes, and clubs... But not as often as with swords.

"Hey, suicider!" the dwarf said when I went into the square.

"That's a contradiction," I said, grinning, "but hi all the same."

"Could you just stick a knife in yourself?" the dwarf continued joking. "I don't want to get my hands dirty."

He wasn't especially solid — more like wiry — but his words and intonation made it clear he was nervous.

"You won't have to."

Competitors are all in place. Start battle?

Well, no reason to put it off.

The dwarf apparently felt the same, and the message changed.

Select your weapon.

Images appeared in front of me, with so many options that I had to scroll. There was even a trident and crowbar!

"What's the holdup?" the dwarf said, provoking me again. "Take the axe. It's easy to chop your own head off with."

Through the menu images, I saw he'd chosen a large axe and shield. I had to remember for future battles not to choose right away so I wouldn't tip my opponent off to what they'd be up against. Although, at our level of mastery, it was more likely that everyone had decided in advance what they'd be fighting with.

You have 15 seconds remaining... 14...

Sword and shield.

"How original," the dwarf said, squinting at me with a sneer.

The battle will end when one competitor dies, loses consciousness, or touches the side of the arena.

So that's how it worked... I'd have to fight closer to the center.

The battle will begin in 20 seconds... 19... 18...

"Hey, I think you're holding the sword from the wrong side!"

"I'll try it this way first, and if it doesn't work

out, I'll switch."

"Sounds good!"

02... 01... 00...

Let's do this!

Chapter 15

THE COUNTDOWN ENDED, and magical barriers appeared around the perimeter of our square. Those were the sides we couldn't touch.

"Suck my dick!"

The dwarf charged at me without a second thought and dealt a powerful blow. Of course, I was still standing three feet away from where it landed. I answered with my own, which he deflected with his shield.

That happened three more times over the next minute. The dwarf flew at me, and I jumped back and answered. He attacked in different ways, but I always jumped to the right. It wasn't very comfortable for me, but it would help me in the future.

Although, aside from agility and my desire to do so, there didn't seem to be anything to it, and just watching his attempts wouldn't get me anywhere. Time to engage.

The dwarf attacked again, and I used Speed to dodge left, immediately hitting him in the shoulder.

"Ow, shit!" he shouted, and the axe fell from his limp hand.

He needed a couple seconds to recover from the shock and figure out that he could fight with his left hand too, but that was enough time for me to get into position. And when he bent over the axe, I leapt forward and cut his head off. The headless body fell to the ground and vanished.

Interesting... I suspected he'd just reappeared somewhere on the tournament grounds, which meant I could run into him again.

Congratulations! You're in the top 64 of participants. Then next battle will take place in approximately one hour. Please exit the arena.

The magical barriers disappeared, and I left the square.

Hm... What about the archery competition? Oh!

318 participants.

Please proceed to Pavilion 46, Position 3.

Time until event begins: 14 minutes, 42 seconds.

Interesting. First of all, the number of participants implied a different scoring system. Most likely, only a certain number of us would advance to the next stage, based on the results of the previous. Or maybe everyone would participate to the end.

Secondly, the timer had started once I'd finished here. This was organized pretty well!

I chose the green route and took a roundabout way to my destination. Excited teenagers were scurrying around everywhere. Some of them were happy, others angry. There were even a few arguments, but heeding the system's warning, no one was actually fighting.

On my way, I'd heard a strange noise coming from a large tent. I had time to spare, so I peeked inside.

It hadn't been my imagination. Inside, surrounded by protective fields, mages were demonstrating their abilities. Judging by the steam coming from all around and flying icicles, these were water mages.

"Excuse me," a quiet female voice said behind me.

I turned around and saw a small, pretty brunette with green eyes.

"Of course."

I moved away from the entrance, shot the woman another glance, and went on my way.

*   *   *

The pin was on a long building that held a shooting range inside. There were 16 sections, and I walked up to the one with a number three glowing above it.

Do you want to begin?
>>Yes

You need to complete three tasks.

Task one: Shoot a target 10 times.

The closer you get to the center, the better. The time needed to complete the required number of shots will also be considered.

20... 19... 18...

I was amused at the clarification regarding the bullseye.

The target was about 65 feet away and 30 feet from the opposite wall of the pavilion. There was a bow on the counter with a bucket of arrows next to it. I picked up the weapon and started turning it around with my left hand to get used to it. It felt comfortable. Just like the sword and shield I'd used to fight the dwarf. The system sure didn't skimp on equipment.

02... 01... 00...

I grabbed an arrow and immediately sent it towards the target, then a second, and kept reloading until I'd reached 10.

The target was completely black, and I couldn't really tell where the arrows had landed, but they seemed to all be densely grouped.

Task two: Shoot a target moving vertically 10 times.

20... 19... 18...

The old target, riddled with arrows, disappeared into the ground and was replaced with a new one.

02... 01... 00...

I paused for a second to judge how fast the target would be moving. As soon as I figured it out, I launched 10 more arrows one after another. The target probably should have hit the bottom range, but it never made it.

Task three: Hit 20 targets that pop up from the ground.

20... 19... 18...

While I waited for the countdown to finish, I glanced around at my neighbors in the gallery and quickly realized that I would have no problem passing the first stage here. The overwhelming majority of my competitors were not only taking a long time to aim, but also managed to miss the target frequently.

02... 01... 00...

The first target popped up 30 feet closer than the previous targets. But that didn't surprise me, since I'd managed to see two other competitors complete this task already.

The arrow sank into the very center of the target, which immediately disappeared, and a second one appeared 50 feet further away. The last two or three minutes reminded me of Whack-a-Mole.

Congratulations! Tasks completed. Your current position: 1/24.

Oh, neat! There was an online tally. And 24 was the number of people who'd completed the first stage. Not bad. I was the last one to arrive at the pavilion, but the first to finish. Pretty good start, but there was more fun to come.

I still had at least half an hour until my next battle, but I couldn't go to the tavern, since I was sure my friends hadn't finished yet. I also threw out the momentary desire to go support Griselda. Most likely, I would just distract her.

In the end, I decided to just walk around. And I had to say, I was pretty impressed.

I especially liked the horseback riding competitions. Chiefly because I wasn't participating in them.

The first step, which I assumed was the easiest, consisted of a serpentine track. The participants had to complete it in an extremely short amount of time, guiding their horse to leap over ditches and go around holes, all while the rider swung a weapon at the life-sized mannequins that popped up here and there at regular intervals.

In the time I spent watching the event, 20 or so participants were brought to tears because they hadn't made it to the finish line. Screw that. If you asked me, there was way too much randomness in it. Although, the horses didn't seem to be part of that randomness, and looked like they were all clones, which was probably true.

Battle with cold weapons. 64 participants.
Please proceed to Pavilion 16, Arena 1.
Time until battle begins: 14 minutes, 59 seconds.

Oh! That was right next door.

I quickly got to the indicated building and went inside.

My opponent showed up four minutes later. Another dwarf.

Hm... Why were there so many dwarves in the tournament? The two I'd faced were definitely not from my guild, so they had to be from the capital or just self-trained. With rewards as good as these, I wouldn't be surprised if they'd come all the way from the Northern Mountains.

"Could you just stick a knife in yourself?!" the bearded man asked as he entered our square.

Well, that was a good start. I hoped he'd fight the same way his predecessor had.

"We can do without the chitchat. I just have to select a regular knife now."

Competitors are all in place. Start battle?
>>Yes

I dragged out the weapon selection again. I only chose mine once I saw the axe and shield I'd expected appear in the dwarf's hands.

The battle will begin in 20 seconds... 19... 18...

The dwarf didn't make any more jokes, instead looking serious and more confident than the first one I'd faced. Well, and he was bigger...

02... 01... 00...

...but he charged to attack the exact same way. I dodged and swung my weapon. He blocked it.

No! On the one hand, I could pull off this one-on-one fight just like the last one. But there was a dangerous possibility that the dwarves had talked during the break, and my opponent now knew my strategy. I had to be flexible.

On the second attack, I leapt to the side and countered. I hit the shield again, and the dwarf didn't even bother to dodge, just switched his shield to the other hand. Hm... He was faster than the first, too, and smarter. Well, it didn't matter. In that case, I'd return to my standard tactics and rely on the fact that I was stronger and more resilient.

The dwarf continued to charge forward, and I leapt aside. I attacked once for every two or three of his, checking for a vulnerable area.

"Maybe we can start fighting now?" he roared angrily.

"I can't fight against an axe."

"Without weapons, then."

"Some other time."

I toyed with him for another five minutes, but he turned out to be smarter than the barons at the guild, and when he felt himself getting tired, he slowed down the attacks and went on the defensive. Good. An axe wasn't as useful for that as a sword.

I made a few test attacks to see what his defensive maneuvers looked like, then activated Speed and Powerful Blow at the same time.

The dwarf didn't catch the changes immediately, and tried to counterattack after my first hit, but I dodged his axe easily and pushed the edge of his shield into his elbow. As I did so, I attacked with my sword from above, then changed my angle and came sharply from below.

The dwarf didn't lower his shield in time, and the sharp blade ripped into his side. He threw his axe up, but before he could bring it down, I closed in and hit him with my shield, then with my sword twice more. This time, I hit him in the hip.

Neither wound was fatal, but they were pouring blood. I moved back to keep a safe distance and continued to land blow after blow. And when my active skills' duration ended, I backed off altogether.

The dwarf was bleeding profusely from the cuts, and he was wobbling. Time was now on my side, and he knew it.

"I'll kill you!" he shouted, and rushed at me.

Dodge, counterattack. Dodge to the other side, counterattack. This time, the dwarf wasn't able to switch his shield hand, and my sword's blade sliced through his shoulder.

"Motherfucker!" He stumbled and sprawled out on the ground.

"Crawl over to touch the barrier," I said, pointing at the edge of the arena that stood less than three feet away from him.

"That would be a dishonorable death!" The young dwarf spat and tried to get up.

"Are you stupid?" I asked, surprised. "It's just a tournament. Dropping out like that is less painful than having your head cut off."

"I don't care!"

He managed to stand and whipped his head around in search of his axe.

Except I spotted it first and went to stand right in front of it.

"Hand it over!" he growled through gritted teeth.

I could have given it to him, but Visilius's voice rang clear in my head: *Thousands of times, an op-*

ponent on the brink of death has taken his killer prematurely rejoicing in his victory to the next world.

"Come and take it."

The dwarf growled again and leapt. His body fell to the ground headless and disappeared seconds later.

Congratulations! You're in the top 32 of participants. Then next battle will take place in approximately one hour. Please exit the arena.

What about archery then?

Oh! Something had changed!

First step completed.

Your current position: 4/250.

Please proceed to Pavilion 118.

Time until event begins: 14 minutes, 53 seconds.

The message produced some unexpected emotions.

On the one hand, I was still high on the leaderboard. On the other, I was three lower than I needed to be. Of course, it was just the first step, and I'd learned I had a chance of winning in every discipline. As well as in the overall ranking.

* * *

The second step in the archery tournament took place in a 65-square-foot pavilion. The furnishings reminded me of Sylvan's house. Here there were also ledges, platforms, awnings, and so on.

Your route will be shown in green. When

you reach the designated area, targets will fly out. They will be illuminated in red. Your task is to cover the distance as quickly as possible and hit as many targets as you can.

The same bow and bucket of arrows from the first step were lying by the entrance.

02… 01… 00…

A 15-foot green line lit up on the ground, getting longer as I moved along it. Then it turned sharply and forced me to jump on top of a crate. As I did so, I heard a bell to my right. I whipped around and saw a glowing red target falling from the ceiling. The bowstring snapped, and the arrow hit the bullseye.

I leapt off the crate and continued to run along the green line.

In total, 20 targets flew out, and I shot the same amount of arrows. I hit all of them, with plenty of running, jumping, and crawling.

Congratulations! Task completed. Your current position: 1/47.

As I now knew from experience, that didn't mean anything. My biggest competitors might not have started yet.

I had to wait almost an hour for my next opponent to be assigned. To my delight, he turned out to be human. A swordsman.

As soon as the battle began, I realized he couldn't have been at level 3 in that ability yet, and I caught him soon enough. I cut his arm off with one blow, and slashed through his neck with a second. It all happened so fast that he probably didn't even realize what was happening.

Congratulations! You're in the top 16 of participants. The next battle will take place in approximately two hours. Please exit the arena.

Great, I had a break coming! I'd been wandering around all over, but still hadn't gone into the tavern. To be fair, judging by the pins, only Russel was there at the moment.

Archery. Second step completed.

Your current position: 2/200.

Please proceed to Pavilion 96.

Time until event begins: 14 minutes, 52 seconds.

The event arena was a shooting gallery again. But this time, we were hung by our feet and swung a little.

They compensated for the higher difficulty and discomfort with slightly bigger targets. I hit all 20. But I wasn't so sure about the bullseye as I'd been before. Oh well. Some participants didn't even try, and just dropped out of the competition.

Congratulations! Task completed. Your current position: 1/35.

The next event will take place in approximately two hours.

Definitely time for a break!

Book Two

*　*　*

The tavern wasn't as busy as I'd been expecting. The system must have arranged for breaks to be staggered. My suspicions were immediately confirmed by the only one of us who was sitting here: Russel.

"I have a two-hour break after the first couple challenges," he said once I'd gotten kombucha, placed an order, and sat down next to him.

"How's it going?" I asked.

"Ugh. Don't ask," he brushed me off. "I chose knife throwing and archery. And I'm in the middle of the leaderboard for both of them. Closer to the bottom for knife throwing."

"Well, the rogues rule the roost there..."

"They what?"

"Have an advantage."

"That's true." He sighed. "They also seem to have a skill that increases accuracy. I saw one jerk sink a knife right into a mannequin's eye from 60 feet away!"

"Who are you calling a jerk?!"

A large palm with hairy fingers landed on Russel's shoulder.

"Be on your way, buddy." I smiled, standing up to approach the halfling. "We're not talking about you."

"That fatass was standing next to me," the hobbit said with a scowl as he pointed at Russel. "He's calling me a jerk."

"Well, he said what he said. You just called him a fatass."

"I was merely stating a fact..."

"So call the fatass a jerk and leave us alone. We can't fight here anyway."

"As if he'd fight me!"

"He's not alone here."

"You're lucky we're not in the city, you fat slob!"

"Fuck you!" Russel said, surprising all of us, and stood up.

"Russ — " I started, but he turned towards me, winked, and mouthed: *Stay out of it.*

"Who do you think you're talking to?!"

The hobbit looked dumbfounded. I didn't know their eyes could get that wide.

"You, half-pint!" Russel took a step forward and leaned down so the tip of his nose was almost touching the hobbit's. "What, you think you're a legend just because you're the best at throwing knives?!"

Once he said that, I understood his plan. He wanted to provoke my major competitor into a fight and get him expelled from the games.

"Russ, quit it!" I took my friend by the shoulder and turned him to face me. "I was just screwing around."

"Quit what?" He frowned, clearly upset by my words.

"What did you say, bitch?!" The hobbit grabbed Russel by his other shoulder and yanked, turning Russel back around.

"No fighting!" came the loud voice of the human tavern keeper, followed quickly by the man himself, carrying my order on a tray and passing by in such a way as to push the two troublemakers apart as if by chance.

Taking advantage of the opportunity, I leaned over to whisper in Russel's ear.

"Knock it off. It's dishonest."

"If you say so." Russel sighed and turned towards the hobbit. "Sorry, man. I confused you for a different hobbit. He pinched my coin purse in the city last night... But I can see you're a good guy."

This baffled the hobbit even more, and he just stood there frozen, opening and closing his mouth.

"Anyway, come have a beer with us!" I said to the halfling. "For friendship among peoples."

"Screw you!" the hobbit finally produced. He left quickly, spitting on the tavern floor.

"I didn't do it for no reason," Russel said, shaking his head. "He really could win the knife throwing competition. His second discipline is archery, and hobbits are strong in that too. Your generosity could cost you skill points."

Or maybe it wouldn't cost me anything at all. The hobbit had attacked us unfairly, and I could have asked my friend to provoke him myself, but... I'd never liked dirty tricks, or the phrase "victory at any cost."

What were the standings now, anyway?

Archery. Third step completed. There are three steps remaining.

Your current position: 1/150.

Break.

Well, there we go. And my conscience and karma were still clear. Three archery steps, four battles, and the crown was mine.

I picked up my utensils and brought the first piece of the intoxicatingly aromatic boar to my mouth.

Chapter 16

THE HORSEBACK RIDING COMPETITIONS took the longest of all the disciplines. My choices, on the other hand, went quickly. Moreover, there was only one more step scheduled for both of them that day. Which meant I'd be free around 5:00 PM.

"Great fight!" Russel clapped me on the shoulder when I left the arena where I'd just battled a human. "Looked to me like you hardly even had to try!"

"That's what you think," I answered, grinning.

It was true. My last opponent had also been level 3 in swordfighting, and I won cleanly on account of my high level, cool head, and Speed ability, which he, like the others, didn't have.

"I just got completely blown out of the water," Russel said, spreading his arms. "Archery next?"

"I'll check, but I think that's all for today."

Battle with cold weapons. You're in the top 8 of participants. Then next battle will take place tomorrow.

Archery. Fourth step in progress.

Your current position: 1/77.

The next two steps will take place tomorrow.

100 participants would be left the next day. I'd enjoyed the latest step, which was held in a tent. I'd had to stand on a vibrating platform that moved in all directions with targets quickly appearing around it. For added difficulty, not all the targets glowed red. Sometimes, blue ones would pop up, which would hurt your score if you shot at them. It was a good thing I wasn't colorblind.

"That's it for today," I said.

"To the tavern?" Russel suggested as we left the pavilion.

"No, I have to go to the city."

"To the guild?"

"No, for something else."

"Bet that 'something else' means tits!" Russel mimed at least D cups to make his point.

No, Linda only had Cs. And I couldn't say I really wanted to use them in the way Russ had in mind.

Of course, there was a chance she wouldn't be home, or that she'd be busy, but since I had some time, I had to make the most of it. I couldn't afford to just hang out in the tavern all night. And if I couldn't see Linda, I'd go to Sylvan's.

Book Two

*   *   *

"What, did you get ousted already?" Linda said, her brows raised in surprise, when she answered the door.

"And hello to you, too," I chuckled. "Not yet. The rest is happening tomorrow, so I decided to stop by for a few hours to boast."

"Flip the sign on the door and come in."

We went down to the cellar again, where Linda immediately changed into a short red dress with a plunging neckline and matching tall boots.

"Is that to work on mental defense?" I smiled.

"No, I just like it. "Here's another matching piece." A whip with a red woven handle and lots of long tails appeared in her hand. "Like it?"

"Only when I'm holding it."

"Shame." The whip disappeared. "Let's go then, raise a shield."

"Done."

She paused for a second and looked at me.

"Release it… Raise it again… Release… Raise. Hm… Now don't fidget." She came over, and a sharp, eight-inch icicle suddenly appeared in her closed fist. "I said don't fidget. I'll heal you if anything happens."

She swung her arm and tried to hit my shoulder. There was a hiss, and the icicle quickly turned to steam.

"Release it and raise it again."

"Done!"

Another icicle appeared, bigger and even sharper-looking, and she swung at me again. There was another hiss and more steam, but this time, the shield couldn't hold out, and her fist with the melted remains of the ice slammed into my shoulder."

Linda exhaled and looked from her fist to me. "Show me your Champions' Guild mark."

I opened my palm and showed her the mark that indicated I was a second-rank champion.

"If it weren't for this and the letter from my father, I would think you were screwing with me..." she said slowly. "And you're really 18... But you progress like an experienced level 20 mage."

"I got lucky with my genetics..."

"Uh-huh. You must the be son of two archmages. Okay. I'm not sure I need to get into this yet... Let me show you something else."

I had to admit, Linda's reaction surprised me. I was expecting more curiosity and probing. At the same time, I had no illusions that she was just going with the flow and had no interest in the background of my mysterious appearance. I figured she was waiting for a more opportune moment, or for me to slip up.

For the next two hours, she used fire, water, and light magic to explain the different ways to use energy to create spells of various schools. Generally speaking, it was all about visualization and the internal desire to produce an icicle rather than a fireball or a heal.

But due to inexperience, a lot of things came

down to the pink elephant you should never think about. So I only managed to feel the cold in my palms and create my first disgraceful excuse for a snowball at the end of those two hours.

"Well... I would have whipped my last student for that," Linda said when she saw the results, and the whip appeared in her hand again. "But it took him a month to get there... Alright, let's try healing. You can practice that in your room safely, too."

Healing turned out to be much harder for me. And that was despite the fact that I was getting better and better at controlling the flow of energy. This was, by the way, the same energy I'd already fully spent several times. In those moments, I felt like I was teetering on the edge of losing consciousness.

Linda's regen buffs and the artifacts she hung on me like a Christmas tree, as well as magical concentration, helped. The last item was an advanced version of focusing on relaxing, which I could already do, but with a few modifications that helped top up my mana supply, too.

"Damn it!" I cursed when, instead of healing, another burst of fire shot from my palm.

"Don't worry, it happens." To my surprise, Linda smiled. "After all, you have to control the energy a little differently. We're rushing now and it's not working."

"I was hoping to get it right today," I sighed.

"Go ahead, I'm not kicking you out."

"But the tournament..."

"I have a magic bed. It gives you an extra 50% rest buff. You'll be able to get enough sleep."

"What about you?"

I involuntarily glanced at her slender figure.

"I have a wide bed. We can both fit," she said, a smile playing on her lips. "Anyway, enough chit-chat, let's keep going!"

* * *

It took me until midnight to finally get it.

"Yes!" I shouted, hugging Linda in the burst of emotions.

"Take it easy, big guy!" She backed away, but her face was pleased. "Let's get something to eat."

Given the late hour, my hostess was really just snacking on... wine and cheese. After such an intensive, energy-consuming day, I devoured everything she offered, starting with smoked meat and ending with vegetables.

"Next time I'll have food to spare," Linda said, watching me eat the last piece of apple pie. "Have more."

I thought for a second, then grabbed a big piece of cheese.

"Can I ask you a personal question?"

"The whip is more of an accessory."

"I meant about Visilius..."

"Ah." Linda moved her gaze to the flame of the candle burning on the table. "Well, you can try."

"What was he like when he was young?"

"How would I know?" she said, surprised. "He

had me late in life. Isn't it obvious?"

She indicated her young face while simultaneously arching her back.

A little embarrassed, I blurted out, "I thought it was magic."

My embarrassment grew.

"Not as much as you seem to think." Linda laughed. "And about my powers... You're not the only one magic comes naturally to. And my father had connections. I was taught by the best specialists."

"Uh-huh..." I dragged out the word, not really believing her words.

"But about what he was like..." She took a sip from her glass. "Well, judging by the letter, he was the same. Smart, strong, domineering, sarcastic, determined, and always certain he was right."

"He treated me well," I mumbled. "Well, aside from his preferred way of waking me up with ice water on the head."

"That was his specialty!" She burst into laughter. "If you look at it that way, he treated us, his kids, well too. He just never asked what we needed or wanted and did everything his way."

"He had three? Children, I mean."

"Yes..." Linda lowered her gaze and started examining her hands, which sat on the table. "But let's not talk about that. Maybe we should talk about you instead. What did my father want to talk to you about by the fire? Or are we going to continue playing this amnesia game?"

"I'm just a goal-oriented guy who wants to

achieve something in life. If you ask me, I prefer to talk about my future."

"Ha... Alright. If you don't want to answer, we'll do as you wish. When it comes to your future, I'm afraid the circumstances are forcing us all to make adjustments to our plans."

"The orcs?"

"Yes. There's a very high probability that this time, they'll make it to the Central City."

"But there are the walls, fortresses, the army..."

"Uh-huh. And someone else rocking the boat from the inside."

My ears perked up, but Linda was quiet.

"Who?"

"Who knows... There are plenty of people dissatisfied with the Emperor, both inside and out. You... These conversations will stay between us, yes?"

"I'm not a kid," I blurted out again, and reached for my wine glass.

Did the witch put something in my drink...?

"I noticed that as well, by the way... You don't speak or act your age at all."

"And acting my age would be staring at your ass and drooling?" I said, trying to switch the focus.

"Acting your age would be not talking back to your elders and looking a wise witch in the mouth."

"And also sweet talking and groveling?" I grinned. "It's not about age, it's about character."

Book Two

"You're right there... Okay, we've been sitting around for too long, and you have the tournament!" Linda drained the rest of her wine and stood up. "Come on."

Her bedroom was behind the office, and she really did have a big bed. There was also a huge mirror across from it.

"Here. And don't make that face!"

She tossed me some clothes she'd just pulled out of her closet. They turned out to be white pajamas.

Shit... That was kind of awkward. At least I could change just by tapping a button in my inventory.

"Ha! They suit you!"

Linda looked at me appraisingly, nodded in approval, and also changed... into a short, semi-transparent nightgown. Over her naked body. Only the weak light from the small candle prevented me from being able to see all the details. Which was a bad thing. The less I could see, the more I'd fantasize! Feeling my arousal growing, I quickly slipped underneath the blanket.

Linda took the candle and left the bedroom, I assumed to go to the bathroom. The most important thing for me then was to distract myself from what I'd just seen and try to...

* * *

"Ilya!"

"What?!"

I opened my eyes and saw it was already light out.

"Time to get up!"

Linda was standing next to the bed.

"What's that?" I asked, indicating the mug in her hand.

"It's cold water, in case you'd gotten addicted to being woken up like that."

"I'm already up!" I smiled and stood up.

A second later, I was wearing my usual armor. I put the pajamas on the nightstand and followed the witch, her hips swaying.

The clock was ticking, so I quickly drank some zoka kindly prepared by my hostess, thanked her for the hospitality and training, and ran out of her shop.

The bed really was magical! I'd slept for five hours and felt amazing. There were no traces of the previous day's hectic hustle and bustle, and the energy boost was noticeable. It was the perfect time to tear everyone apart!

* * *

Twenty minutes later, after I'd arrived on the tournament grounds, I learned who my next opponent would be. A hobbit. And not just any hobbit, but the exact same one Russel had almost gotten in a fight with the night before.

"Oof," my ginger friend murmured as he followed me into the pavilion. "You shouldn't have stopped me last night."

Well, now this was a game with two outcomes. I couldn't rule out that he was my biggest competitor for the overall reward. According to Russel, he was good at knife throwing, and if he could beat me, he'd be in the top four at least.

I was desperately lacking experience fighting halflings, since there weren't many of them at the Champions' Guild. Although, Nikos knew that was a weak spot for me and sometimes arranged for me to spar with them, but this pipsqueak probably came across people more often.

On the other hand, what better time than now to test my strength? After all, in a real battle to the death, you didn't get to choose your opponent.

"Fancy meeting you here," the hobbit said, baring his teeth when I entered the square. "It's a pity I won't get to slice up the ginger."

I didn't see the point engaging in a petty insults, so I just confirmed that I was ready to fight.

I lingered on the weapon choice until the last minute, picking one when there were only two seconds left on the timer. The hobbit chose his simultaneously, and two shortswords appeared in his hands. Fucker. I'd only ever fought against shortswords twice.

The battle will begin in 20 seconds... 19... 18...

"Should I dice you up quickly or cut off piece by piece?"

The hobbit showed his teeth again, and I...

And I what? The phrase "we're not playing for keeps" didn't apply, since that's exactly what we were playing for, and the stakes were high. But I couldn't care less about that. Every second that ticked away on the countdown, my excitement and anticipation for the battle grew. It was unlikely there'd be any long, tactical games here, and it was an excellent opportunity to show myself first of all what I was worth.

02... 01... 00...

The hobbit charged at me immediately, ducked under my attack, and dealt his own. I blocked it with my shield, and he darted to the side with a carnivorous grin and slashed at my side with his second sword.

But he had a surprise waiting for him: Speed, which allowed me to not only dodge the attack, but also counterattack. The swing wasn't enough to completely slice through his wrist, but the tendons were severed, causing one of his swords to fall to the ground.

"Ow, shit!" The stunned hobbit leapt back and stared in disbelief at his profusely bleeding hand. "How the fuck did you do that?!"

I could have made some snide remark or even run from him while waiting for him to weaken from blood loss, but since I'd started training for a real battle, I had to simulate conditions where I needed to act quickly. I also really wanted to take him down before the Speed duration ended.

I attacked, using my height and my long weapon to my advantage and paying close attention to make sure he didn't counterattack. He did exactly that after parrying my first swing and dodging the second. Luckily, my speed was still increased, and I was able to move to the side and block his attack with my shield, then stab at his stomach.

He almost got away. But "almost" didn't count. The blade plunged 2 inches into his flesh.

"Fuck!" he shouted, and quickly attacked, realizing it was his last chance. But I'd been expecting that, and I jumped back twice, waited for the right moment, and slashed at my opponent's good arm.

"I'll find you!" the hobbit bellowed, hatred filling his voice.

Turning around, he jumped into the barrier... and vanished in a flash.

Congratulations! You're in the top 4 of participants. The next event will take place in approximately two hours. Please exit the arena.

"That was fantastic!"

Russel pounced on me the second I left the arena. It had turned out really well. Though, I had to admit, the halfling was good. He was incredibly nimble. If I hadn't had the Speed skill, the battle would probably have ended faster, and not in my favor.

Russel said he wanted to go with me to the next competition, the countdown for which had already started.

*   *   *

The second-to-last step of the archery competition made us sweat and really exert ourselves. Mainly our legs, since we had to stay in the saddle.

The track, along which targets regularly appeared, was a complicated one. It had raised embankments, ditches, mud that my cloned mare got stuck in, and so on.

I finished my run with the thought that this aspect of my training had been wrongly forgotten. And since hadn't given us any training like it at the guild so far, I'd have to find time to rent a horse and ride around the city. Ha... Except where would I find the time? I was up to my eyeballs in things to do.

*   *   *

"How's it going?" Griselda asked as I sat down at the table and ordered breakfast.

It was just the two of us at the moment. Immediately after my competition, Russel dashed off to support Brun in horseback riding.

"I'm currently first in archery, but there are still 30 people who haven't finished," I answered. "Fourth in offensive weapons."

"Congrats! You've already won at least a level 3 elixir!" She hugged me and kissed my cheek.

"Thanks!" I smiled and took a sip of beer. "What about you?"

"I'm 35th in archery right now..." She smiled humbly.

"Hey, that's awesome! You should make it to the last step!"

"I hope so... Where were you last night?"

Griselda asked this question in a casual way, but it was clear she really wanted to know.

"Jealous?" I grinned.

"Of course not!" She scoffed and turned away. "It's just dangerous at night, so I was worried."

"I was training."

I didn't want to worry her more, so I stalled with a sip of beer and thought about it.

The young body I'd ended up in was actively producing hormones, which led to increased desire. I could suppress it somewhat with grueling workouts, but it built up all the same... It was distracting, and I had to do something about it. And it seemed like hooking up with Griselda was one of the most obvious ways to handle it. She clearly liked me, and I liked her, too.

My gaze glided across her lovely profile, the blonde hair tucked behind her ear. Along her elegant neck and down her neckline to her breasts, quite impressive for her slender figure and short stature.

My body reacted very strongly to her... But she wasn't a stranger. Getting involved with her wouldn't just be about sex, but a relationship. And relationships were costly, both in time and on an emotional level. What if something happened? She'd be upset... It was a tricky situation. At the moment, the option of more casual connections seemed more logical. This was, again, the kind of feeling described in books: a spark, a flame, the all-consuming passion... There was nothing that even came close. Pure chemistry and sexual attraction...

"Brun came in fourth in the overall horseback riding standings!" Russel shouted as he ran into the tavern.

"Keep your voice down," Brun shouted back as he followed Russel in. "First of all, not everyone's finished yet, and secondly, there are still two more steps."

"It's still cool!" I said.

"Well done!" Griselda joined in.

"I know!" Brun clapped his hands and smiled happily. "Now let's order and talk about how everything's gone."

Our spirits at breakfast were high, and we eagerly awaited the last steps of the competitions that would decide the fate of the valuable prizes.

Chapter 17

MY OPPONENT IN THE NEXT BATTLE was a dwarf, but I didn't even have time to be nervous.

He decided to take me on with a quick and powerful onslaught, which had apparently proven to be a good approach in previous battles. And it might have borne fruit if it weren't for my Speed skill and well-timed activation of Powerful Blow.

The battle was over in all of 15 seconds. The dwarf only had time to open his eyes wide in surprise to look at the perforating wound in his stomach before I ended his suffering with a blow to the neck.

After that, we were all in for a surprise. The final steps of all the competitions were held in a separate large arena. And they all happened in front of spectators.

"There's so many people!" Griselda whispered

nervously as she looked around at the packed stands.

We'd come out onto a round field and were waiting for the order to get into formation and begin.

"It's nothing for you!" I smiled and put my arm around her supportively. "Look at it like practice. You have to learn how to shoot in any situation. Then it'll be easier."

"That's true."

She took a deep breath and offered an uncertain smile.

50 people had qualified for the last step, and I was still in first place. But I didn't know how big of a gap there was between me and second place. Or third. Maybe all 10 places were neck-and-neck, and any mistake could drop me down who knew how far...

Damn it! I wasn't Griselda! What was I having these destructive thoughts for?! I was good. I was leading! And now I'd show class to hundreds of humans, dwarves, and hobbits! Besides, almost everyone sitting in the stands had already been eliminated from their competitions.

ATTENTION: Archery, final step! All participants, take your positions.

You are position 5.

In the middle of the massive field, a circle divided into 50 sectors began to shimmer, and the finalists hurried to their places, forming a complete ring. What, were we going to shoot each other from 30 feet?

Turn your backs to the center.

Apparently not. Everyone turned to face the stands.

Your task: Stand in place and kill the approaching enemies.

The competition has begun!

And it did, without any countdown.

Something like a magical shield or screen began to flicker around the field, and orcs came rushing forth towards us.

Now that's what I call a finale! Total immersion!

I stood as though spellbound, watching the approaching wall of enemies for a moment before pushing my wonderment aside and focusing on just the ones running directly through my sector.

They were green, with fangs and axes. But their armor consisted only of loincloths and boots.

I let the first one get within 6 feet, then shot my first arrow. It hit the orc in the chest, who collapsed silently. I wondered if landing an arrow in the heart was worth more points than in the stomach. Most likely, it was.

I shot again. The second orc collapsed. And again. The third rolled on the ground.

With a smile on my face, I instinctively pulled the bowstring taut and loaded one arrow after another, noting with pleasure that the orcs stopped moving after I shot them.

The stands were going wild, but the enemies roared so loudly that I couldn't even hear my neighbors in the ring. Whether the spectators were cheering for the participants or the attackers, I personally couldn't tell.

Of course, this wasn't just going to be an endless free-for-all, and it soon became clear what the difficulty of the final step would be. Orcs continued to stream from the glimmering screen surrounding the field. And each time a new one appeared, it had more armor than the last.

First, greaves, shoulder pads, and bracers were added to the loincloths. Then helmets. Then leather pants, followed by jackets. None of this really got in my way, though I could see out of the corner of my eye that some of my competitors were having trouble holding the greenskins off. And if they weren't finished off quickly, they'd continue to rush towards the center, and it would take additional time to kill them.

Then it got really tough. Round shields appeared in the orcs' hands, which they could use for cover. I couldn't shoot mindlessly now, but had to wait for them to be unprotected or use two arrows to hit them first in the leg, then finish them off.

This was the wave that began to claim victims from the participants, hacked to pieces by the large axes of the snarling greenskins. I noticed that once they'd done their job, the orcs immediately vanished, and the lighting on the fallen participant's sector went out.

Meanwhile, the competition neared its climax. The orcs' shields got even bigger, and their leather armor was reinforced with inserts that could only be pierced at close range, and only if your aim was good.

I managed it with some difficulty, but now the elimination rate had skyrocketed. It took a lot of effort for me to not pay attention to the fact that less than seven feet away, two greenskins were chopping up my neighbor, growling as their axes sunk in with a squelching sound.

The orc running towards me lost its rhythm slightly when it jumped over the body its predecessor, and I released the bowstring. The arrow flew just centimeters over the edge of the shield and hit the greenskin right in the face.

It fell 30 feet away from me, and two others quickly took its place. The first took an arrow in the leg, and I managed to shoot the second in the side.

There wasn't time to finish them off, and I just kept shooting, my mind clear. The growling, the noise of the crowd, and shouts as competitors were killed behind me all became white noise. The orcs pushed forward relentlessly, but I didn't give up.

Another arrow landed, and the enemy began to fall, but didn't even hit the ground before it was shoved aside by the next, whose sturdy shield almost completely covered it.

There was no time to analyze. I just pulled back and shot. I couldn't miss from 15 feet away, and the orc, hit in the leg, fell to the ground... And was replaced by another. I pulled back and shot. It roared and fell, but kept crawling towards me. I shot again, and...

Congratulations! You are the winner of the archery competition!

The orcs disappeared, and I turned around. 49 chopped up bodies were lying in the center of the ring, including Griselda. I was the only one left standing.

First place reward: A level 1 elixir of your choice. You can get your prize any time after you leave the tournament grounds.

While I couldn't use the reward yet, a list appeared, and I scrolled through it without thinking. Holy shit! So that's where you could get them!

There was even the Night Vision potion I'd heard so much about, and which cost an arm and a leg at the market. Though, actually, it was more like three arms and a leg. There was also a large General Body Upgrade potion and, of course, the blue bottle Visilius had given me.

Which meant I could significantly strengthen my magical potential! Fantastic!

Please exit the arena so it can be prepared for the next finale.

You have 00 minutes and 59 seconds.

I looked around again and realized that the bodies had disappeared, and I was standing in proud solitude in the center of the arena. I had to hurry, or I would get transported to the respawn area, where the dead were resurrected, and that was a long way away.

"Awesome!"

"Garbage!"

"Well done!"

"Jackass!"

I heard these and other interesting words as I walked towards the stands.

"You're a jackass!" I answered one of the spectators, and I opened the map.

Russel and Brun were in the stands, and Griselda was hurrying back from the respawn point. What was next on the agenda?

Let's see... The magic finals were taking place in a different arena, so the only things before my next competition were knife throwing and the horse race. It would all be held where I already was, so I could go hang out with my friends in the stands for now.

*   *   *

The knife throwing finals were similar to the archery competition. Except that there were far fewer orcs to account for the difference in weapons. It looked just as epic from the stands as it had from the field.

First came a bunch of orcs running and waving their axes, who quickly died. Then, as their equipment improved, the ring shrank more and more. And then the first casualties came among the finalists.

Those casualties began to increase, and soon enough, there was a turning point, and only a few of the most skilled knife throwers remained.

It was fascinating to watch, and very impressive. After all, something similar could happen in the real world, and considering the alarming news rolling in, it was imminent.

"Three left!" Russel said, pointing out what we could already see.

But this didn't last long. Greenskins reached the competitors in two sectors simultaneously. They raised their axe blades, and...

The knife throwing finals are over.

The orcs disappeared, and the winner threw his arm in the air, then began to bow dramatically, turning to each section of the stands in turn.

"Is that...?"

"Yep." I nodded at Russel. "And it's terrific that he won this competition."

The winner was the hobbit who'd bothered Russel the day before, and who I beat in the sword-fighting quarter finals. It was terrific that he'd won here because it meant he couldn't beat me in the overall score, even if I immediately lost in my next finals. My chances increased with his win.

"Well, gotta go!" Brun got up from his seat.

"Let's go!"

"Good luck!"

Griselda, who'd now joined us, hugged him and kissed him on the cheek, then Russel jumped over two steps and rushed towards the field.

The field, meanwhile, was being quickly reset, and soon it started looking like a racetrack.

"The course doesn't look too hard," Russel murmured thoughtfully.

I'd had the same thought, which hinted that it

wouldn't be so simple.

The main part of the arena became a rectangle separated into 10 tracks about 350 yards long, and there were horses in a stall at the beginning of each. Numbers from one to ten glowed above them.

It was clear that the riders would race in five sets. But so far, there were no major obstacles visible.

ATTENTION: The first group will begin in 20 seconds.

The first group mounted their horses and got ready to start.

02... 01... 00...

The riders burst out of the starting gate, and orcs simultaneously appeared along the entire length of the track. Of course.

"That's not fair!" Griselda shouted in my ear above the noise of the crowd. "The first group didn't know what would happen, but the rest can prepare for it."

"They probably got personal messages about it," I suggested.

In the meantime, the participants were cutting down greenskins, trying to break through. And with every second, my confidence grew that they weren't expected to finish successfully.

Only one had made it to the midway point, but he was finally knocked off his horse by one orc's huge axe.

ATTENTION: The second group will begin in 20 seconds.

The "organizers" weren't going to dillydally. The corpses vanished in an instant, and new horses appeared at the start.

"There's Brun!" Russel shouted. "The second from that side!"

Oh yeah! Looking closer, I recognized the dark-haired head of our friend standing next to his horse.

"You think he has a chance?" Griselda asked excitedly.

"There's always a chance. But I think there's still more randomness here than in the other challenges."

"Maybe that's for the best!" Russel shouted.

"It's possible."

02... 01... 00...

The riders charged forward, and out came the greenskins.

"Let's go, Brun!!" Griselda shouted, nearly deafening me.

"Kill the bastards!" Russel shouted in my other ear.

I had to say, our friend was doing well. Of course, it was hard to see from where we were, but he killed the first three orcs without slowing down and managed to slip between the next two.

"Step on it!!"

Damn! He was really good! We had to remember that if we needed to send someone from battle and break through for backup, Brun was an excellent candidate. He could duck and evade the large axes while still taking down enemies with skill.

Three competitors from this group reached the midway point. Almost immediately, the guy on the track nearest us was knocked out of his saddle and quickly eliminated. Brun managed to fight off an axe blow and knocked the greenskin back with a kick to the head. It wasn't likely that the others caught this maneuver, but I'd already gotten two vision upgrades.

I also saw my friend deftly redirect his horse and run an orc over while simultaneously cutting down another.

Unfortunately, he didn't make it to the finish. He got caught about three-quarters of the way down the track.

"He's in first so far!" Russel turned away from the arena for a moment so he wouldn't see the bloody end of the fight.

"He has a chance, but let's not talk about it yet," I said, not wanting to bring bad luck.

That was how we ended up rooting for the orcs in the rest of the races. And they were worthy fighters. Until...

No one in the third group was able to surpass Brun, but the two from the fourth group did.

"Third..."

Russel's voice carried concern. He realized that the next group had the biggest advantage and could adopt the most successful tactics.

02... 01... 00...

The riders started.

"That's so unfair, damn it!" Russel suddenly shouted, pointing towards the arena. "They're avoiding fights."

He was right: six participants from the last group had immediately decided that they didn't need to kill any orcs, and the best strategy was just to break through.

Five of them reached the midway point. Two were then knocked down, but the other three managed to get a little further than Brun.

"Shit!" Russel kicked the wooden bench we hadn't sat down on once during all five races. "He's sixth now..."

"Come on, don't make such a fuss!" I smiled and clapped Russel on the shoulder. "They still haven't calculated the results for the other sets."

The results hadn't been announced. Everyone had found out I won my competition because the rest had been chopped up and sent to the respawn point. Everyone died right there. Brun had already hurried back to the arena from the respawn point, but I didn't have time to wait for him.

Please proceed to the arena.

Time until battle begins: 01 minute, 59 seconds.

This time, the system didn't show off and reorganize the arena. Instead, a 50-foot circle appeared in the middle of the field, fenced in by a shimmering barrier.

"Tear him up!" Russel said, grasping my hand.

"Good luck!" Griselda pressed her firm chest to me and stood on her tiptoes to kiss me on the lips.

"Thanks!" I smiled and walked down the steps.

My opponent got there first. He was a towering

human who exuded confidence. The crowd greeted him with an eruption of cheers. But when I appeared, the noise died down quickly. The spectators clearly hadn't expected to see the winner of another discipline in the finals.

Everyone understood that, regardless of the outcome of this battle, I would most likely win the overall prize. Which meant I'd get at least level 1 and level 2 elixirs, as well as a skill point. And that meant I'd quickly surpass all of them in terms of my development. They had reason to be envious, and most people were obviously going to root against me.

"Hi!" I waved to my opponent as I entered the circle.

"Hi to you, too!" The tall man grinned and scrutinized me. "You shoot well."

"I can cross-stitch, too," I muttered, but I stopped joking after that, since the weapon selection menu had appeared in front of me.

As always, I drew out the decision, but so did my opponent.

03... 02...

My usual sword and shield appeared in my hands, and the other guy chose... God damn it! A shield and a 10-foot spear. Well... I'd have chosen that too if I were level 3 with stabbing weapons.

Time until final battle: 19... 18... 17...

Fine, then. It wasn't pleasant, of course, but that was what a tournament was for: to see everyone. Or rather, to beat everyone. I looked at my opponent in a new light and realized he was physically quite strong. And if he was also, for example, level 6 or even 7 (which was, in theory, possible if he were the son of some rich man), then he might have some higher-level skills...

In any case, my strategy was clear: wait for the right moment to speed up and shred him like cabbage... Or hope he'd get sunstroke.

02... 01... 00...

We moved in a slow circle. My opponent tried to get a little closer, but I kept my distance.

"You like it?" He nodded at his spear.

"Sure. Throw it over, I'll take a closer look."

"Don't move, I'll bring it myself."

He was dripping confidence, and it wasn't just for show.

There were three things I needed to do here. Force him to try a strong blow, evade that, and then before he could try another, close the distance and deal my own. A single, fatal hit. Except he was probably well aware of it.

The stands were roaring at first, but the longer we continued to circle, the more the sounds turned to whistles and jeers. I'd like to see them when a level 1 upgrade elixir was at stake.

This was where the difference in age and background came into play. I really didn't give a shit about how my behavior looked from the outside, but my young, hot-headed opponent couldn't handle the pressure from the spectators as well and decided to leap into action.

He took a few quick steps forward and dealt the first blow. I blocked it with my shield. Another hit. And another block.

"Your spear is dull!" I grinned, trying to make my voice sound mocking.

I couldn't tell if it worked or not, but the blows started coming faster, and my opponent took another step closer.

I wondered how long he could swing his spear around for.

As if he'd read my mind, he gave me a very unpleasant surprise. Barely striking a blow, as he returned his weapon to its original position, he switch his spear and shield and jabbed again.

I hadn't expected that, and while I managed to hit the shaft with my sword, the tip tore through my jacket and left a deep scratch in my shoulder.

The crowd erupted, and my opponent flashed a predatory grin.

I pulled back and quickly reevaluated his capabilities. Not only was he level 3 with a spear, but he also seemed to be ambidextrous. Shit. At this rate, he'd give me scratches all over, and sooner or later he'd catch me and finish me off. Which meant I had to change my plan to exhaust him.

He closed in and started poking my shield with his spear again, waiting for the best moment for a real attack. It was risky, but I had to give it to him.

I parried a few more attacks, but didn't take another step back. My opponent immediately came closer and jabbed, then repeated the maneuver that had already worked once. I was expecting it and sped up a little earlier. Fuck! He also made adjustments to his strike, and even with evasive maneuvers, my jacket and side took damage.

Ignoring the pain, I jumped forward and dealt a powerful blow. At the last second, he deflected it, but then I used his technique and switched my sword and shield.

The blade flashed and pierced below his ribs. I immediately leapt back to avoid any accidents.

My opponent froze and looked down at the blood gushing from the hole in his stomach.

"Shit!" he mumbled, shocked, and fell to his knees.

The stands fell silent.

"Another time, my friend…"

I watched him without lowering my sword, and didn't even think of trying to finish him off. Even in the hands of a mortally wounded enemy, a spear was dangerous.

And he did throw the weapon, but I was ready for that and blocked it easily. Then I picked up my trophy, walked around my opponent, who'd fallen to the grass, and plunged his own spear into his heart.

Congratulations! You are the winner of the offensive weapon competition!

First place reward: A level 1 elixir of your choice. You can get your prize any time after you leave the tournament grounds.

I walked towards the stands to only occasional clapping, and half of that noise was made by my three friends.

From Brun's wide smile, I realized Brun had taken a prize place, too. But before I could even ask him about it, Griselda came flying up to me.

"Hooray!" she shouted, hanging herself around my neck and kissing me on the lips again.

Was I imagining it, or did I feel the tip of her tongue?

"Let's go."

Feeling uncomfortable with so many hostile eyes on me, I waved at the stairs leading away from the stands.

Once we were outside, I let my friends congratulate me, then turned to Brun.

"How'd you do?"

"Second place!" He laughed.

"Hell yeah!" I clapped him on the shoulder. "Let's hear the details! Five people got further than you."

"I know. They rolled out the statistics. First of all, the score was calculated not just on distance, but on damage dealt. And I got lucky. The ones who were ahead of me up to the finals couldn't manage. Well, aside from one."

"Ah. Well, anyway, a level 2 elixir is pretty cool!" I grasped his large hand. "What are you going to do with it?"

I wasn't asking for no reason. Brun's family had major money problems. His father had started a long-distance transportation business, but he didn't fully understand how to run it and didn't deliver the goods to his customers. In short, first his caravan was plundered, and then he was murdered. His debts fell to Brun's mother, two older sisters, and Brun himself, who had still been a child then.

He didn't like to talk about it, but from snippets here and there, I pieced together that the situation was rapidly getting worse. The interest was piling up, and the debt was growing. And the worst part was that some shady characters had started hanging around his mother, offering to fix the problem... if she gave them Brun's younger sisters.

"I'm gonna see what kind of level 2 elixirs cost the most at the market, then pick that one and sell it. I'll buy a level 3 for myself, and I'll settle my father's debts with the difference!" He was talking a mile a minute, and it was the first time I'd seen someone beaming with happiness like that.

"That's a great plan!" I clapped him on the shoulder again and turned to the others. "Well, shall we go?"

"Don't drag your feet!" Russel laughed. "You're planning to get drunk today, aren't you?!"

"That's why I was wondering why you were rooting for us like you were going to get the prize yourself," Brun said, and elbowed Russel in the side. "Alright. We can today!"

We activated the exit from the tournament grounds and almost got hit by a cart rushing off somewhere.

"Watch out, for fuck's sake!" Russel called out, but the man on the cart didn't turn around.

"There's something wrong," I said, indicating the people running all around. "Yesterday and this morning, things were much calmer."

"Excuse me!" Russel approached a plainly

dressed woman walking quickly in the direction of the city.

"Move it, kid!" She brushed him off.

"What the hell's going on?!"

Russel persisted and went around the tight-lipped woman to stand in her way.

"What happened?!"

"What rock did you just crawl out from under?!" she snapped, trying to go around the unexpected obstacle.

"We just came from the tower, lady!" Russel was starting to get anxious. "In the time you've spent arguing, you could have just told us what was going on."

"What is there to tell?!" Suddenly, she froze, as though deflated. "The orcs are storming the walls."

There was a pause, which the woman used to hurry away.

Griselda broke the silence. "We have to get to the guild."

"Yes. Go!" I nodded.

"What about you?"

"I'll come a little later."

"Let's go together..."

"Griselda!" I walked up to her, took her by the shoulders, and looked her in the eyes. "You're in charge. Run to the guild. If anyone asks about me, tell them I'm getting my reward and am on my way."

My friends exchanged glances, surprised at my tone, but decided not to argue, and soon ran off towards the guild.

The Last Portal Jumper

As for me, I had a ton of plans for the rest of
the day. And the first of them was to find out if the
Rogues' Guild was recruiting.

Chapter 18

THE ROGUES' GUILD was located at the other end of the Central City, and I'd have to run if I wanted to have even a theoretical chance of accomplishing everything I was hoping to.

I kept my head on a swivel, and I'd slow down whenever I heard an intriguing conversation.

"If you look from the walls, it's just green all the way to the horizon..."

"Thousands of catapults, and all the size of city hall! No, the size of the Champions' Guild!"

"The Ziranians sold to the orcs!"

"They've already broken through the wall in several places!"

"And they're all on elephants!"

I burst out laughing at the last sentence, because everyone know the orcs and local elephants had an intolerance to odor. And also that elephants didn't live on this continent.

But even despite a few obvious exaggerations, a discouraging picture emerged. The orcs really had gotten to the walls protecting the southwestern border of the empire of Shrinanth, and it seemed like there were a lot of them.

The border clearly couldn't be taken by storm. After all, they were expecting the enemy, and the walls had been built specifically for times like this. But all the same, the climate was putting pressure on people's psyches, and most importantly, a ton of soldiers were now being sent to the border, including guards. Which meant the already shitty situation of crime and robberies in the city was about to get worse.

I tried not to think about what would happen if the orcs did break through the walls. My task was to get as much done as possible before then, if it did happen.

The two high, round towers of the Rogues' Guild were getting closer, and... Fuck! I was human! Not to mention I was in the ranks of their competitors. I had to change my appearance immediately.

I didn't know any taverns suitable for that purpose in this area, but luckily, I quickly noticed a narrow alleyway between houses with no one around. I slipped into it, changed my skin and clothes, and came out the other side.

On the outside, the Rogues' Guild was essentially the same as the Champions' Guild. It had the same tall fence, and the buildings, as far as I could tell, were similar, except that they were rounder and less... severe. There were four guards at the gate. Naturally, there were hobbits here.

As far as I'd managed to find out, halflings made up at least 90% of the population here, the rest being humans. Dwarves considered joining the rogues to be beneath them. Though it was more likely a matter of their build and general lack of predisposition to this development path.

"Whaddya want?" one of the guards asked lazily.

"Here for admission!"

"Why didn't you show up at night?" he continued, casting an appraising look at me.

"I go to the brothel at night."

"Well, come back after the brothel." He didn't appreciate the joke.

"Come on, Vic," another hobbit said, joining the conversation. "The new period starts tomorrow. Kid might end up in the accelerated group, you never know."

Yes! That was what I was counting on. After the conflict, both guilds had reconsidered their training, and one of them probably took the idea from the other. Or maybe the practice was common and had been put to use before.

"Costs gold for everyone," Vic said, yawning, and held out his hand.

"How about this: if I hit that announcement on the notice board over there, you let me in for free."

"Even a champion could hit it from here..."

I'll back up 10 feet."

"Make it 15!"

Bastard.

"Okay!"

I backed up, activated Eagle Eye, and hurled a knife.

"Hey! You can't use a skill. Just throw it."

"Come on!" I couldn't resist. "Does your commander know you're taking level 5 recruits for a spin right on the verge of a war?"

"Quit screwing around, Vic!" the second guard said, the others nodding in unison.

"Hand on the ball," said the guard holding me up, displeasure clouding his face.

The ball flashed green so brightly that I was afraid my actual level would be revealed.

"20 yards ahead and 30 to the right."

The gate finally opened, and I went inside. Wow. It was like a clone. The arenas and training grounds. The canteen, the barracks, the instructional and administrative buildings. The only difference was that, instead of the sparse tall trees the champions had, there were mostly bushes here.

"Here for admission!" I told the guard at the entrance to the building.

"Ball color."

"Bright green!"

"First room."

Inside was also nearly identical, which wasn't surprising, since the system had created both guilds.

In the office was the first female hobbit I'd encountered here. I wondered if she'd also suggest I hit the wall or stand on my —

"Jump," she said, looking at me indifferently when I approached the desk.

Hm... Maybe we could skip the standard program of torturing the newbie? Besides, I was aiming for the special group.

I took a quick glance around, got my bearings, and...

Took a short run to jump onto the wall. I pushed off from a stone that was protruding slightly, then even harder off another one on the wall next to the door. I made a 360-degree turn in mid-air, adjust myself a little with my hands on the ceiling, then touched the third wall and stuck a perfect landing in front of the hobbit's desk.

"Did you come from the circus?"

Her voice and facial expression hadn't changed.

"Something like that," I mumbled, unable to come up with an original joke.

"You'll be separated into groups tomorrow morning at 6:00. Classes start at 7:00. You can leave today if you have things to attend to. Between tomorrow and the end of the course, leaving the campus is forbidden. You'll be housed and fed for free. We'll give you clothes. If you agree, sign here and hand over 100 gold."

Geez! Taking courses at both guilds clearly wouldn't have worked anyway. But having to be locked up here... I hadn't expected that. But, shit... I didn't have a choice. There was nowhere else I could get two skill points in a little over two weeks. And in light of recent events, time was now the most valuable resource.

I marked the paper and left the office as fast as possible, then left through the gate, accompanied by Vic's jokes.

* * *

I rushed back at full speed. I only stopped once to pop into a tavern and change back into a human.

I got to the gates of the Champions' Guild just after 9:00 PM. Luckily, my acquaintance Dickens was on guard duty tonight.

"Hey!" I said, still panting a little from my sprint. "I need to talk to Nikos. Is he inside?"

"Yeah," he said, raising his eyebrows. "What, did you find another 'item'?"

"Not exactly... It's personal, but really important."

"Well, I won't keep you, then. He's been in a meeting at the lecture hall for four hours already. I don't know how long it'll be. You get it."

"Thanks!" I gave him a sincere smile and went through the gate.

The bald warehouse assistant might have been right about reputation. It wasn't as useless as I'd thought. As long as I didn't lose it now.

Checking that the meeting was still going on in the lecture hall, I first stopped at my room and took everything valuable from the safe, then hurried to the canteen.

Of my friends, only Griselda was there, and judging by the way her face lit up, she'd been waiting for me. Well... Alright. We didn't have anything serious between us, but it still wouldn't be nice to just disappear.

"Finish what you needed to do?" she asked when I collapsed in the chair next to her.

"Not yet... Listen. I need 15 minutes to eat all this," I said, indicating the dishes on my tray. "There's a meeting going on in the lecture hall, and I need to catch Nikos after it. Can you help me?"

"Of course!" Griselda smiled warmly, which made me feel pretty awful. "You want me to keep an eye out for him?"

"Yes. If they finish their meeting, come back here. If they don't, I'll find you once I'm done. We can just sit and chat then."

"Okay!"

She stood up and brushed her hand over my shoulder as she left.

*　*　*

"They're still in there," Griselda said, turning to me as I came up behind her.

It was already completely dark.

She was sitting on the grass under a tall pine tree with sprawling branches not far from the entrance to the lecture hall. Okay... Since we were about to be separated for an unknown period of time, I could close the book on a few questions.

"Here."

I held out two clay mugs, then took out a pitcher of wine and filled them.

"What's this?" she asked, surprised.

"A wine purchased especially for this purpose. For the record, the seller assured me that the woman, meaning you, would like it so much that I'd definitely get lucky tonight."

"Haha! My aunt used to make this kind of wine, so I doubt you'll surprise me with anything."

"In this case, I also went to the pharmacy and bought a female arousal powder. That's also in there."

I raised my mug and took a sip of wine. It was pretty good, actually...

"So, what's the occasion?" Griselda hadn't taken her eyes off of my face.

"I have to leave for a little while."

"For how long?"

"Anywhere from a few days to a month."

"I see."

Griselda drained the contents of her mug in one gulp and turned back to me.

"And then?"

"Then I'll come back and continue training... If the orcs haven't made it over the city walls by then."

"The Central City doesn't have walls."

"Well... Yeah..." I emptied my mug as well and refilled them both. "Where will you go if the orcs make it here?"

"My mom, first. I'll send her and the kids to the border of the hobbits' land, further if needed, depending on whether the champions have any need for a low-ranking, useless fool like me."

She sighed and wrapped her arms around her knees.

"You're not useless."

I moved closer and hugged her.

"Yeah..." she whispered. "What about you?"

"I have something I need to do at the Sea Forest..."

"If I didn't know you, I'd think you'd gotten scared and decided to get away from me..."

"Well, it's a good think you know me."

"That's true." She gulped her wine again. "Except I don't know how you feel about me..."

There we go! The six million-dollar questions had begun.

"Griselda... I really like you. You're a beautiful woman, and my friend."

"You can stop there..." she said, and tried to stand up.

"Not yet, just listen." I held her back. "So, you're my friend. Today, when we were at the tavern during the tournament, I was thinking about you, about my feelings..."

She winced, barely perceptible.

"And... Then I thought some more, and more when I was coming here. And I realized that they don't matter. I can't commit myself to a relationship. I can't even afford to have feelings..."

"Why?" She turned to me, our faces almost touching.

"I might be drafted into the war at any moment. But I have a plan."

"A reliable one?" She grinned, repeating one of my favorite expressions.

"Like the clock on the that tower."

"Must be nice to be able to suppress emotions with reason..."

"Oh, don't start." I took my hand from her shoulder. "You're a pragmatist, too, and other than that time we were drunk, you never showed anything, either."

"I'm joking!" She smiled widely and held out her mug. "Refill me! I'm sitting here making fun of him, and he's almost changed his mind about leaving... He sits there making excuses! I like Brun better, anyway."

"You don't need to take it that far!" I smiled and took out the wine.

"Okay, okay, I'm done." She raised her mug and turned towards me again. "You... I like you, Ilya. You're strong, confident, and... strange. You're not like the others. It's... alluring. But you're right. Now isn't the time. But can we just have sex already?!"

"Uhh..."

"Kidding. Relax!"

She laughed loudly and turned to take a sip from her mug. But in the light of the two moons, something odd glimmered in her eyes.

We changed the subject and talked about the tournament, and 20 minutes later, the doors to the lecture hall opened as the meeting participants began to leave.

I recognized Nikos easily by his silhouette, but he was talking to someone, and I had to hang around in his peripheral view for a while to get his attention. Eventually, he nodded to indicate he'd seen me, and showed me five fingers.

It took 15 minutes for him to be free, though, because two more people came up to him. Finally, the champions dispersed, and Nikos came over to the tree I was standing under.

"These nighttime visits from students are more concerning than what we just discussed," he said in place of a greeting. "Go on, tell me you want to go fight the orcs at the wall. Then I'll know you're an idiot and have no problem letting you go."

"I have to go, but not to the wall."

"Then where?"

"I have something I need to do..."

"You'll fall behind the special group."

"I'll catch up."

"The training period will most likely be cut down even more. The intensity will be exorbitant. Even you can't — "

"I can. I'm not going on vacation."

Nikos examined me for a long time, then held out his hand.

"My personal code for mail is 12654-kri-8. Write me if there's an emergency."

"Thank you." I shook his large hand.

"If it weren't for your actions, I'd think you were running away."

"You're not the first one to tell me that to-night."

"I see."

The instructor smiled, turned around, and left. I went back to Griselda.

She was standing under the tree, twirling her empty mug in her hands.

"Are you leaving?"

"Yeah, I have to go..." I took a step forward and hugged her tightly. "Take care of yourself."

"You too!" She pulled back a little and put a hand on my cheek. "Maybe someday, I can fit into your plan."

Saying this, she stood on her tiptoes and kissed me on the lips... Then she quickly turned around and hurried away.

I watched her for a moment, then picked up my bag and ran to the gate. Of course, I'd have to say goodbye to Russel and Brun, but I wasn't finished with what I had to do today.

* * *

"You're becoming a frequent visitor!" Linda looked surprised as she opened the door. "You liked my bed that much?"

"I liked it a lot. But I'm here to let you know that I most likely won't be able to come for the next three weeks."

"Why?" Her eyes narrowed.

"Business."

"Don't tell me you've decided to — "

"I'm not going to fight the orcs at the wall, or run away to the hobbits or anywhere else. I'm going to grind on an individual program, but not here. Barring force maj... Unless circumstances prevent it, I'll be back in three weeks."

"Well, alright..." For the first time, the sorceress looked flustered. "If you need anything, my personal post office number is 71994-slv-2."

"I'll remember that!" I held out my hand. "Thanks."

"Come on... You're like family. We shared a damn bed."

To my surprise, she took a few steps forward and hugged me. She smelled like fresh forest air and flowers... And I very much wanted to take her hand, lead her to the bedroom, throw her down on the bed, and...

"Are you controlling my mind again?" I asked, not pulling away.

"No..."

"I have to go, then."

"To the brothel?"

"Yeah."

She pulled away and looked me intently in the eyes.

"You're wise beyond your years. Too far beyond."

"I have good genetics... And a good teacher."

I turned around, and first heard the sound of a bell, then the door closing and the lock turning.

The Last Portal Jumper

* * *

In one day, with some effort and the right words, I could definitely have slept with Griselda, and maybe even Linda... Except that both of those actions would have unpredictable consequences. Anyway, it didn't matter. I'd think about that when I left the Rogues' Guild, but for now...

For now, I needed to relax. And if I recalled correctly, there was an excellent, albeit expensive, place to do so nearby called Nocturnal Paradise. Quiet music, drinks, and dancing girls, any of which I could take to a room with me.

I didn't know if it would get to that point, but my eyes at least needed something nice to look at before I was voluntarily locked in a place where there were only hobbits for three weeks...

* * *

One week earlier

The senior investigator of the Department of Rumors had long since stopped caring about his beloved's expectations. He'd sent his last handwritten letter the day news arrived of the attack on veterans in the Central City.

Pinter had almost forgotten that he even had a beloved, since these days, he never saw anything outside of the administrative building.

New information was added to the developing

picture every hour, almost always destroying the theories built on the basis of the previous data. Command had already directly accused the Department of Rumors in general, and its "head jerkoff" in particular, of being a waste of government money. And the senior investigator was starting to believe that, too. He was especially discouraged by his last conversation with the Head Thinker four days earlier.

"Disaster?" Pinter had asked as he sat down.

"Completely," the Head Thinker said, pursing his lips.

His disproportionately large head shook, and his seven-fingered hand grasped for the glass of clear liquor.

He looks normal, the senior investigator caught himself thinking. *The bastard demanding reports from me is a much bigger freak. At least this one's smart.*

"A setup?" Pinter asked.

"I told you this could happen!"

The Head Thinker poured the liquor into his huge mouth and chased it, munching on a stinking fish head.

He was right. The mutant, being the brains of the organization, had warned more than once that if the public were to learn how they worked, the Department of Rumors would become easy prey for attackers, since they could just falsify the raw data.

"Taking this all into consideration," the Head Thinker started, "I can say that there is an equal probability that the situation has been organized by the Rogues' Guild, the champions, you, me, a council of hobbits, elves, our Emperor, direct descendants of outsiders, descendents of the executed members of the previous conspiracy, dwarves, residents of the southern continent, hunters looking for the dragon Zurantan, a large magical circle, a small magi — "

"I get your point..." Pinter grimaced and looked sadly at the empty glass of alcohol on the desk. "What are your recommendations?"

"Only count very fresh data."

...

With that, their "lovely" conversation had ended, and Pinter's head had been spinning with all the fresh data over the last four days. Even just Vinus's latest report.

Leaving out information about all kinds of bastards like the now former treasurer Ninx and the still (what a shock!) unsuccessful searches for the featureless creature, it also contained contained information that could be related to the current events.

The agent reported that she'd found a camp destroyed by magic near the edge of the Sea Forest, and had managed to find out from circumstantial, minute details that at least three dozen elves had lived there.

She'd also reported that monster activity was increasing in the area.

It seemed like nonsense (if you could call a band of elves in Shrinanth nonsense!). But still...

Without the most important element, this could be ignored.

That element being the brand-new order to remove half of Ninx's garrison from the fortress at the southern border and send them to the walls, where the number of orcs was growing by the day...

With some imagination, it was possible to see this pointing to a joint global sabotage by the orcs, hobbits, and elves.

Pinter crumpled up the report and tossed it into the trash.

Damn it! All he needed to top off this shit sundae was the second coming of the dragon Zurantan or the featureless creature! Well, at least the latter seemed to be going smoothly, and Vinus's speculations hadn't been confirmed.

Although, knowing his agent, Pinter had no doubt that as soon as she resolved all the priority issues, she'd immediately return to that investigation...

Chapter 19

THE FIRST STAGE OF SELECTION for the super group at the Rogues' Guild took place on an obstacle course. The most difficult one. It was basically the same as the one at the Champions' Guild, except that this one had more obstacles requiring dexterity to overcome. Like running across a long, narrow log or jumping from rope to rope.

"My name is Berins, and I will be the instructor for the special group," announced a trim, slender hobbit who looked to be somewhere between 40 and 60 (I'd have to learn how to estimate their age). "Those of you who complete three laps and meet the standard will be advanced to the next stage of selection. If you fall off the course, you'll need to start from the beginning. Any smartasses trying to cheat will be expelled from the guild. Questions?"

Not for now.

Until then, I hadn't been able to decide how to use the skill points I'd gotten for my second rank at the Champions' Guild and from the tournament. I didn't want to spend them on my human form, since I wouldn't be able to use it under any circumstances in the near future, and I was torn between three choices for the hobbit: Rain of Arrows, Dagger Fan, and Speed.

The first two looked much cooler, of course. The menu showed an image of me heroically striking 10 attacking orcs with one arrow... But that was just a fantasy. If I wanted to learn that, I'd also need to improve my shooting ability and throw a lot of points into a whole range of skills. Speed, on the other hand, had already proven useful as a human.

So I threw a skill point into that one, mentally waving my hairy hobbit hand, but saved the second point. Of course, I could always upgrade one of my current skills, but that wouldn't be much of a boost at the moment, so I'd let it be for now. You never knew when it might come in handy.

I'd also chosen my elixirs from the tournament, but hadn't used them yet. Firstly, they wouldn't help me right now, and secondly, the effects were unpredictable, so it would be better to drink them at night, before bed.

"Step up to the link one by one in a column," Berins commanded, not waiting for questions. When we'd lined up, he continued, "The first dozen of you will begin at my command at 10-second intervals. On your marks! Get set! Go!"

I was lucky, standing 12th in line. Since I had time, I thoroughly examined the course to see what the obstacles were and why they were the most difficult for special group candidates.

One by one, the hobbits set off. And frankly, it was a so-so show. Something I hadn't taken into account was that these were mostly newbies, averaging level 3 or 4, and without many skills. Well, it had been similar for me at first at the Champions' Guild, too, but in the last two weeks, I'd gotten used to hanging around with the best, and what I was seeing now, to be frank, did not impress me.

Most of the challengers were slow runners. On top of that, they were constantly falling and not landing jumps. Only two of them managed to complete the first lap without having to start over, and one of them couldn't keep up the pace and plunged from a rope into a huge puddle of mud right at the start of the second lap.

I mentally made a bet with myself for beer on whether the last halfling could go the distance perfectly. He got close. But in the end, he ran out of steam on the third lap and wasn't able to jump over a trench of water on the first try. He collected himself, though, and finished first, well ahead of the others.

Our group didn't even have to wait for everyone to finish. To save time, the five who were lagging way behind were removed from the competition after they finished the second lap.

"Second dozen! On your marks!" Berins shouted. "Get set. Go!"

I took of second, but after just 50 yards, I passed the hobbit in front of me and took first. The fact that I rarely used my hobbit skin did hinder me a little, but with my upgraded stats, abilities, and skills, I didn't have any real trouble completing the course. I leapt over ditches and other obstacles with ease, ran across narrow logs like they were wide roads, hopped along the ropes like... Well, like Katie.

On the second lap, I started catching up to the tail end of the previous group. And in the middle of the third, I passed the hobbit who'd started first again. I didn't need to use Speed, which was a good thing, really. No need to immediately reveal my high level. I'd stick to the story that I was already almost 19, and had trained hard to join the guild in my village.

Visilius had also made me learn the basic geography of the area around White Water, and we'd chosen a neighborhood where I'd been born in my fictional biography. There was always the possibility that I'd come across someone from there, but in that case, I could just say I didn't want to talk about it, or bring up my amnesia.

"You!" Berins pointed at me, then indicated the area where two halflings who'd met the requirements were standing. "Over there."

Well, alright then. I'd done well. We'd have to wait and see what was next.

* * *

What was next was archery, knife throwing, and a general fitness test ending with push-ups and sit-ups.

At the end, I made it easily into the top 20, landing myself in the special group. The rest were split up and sent for warm-ups, while we were sent to the lecture hall.

Before that, though, there was one unpleasant event.

"I did the obstacle course faster than half guys here!" a light-haired human said, outraged when the participants in the special group were announced and he wasn't one of them.

He was one of three humans in the group, and the only one who'd finished the first stage. And in the subsequent stages, he had actually surpassed at least two-thirds of the halflings.

"We evaluate based on a set of parameters," Berins said, brushing him off.

"And which of those did I stumble in?!"

Filled with righteous anger, he ran up to the instructor and towered over him.

"In the aggregate and in potential," the halfling said, craning his neck. "And if you raise your voice to me again and don't get back in order right this minute, consider yourself dismissed."

He had two options, and he chose the one I probably would have in his position, too. At this stage, before getting first rank, he still wasn't considered a rogue and could go to the Champions' Guild.

"Go to hell! Fucking racist!"

He spat on the ground and started to turn around, but wasn't able to. I didn't even see the moment of impact. The human suddenly buckled over, turned red, and fell into the grass.

"Dismissed," Berins said with disdain, then stepped over the would-be student and came up to our group.

What I'd seen bothered me both because of the injustice itself and because I couldn't intervene. My mind was only put at rest by the fact that if this was how humans were treated here, he really would be better off going to the champions. Besides, I hadn't seen any kind of racial segregation there.

Could that have anyhting to do with the recent unrest? In theory, no. The rogues and champions seemed to have settled matters. Although, as far as I knew from overheard snippets of conversation, the investigation into what had happened was still ongoing.

*　*　*

"Now then!" came Berins's already familiar bark to get our attention once we'd taken our seats in one of the lecture rooms. "You've shown a high level of basic training, so you have a chance to complete the accelerated program. Three days have been allocated for first rank. Two weeks for second rank. One more day for two exams. There will be no off days. Leaving the campus is forbidden. Questions?"

His tone and behavior did not invite inconsequential questions, but the essence was clear.

"You!!" Berins pointed at me. "Name?"

"Ilyenis!"

I tried out my pseudonym for the first time, and realized it didn't sound very good and I'd have to think of another.

"You're the prefect! Pass these out!"

A stack of papers appeared in his hands, evidently the schedule.

Damn it. I hadn't wanted to take on any extra obligations this time, or make friends. That would just distract me from my studies. But it seemed I'd stood out too much during selection.

"Ilyenis, your task is to beat the hell out of anyone who can't stick to the schedule and is late to classes," Berins continued as I handed out the papers. "If you can't handle that, I'll beat the hell out of you. Understood?"

"Yes."

"You have a minute to look over the schedule and get to class."

I looked it over.

06:30–08:30: Morning exercise (that sounded even worse than the champions' "warm-up")

08:30–09:30: Breakfast

09:30–10:50: Classes

11:00–15:00: Combat training

15:00–17:00: Lunch.

17:00–21:00: Grinding secondary abilities

(woah, that could be cool)

21:00–22:00: Dinner

22:00–23:00: Theory

Yes, someone was definitely stealing information from the other. Everything was so similar both generally in the length of the course and in the schedule. Well, so much the better. I wouldn't have to build a new routine.

*   *   *

Fortunately, Berins had made a major impression on the other members of the group, and no one wanted to risk being late, so my prefect duties ended with handing out the schedules.

The four-hour combat training was essentially the same as at the Champions' Guild. And with my superior stats, it was even too easy. I'd to take the initiative and make things harder for myself.

The theoretical part was also mostly the same, except that they hadn't dropped the "History of the Guild" subject like the champions had to focus on more practical courses. I also noticed that this history put a heavy emphasis on the fact that the Rogues' Guild was a hobbit guild.

"Why do we accept humans at all?" one of my classmates asked.

It looked to be the hobbit who'd done well in the first stage of selection. I couldn't be sure, though. In the same uniform, the young hobbits all looked to similar to me.

"Excellent question," the gray-haired instructor said. "It's a system directive. We have to take them. And mostly, they can't handle our requirements. They rarely get to third rank."

Hm... We'd seen that "inability" today. This was increasingly smacking of outright racism. Moreover, the instructor's explanations were met with smiles and approving nods from most of the hobbits. I didn't like it, but oh well. My goal was to get second rank in three weeks, get two skills, ideally complete two or three exclusive quests in the dungeon, and get the hell out of here.

Also, Sylvan was a rogue! And he was definitely high-ranking. I'd have to ask him how long this crap had been going on here. Had it started recently, or was he just so good that they couldn't expel him? Curious.

*　*　*

During the lunch break, I still didn't dare to drink the elixirs, so I kept practicing magic, waiting impatiently for the "grinding of secondary abilities" part of the schedule. My curiosity was so great that I got to class first, 15 minutes before it started.

When everyone had arrived, the instructor led us to a small, nondescript house by the wall that divided the guild's campus from the city. Except it turned out not to be a house at all, but the disguised entrance to the enormous dungeon.

Magical lamps were few and far between on the walls, so the gloom reigned.

"Here you will sharpen your rogue-specific

skills," Berins said in his usual manner as he walked along our ranks. "For now, that means Stealth, Quiet Steps, and Detection. At higher ranks, you'll work on Disguise, Attacking from the Shadows, and so on. Questions?"

Everyone was likely interested in how things would go from a technical perspective, but of course, no one asked. Speaking of which, though, I wondered if the Champions' Guild also had a dungeon like this. If so, what could you do there?

"This area is divided into various zones," Berins began. "Today, we'll be working on what's called Finders Keepers..."

A long explanation followed on the principles of grinding, and the longer I listened, the more I admired the awesome plan the rogue's had come up with.

Everything was run in game format.

For example, Finders Keepers involved all of us going into a huge labyrinth from different entrances. Then, using all possible means of remaining undetected, we had to search for and collect various artifacts. Extra points were given for detecting, sneaking up on, and hitting one of your competitors with your sword.

The labyrinth was set up so that the instructor could arrange it however he wanted and could control the number of traps and obstacles, or even release monsters into it. The last option hadn't been used on us yet, though.

"So... Questions?" Berins finished.

Definitely. I took a step forward.

"How do you account for the fact that one of us might have level 3 of Stealth, but others have level 2 or even 1? It'll be easier for the first, and the experience won't accumulate as fast."

"Good question!" Berins nodded. "Have you heard anything about mass spell artifacts?"

I had, but that had been in classes at the Champions' Guild after getting first rank, so I kept quiet.

"Those artifacts apply a spell in an area around you!" one of my classmates said, showing off his knowledge.

"Correct! Follow me."

Berins led us further into the dungeon and stopped next to a large, round stone covered in glowing runes.

"This is a stone that lowers stealth. Everyone who gets within 15 feet of it will have their stealth level lowered to 2. The effect lasts a little less than an hour."

"And if someone's only level 1?" another class-mate squeaked.

"If you're level 1, you'll stay level 1."

Interesting. It was a cursed stone, to put it simply. Well, a debuff stone. There were others like it that increased stats, as well as more powerful ones. They were regularly used in battle.

No one had any other questions, so following Berins's instructions, we ran around the perimeter of the labyrinth and took our starting positions.

"Enter!" Berins thundered, shaking the cave with the echo, and I walked into the darkness.

The black walls were sparsely covered with the familiar bluish moss, providing very little light. Although, with my twice upgraded vision, I could probably see better than most.

The task wasn't to just hide, but to search, so I tried not to drag my feet and moved briskly along the dark corridors, for which I was quickly rewarded. Something glimmered, barely noticeable at the edge of my vision. As I got closer, I noticed a small green pebble on the ground.

It was one of the items we were supposed to find and keep — or rather, take wherever we were told after we picked it up.

Pressing myself to the wall, I cautiously approached the item. I was right to be on my guard. When I'd gotten within 10 feet, it suddenly appeared to flicker. Which meant that, most likely, someone hidden had just passed in front of me. And *that* meant that this "someone" was taking my loot.

I raised my shortsword and took a couple steps forward. The stone flickered again, and I jumped forward and swung.

A hobbit appeared and collapsed silently to the ground. Silently because the swords we'd been given weren't regular swords. They were blunt, but they paralyzed the victim for 30 seconds. I leaned over and grabbed the loot that had fallen from the hobbit's hand.

Okay... Now, where was it supposed to go? Ah, over there!

A narrow beam of light struck the ceiling of the

cave about 60 feet away, apparently visible only to the person holding the stone. Now I just had to take it over there without running into someone on the way.

I clasped my hand around the stone so it wouldn't give me away with its light, pressed myself against the wall, and carefully moved forward... Then froze after just three feet. Something wasn't right. I looked at the seemingly empty dark corridor, but I felt confident that there was someone right in front of me.

I had enough experience, and the right abilities, to be able to trust my gut. And if I was right, whoever it was had seen the stone disappear, and was now lying in wait for me.

Of course, I could just swing blindly, but there was no guarantee that my opponent was within reach, and any sudden movement would give the game away...

I walked as slowly as I could towards the opposite wall of the six-foot-wide passageway, then pressed myself against that wall and started to sneak along it.

When I'd covered five feet, I sensed moreso than saw movement, and leapt to the side. Sparks flew from the wall as the sword struck the exact place I'd just been standing. And finally, I saw the silhouette of my opponent. The rest was a matter of technique. I was much better with a sword, and I got it out in a few seconds without even using Speed.

Then the immobilized hobbit fell to the ground.

I crouched and waited a few seconds for Stealth to activate again, then crawled to the other side of the corridor.

After another 30 seconds, I moved in the direction of the light again. This time, I made it. I felt someone nearby a few more times, and once, I even clearly saw a flash of a silhouette in the distance.

In the end, we spent all four hours playing combat hide-and-seek. And I had to admit, I really enjoyed it. There was no way to know how much it increased my stealth, but my abilities to detect unseen things and sense them from the smallest movements or even variations in the air definitely progressed.

Unfortunately, they wouldn't let us into other parts of the dungeon until we got second rank. I really wanted to see what the halflings had thought up there, and take advantage of it as much as possible. It was almost a shame I wouldn't be here for long.

Although... Today I'd stood out during selection, in combat training, and now in the dungeon. Maybe, if I kept going like this, I'd be able to get myself some kind of exclusive advanced program. That would be amazing. And made me want to see the local dungeon even more. There were rumors in the Champions' Guild that it was really fun... Though what constituted "fun," no one knew for sure. No problem — I'd find out for myself soon enough!

The Last Portal Jumper

*　*　*

In the evening on my first day, after a hearty dinner, I rushed to my room and did what I'd been thinking about all day: I drank the level 1 enhancement elixirs.

First the blue one that increased my mana reserve and expanded my magic channels, the same one Visilius had given me.

The effect was exactly the same as the first time. It felt like I could hear a train approaching from far away, and a few seconds later, it hit me full force.

I came to fairly quickly, but I couldn't drink the second elixir immediately. I decided to wait until the minor dizziness passed. To make the best use of my time, I started checking the changes to my magical strength.

I couldn't say it was too noticeable, but it seemed like I could move energy through my body more easily. On the other hand, it could just have been in my head.

As far as I understood from Linda, the potion would soon give me the ability to use stronger spells. I was already pretty good with the simple ones.

Once I felt completely normal again, it was time for the second elixir: Night Vision. An extremely useful thing to have, allowing you to see in the dark well. And as an added bonus, it allowed you to detect enemies more easily using Stealth and other forms of camouflage.

Just in case, I laid back down on the bed. I lifted the vial to my lips with gleeful anticipation and gulped down the bittersweet green liquid. Nothing happened for 30 seconds, but then my eyes got itchy, almost immediately followed by a solar flare in my head, and I passed out.

When I came to, the candle on the small table had burned down, and dawn was breaking. Actually...

I stood up from the bed and walked over to the window. I could see one of the two moons, and judging by its position, it wasn't even three in the morning.

Trying not to make noise, I went into the hallway and walked over to the window that looked out on the clocktower. Yep — it was 2:30 AM. In other words, it was still fully dark, but it felt like morning. Not as bright as daytime, but still... Very, very cool!

I'd have to get used to my new level of perception, of course. I would probably have trouble telling time at first, since I wouldn't notice when it was getting dark or light, but I figured I'd adjust quickly. Holy shit!

Visilius had been right. I had to get these elixirs, regardless of the cost, and sleep with or kill whoever I had to.

My new ability could cause trouble for the dungeon games, but since they equalized our stealth, they'd probably disable things like this, too.

The Last Portal Jumper

I went back to my room, extremely pleased, took out an egg I hadn't been planning to give Viza yet (I'd bought a supply of them in the city), and crashed into bed.

Chapter 20

AS I'D EXPECTED, Night Vision didn't cause any issues in the dungeon. As soon as I went down there, it was disabled. I remembered how I wasn't able to take out any weapons at the local police station, and I made another mental note not to get into fights in the enemy's territory.

The first three days were packed, though that was mainly because I spent all my free time in my room (identical to the one at the Champions' Guild, but with less furniture) talking to Viza and practicing magic.

I was getting much better at Healing, by the way. At first, fireballs would still sometimes shoot out, but I consciously put in less energy and practiced next to the washbasin, far away from anything flammable so I didn't set any fires. But I'd started to feel the difference in the flow of magic on the second day, and I didn't conjure any more accidental fire.

That was when I switched to real-life practice, on Linda's advice. And I cut my hand before using magic.

Where do you hide that all the time?!

Viza, almost fully-grown now, was sitting across from me, her fangs dripping with saliva. Her question was referring to the fact that I collected my blood, which was leaking from the cut, in a special vial, then hid it in my inventory.

"It's for Christmas!"

What?!

"For a special occasion," I clarified. "Do a really good job, like saving me in a critical situation, and then I'll give it to you."

Come on!! Give me a little sip now! Did you hear what that blind guy said? You have to spoil your pet, and it'll get new abilities!

"I don't think he meant my blood. So be patient. Look, we're going to the dungeon soon. You'll probably get a chance to make a difference there."

Cheapskate!

On the third day, once I was confident with Healing, I started alternating it with the fire shield so I could feel the energy flow even better and not screw up in a decisive moment.

* * *

Time flew, and exam day arrived.

And, of course, everything was familiar. The theoretical portion was done outside by the statue of the First Great Rogue. I answered 44 questions correctly out of 50 and was the first to run after the dungeon key.

Without waiting for anyone, I quickly checked my inventory and went confidently into the huge portal.

Do you want to enter the first level of the Rogues' Guild dungeon?

>>Yes

Select the area you want to transport to. Near/middle/far.

>>Far

ATTENTION: A new exclusive quest is available: Find the Sword of Fate.

Reward: A free body upgrade.

This offer will be active for one minute.

Accept/Decline

I accepted without hesitation, then looked around. Despite the fact that I could hear the dungeon was completely different, what I saw still surprised me, to put it mildly.

It wasn't a dungeon at all. The place reminded me more of an abandoned, overgrown ancient city. Or a labyrinth made of both relatively intact and half-destroyed walls of stone buildings of varying sizes and stories. One had holes for windows and doors, through which streets could be seen. Others were solid.

Dark clouds swirled over the city. It looked like rain was about to fall.

The enemies here were different, too. Currently, three five-foot-long green lizards with fangs and sweeping, spiny tails were scurrying at the edges of my vision. And in two window openings sat hairy monkeys with fangs just as terrible.

One of our lectures had given special attention to those brown monsters. They didn't drop anything useful, but they posed a serious danger. Firstly, because they could jump far and high, and secondly, because in addition to their sharp teeth, they also had long claws.

I started with those.

As soon as the defensive barrier fell, my bowstring snapped and the arrow plunged into the chest of the nearest monkey. The second one shrieked and leapt. I took a step to the side, slashing its head off in mid-air.

The lizards also came charging at me, but their behavior wasn't much different from the ants at the Champions' Guild dungeon, so I didn't have any trouble with them.

That seemed to be all of them. Was that how things worked here? Apparently, there were fewer monsters here overall than at the Champions' Guild, but the woolly brown beasts could leap out at any moment from any window or door. And if that happened behind your back, it could be dangerous.

Book Two

So then, what did I need to do? Walk quietly with Stealth, of course! It was a place created for grinding rogue-specific abilities.

My financial position allowed me to not bother with nonsense like collecting loot from common mobs. My time would be better spent using the same amount of effort to kill more monsters and grinding Stealth.

Though it'd be worth the time to examine the bushes, flowers, and vines creeping along the walls. Some of them contained potion ingredients that were in high demand and expensive.

The exclusive quest marker pointed the way, and I followed it. But soon enough, I realized that this place wasn't set up to be traversed quickly in a straight line. Walls constantly stood in my way, with no doors or windows, forcing me to go around them.

I also regularly came across fences seven to ten feet high that I had to climb over. In some places, there was no way through at all, and I had to sneak through a house, where the monkeys really liked to hide. But soon I was able to detect them ahead of time, by sound. They had a characteristic snort, and their claws clicked loudly on the stone when they moved.

I always killed the first leaping monster with an arrow. And the second, if I had time. The rest I took down with my sword or spear, since I really wanted to get to level 3 with those weapons, too.

I also had my shield out all the time and tried to catch the jumping beasts on it. Not that it was necessary, but level 3 in using a shield, if a few more conditions were met, would unlock an awesome higher-level champion ability: Battering Ram.

In general, I used as many abilities and tricks as I could, trying to get the most out of the time I had. Aside from the lizards and monkeys, there was another very unpleasant monster here: 15-foot-long snakes that camouflaged themselves in the vines. They weren't venomous, but their bite could cause considerable weakness that lasted almost an hour. And serious injury, of course, since their fangs were two inches long. They were also lightning fast.

My first encounter with one almost ended in disaster. I just barely managed to get my shield up at the last second, and the monster's head bashed into it with a thud. I immediately cut its head off and doubled my caution.

After that, whenever I saw something even remotely resembling that type of monster, I'd charge a fireball just in case. Of course, more often than not, the victim would be a harmless vine, but it was better to be safe than sorry, and I killed four of the slithering bastards that way.

Sometimes, large birds resembling owls would attack me. But that was rare, and Viza always alerted me to them. She usually struck them down, too (what she wouldn't do for a vial of blood). There was only one time her attack just wounded the bird and I had to finish the job with an arrow.

But she helped me with more than that. The

skill she'd gotten during our first trip to the Champions' Guild dungeon finally kicked in.

Stop! she shouted mentally, and she appeared on my shoulder.

She hadn't chosen the best time. I'd been trying to determine whether there was a snake in front of me or yet another vine.

I nearly jumped out of my skin from surprise and threw such a big fireball that it burned up every plant within a six-foot radius of the supposed threat. It turned out not to be a snake.

"What're you yelling for?!" I hissed, looking around to make sure my spell hadn't attracted the attention of any monsters.

My bad, I'm just so excited!

"Why?"

I smell a stash!

A stash? In the later lessons at the Champions' Guild, they'd told us that the system sometimes set up caches. They were hard to find, but they contained valuable loot. I didn't think they'd be on the first few levels of the dungeon, though. Either I hadn't gotten lucky before or they were only in the rogues' dungeon.

"Go get it!"

Get it? I can only show you where it is.

"Well, show me, then."

Viza led me to a nearby house, then waved her wing towards one of the corners.

It's over there, right under the ceiling. Behind the second stone from the top.

"The one with the crack?"

No, to the right of the corner.

I took out my spear and put out a hand to tap on the stone.

Yeah, that one.

"How do I get it?"

Fuck if I know. You're expecting a lot of a little bat.

Alright then... That "little bat" already had a wingspan of almost three feet, and when she was a considerable weight sitting on my shoulder.

I looked around, saw a couple large stones, and hauled them over to the corner. Soon I had a pretty nice pyramid. I clambered onto it and tried to slide the stone out. It didn't budge. I tried getting my fingers into the grout space for leverage. Nothing. I pulled out a sledgehammer (that I'd picked up just in case) and swung it with all my might. Damn it. Not even a tiny piece fell off the stone, which hinted that it was magical in nature.

The fireball hadn't attracted enemies, but the sound of the sledgehammer reverberated widely. Viza and I spent the next minute fighting off a dozen monkeys and lizards that came flying from all the window and door openings.

"Now then," I mumbled, wiping my sword on the hair of the last decapitated monkey. "There has to be another way to open this thing."

Such as?

"Such as saying a password or tugging on some other shit in this room."

Can I make a joke?

"If it's about shit, let's not."

Well, if it's not shit you're after, then tug on that rope over there.

"What rope?"

Over there, the blue one glowing in the other corner.

"I don't see it."

You need better vision. Motherfucker!

She'd added that last part because she'd flown over to the right corner, but had miscalculated, snagged a wing, and crashed into the wall at full force.

It's all your fault. Heal me!

I healed her and looked at the area she'd hit.

"I still don't see shit."

Lift me up.

I scooped Viza up carefully and held her up. Her wings got in her way, but after a little tinkering, she was able to latch her tiny claws onto something I couldn't see.

Pull down.

With an odd feeling like I'd won a giveaway, I carefully pulled the wight down.

There was a loud click, and the stone I'd been picking and hammering at unsuccessfully vanished, leaving an empty space with something shimmering inside.

Fascinating. I knew caches could be found if you had certain high-level skills, abilities, or spells. But the fact that the mechanisms that opened them could also be invisible was a revelation for me. Good thing I had Viza with me!

"Seems like your radius of detection is about

12 feet, then?"

Something like that. Progress is slow-going without blood... Anyway, what're you standing there for? Don't you want to know what's in there?

Of course I did. I climbed up the pyramid of stones and stuck a hand into the crevice, hoping there wasn't an unpleasant surprise like a venomous snake waiting. All clear. There was a little ring in the stash. As soon as I picked it up, the blue glow around it went out, and it looked completely plain. Just cheap silver... What about its properties?

Small Trickster's Ring. Rogue branch skill efficiency: +5%.

Hm... Not bad. If I was remembering correctly, this item cost over 300,000 gold at the market. Considering I had 10 fingers, it was absolutely beautiful. Of course, this was one of those artifacts you'd be the first to lose if you found yourself getting hit on the head in a dark alley.

I thought about the two burnt corpses I'd left on the street the night the veterans were attacked. They'd probably had better rings... It was a shame I'd been in no condition to go poking around in burnt flesh.

I put the new item on, pleased.

"If you find more like this, I'll give you the blood!" I winked at Viza.

Cheapskate! she shouted, and went back into my inventory.

Chuckling to myself, I checked to make sure there were no more trinkets in the stash, then continued on my way.

*　*　*

I hadn't bothered to dissect the monsters, and useful plants were rare. In the two hours it took me to get to the exclusive quest location, I only picked three red flowers that looked like poppy (100 gold each) and 30 plum-like fruits that grew on shrubs (60 gold each).

Stage 1: Find the palace. Complete.
Stage 2: Find the Sword of Fate.
Do you want to enter?
Yes/No

A portal opened in the wall of a fairly large building that, despite its size, bore no resemblance to a palace. But there was magic here, right? It could be much bigger on the inside.

I looked at the skill point I'd been holding onto, and decided to keep it still.

I wondered if there were hordes of monsters or a boss inside. It could be either one, but in any case, it wasn't likely to be more of a challenge than the scarab. And I'd leveled up a lot since that encounter. So as I entered the portal, if I was nervous at all, it was minor.

The inside of the palace did, in fact, turn out to be bigger, and perhaps at some point had belonged to a sultan. There were thick carved columns, a marble slab floor, a narrow staircase leading to the second floor, and long, dark corridors stretching out on two sides. I assumed they were dark anyway, since I could see through them easily with my night vision.

Although... I couldn't rule out the possibility that it was nighttime in the city I'd just been walking through for the last two hours. It was just that time of day didn't matter as much for me now. Though that didn't seem likely. Considering the monkeys, snakes, and eagles, that would be a bit much for small hobbits with only first rank or below.

Anyway, it was time to get started.

A sword and shield appeared in my hands. Assuming the real fun would be upstairs, I started on the ground floor and turned into the left corridor.

What could be living in an ancient, abandoned magical palace? Anything, according to our classes. Even eagles, as paradoxical as it might seem. But I got the sense that there'd be something a little more interesting here, like... MUMMIES!

That was what suddenly leapt out from the room I'd been walking towards on the left-hand side.

A desiccated, seven-foot-tall skeletal frame wrapped in something like yellowed bandages. A classic mummy, basically.

It took me a lot of effort not to leap back. The mummy was standing 10 feet away from me, twisting its head around in an attempt to figure out where I was.

Well, if we were going to grind, then let's grind. The bow that had appeared in my hand was replaced with a spear. Trying not to make a sound, I took a cautious step forward. And another. And another.

The mummy flinched and slowly turned towards me. I couldn't wait any longer for it to make a move, so I thrust my spear forward, plunging it into its bandaged face.

The body fell silently to the marble floor and crumbled into dust.

That was it. Big deal! It looked spooky, but died from one —

I heard footsteps behind me and turned around. Holy shit!

At least 15 more mummies were racing my way. I heard another sound. This time, on the other side. I looked, already knowing what I'd see. An equal number of enemies was rushing towards me from that side.

I should have been scared or even shit myself, but instead, as often happened in critical moments, I was overcome with a wave of euphoria and excitement. Without hesitation, I launched a huge fireball at one of the rapidly closing in groups and ducked into the room the first mummy had jumped out of.

It turned out to be a crypt with an open sarcophagus. Luckily, it was the only one.

I stood next to it and equipped my bow and a fire arrow, then felt a familiar weight on my shoulder and the touch of a membranous wing on the back of my head.

"If I survive, the blood is yours."

Deal!

Viza's deafening shriek filled the crypt, and she pushed off from my shoulder. As soon as she did, I shot the first mummy to appear in the head.

Chapter 21

VIZA SPLIT THE NEXT TWO IN HALF and disappeared into the corridor. No new enemies appeared from the direction she'd flown in, but they kept pouring in nonstop from the other side. Though the first mummies were either on fire or smoldering, so they couldn't move as quickly, and I shot three of them in the head without issue.

Then I launched another fireball and backed up to the wall furthest from the door, since the smoke was making it hard to see. It wasn't much better at the back, and I crouched down so I could at least see the legs of any approaching monsters. There was no point shooting them anywhere but the head; the mummies didn't feel pain. So I aimed for the approximate location of their heads.

About one in three arrows hit the mark, which wouldn't have been much help if it weren't for the smoke, which, as it turned out, was also hindering the enemies. When they ran in, they couldn't charge straight at me, but had to wander around the room.

I kept shooting, and when two monsters got too close, I grabbed my sword and swung in a wide arc to hit both. One collapsed. The other just got thrown off balance, but stayed on its feet.

Realizing that things would depend more on luck and on Viza, I hurled a fireball as big as I could make towards the part of the room where the groaning of the mummies was loudest of all, then just started blindly waving my sword and hoping it made contact.

The sword whistled through the air, the smoke burned my eyes and lungs, and the monsters kept screaming and wheezing. Which actually helped me figure out where to swing my sword. A few times, increased resistance showed me the blade had hit its target.

But I still missed one bastard. It was unexpectedly quiet and able to sneak along the wall unnoticed. Its head was smoldering from a fireball, though, which apparently affected its "vision." So, when it leapt from the black smoke, it grabbed me not by the throat, but by the shoulder.

"Ah, fuck!"

I whipped around and hit it in the face with my forehead. Its ancient bones had clearly decayed quite a bit. There was a crunch, and the mummy dropped to the floor with a cracked skull.

My sword appeared in my hands again, and

right on time — a growl came from far too close. I fought off the attacker and sliced it in two.

I didn't hear any more sounds, but I kept going anyway, closing my eyes against the smoke and swinging my sword right and left relentlessly.

That's all of 'em! You won!

"Are you sure?!" I shouted, coughing immediately.

Yeah, definitely! Cast some Healing and go along the wall back to the main hall. The smoke's not as bad there.

I followed Viza's wise advice and, got out of the room as fast as I could, feeling much better. I somehow made it to the entrance hall, collapsed to the floor, and cast Healing three more times.

The very simple healing spell mainly helped treat injuries. But if you directed it right and used a lot of mana, it could also partially reduce other negative effects. I was able to see fairly well again after a minute, and my lungs were no longer burning. But I still felt awful and seriously nauseated, possibly from using too much mana, so before I moved on, I had to rest for a while.

"Do you know how many more there are here?" I wheezed out, coughing again.

What, that wasn't enough for you?

Viza flew over and sat on the floor next to me.

"I have... But we still have to kill them all, don't we?"

Relax. There's no one else here.

"You're sure?!" I looked into her small black eyes.

Guaranteed!

"Why the hell is this place so big if all the monsters were in one place?"

No freebies.

I thought I heard sarcasm in Viza's thought.

I think there were a set number of those assholes here. But the system knew your level and placed them in the least convenient way.

Okay... That sounded logical. And if I'd been in any shape to think, I would have come to the same conclusion.

"So, I could sleep here?"

Yeah. But don't forget that classes start tomorrow, and there are still a bunch of monsters.

"Wake me up in an hour?"

Sure. And you're forgetting something.

What now? Ah...

The vial of blood appeared in my palm. Viza immediately flew onto my stomach and put her face close.

Smiling, I pulled out the cork and spilled the contents right into her open, toothy mouth. Then I drank an antidote potion and let my exhaustion win and take me to dreamland...

*   *   *

Dreams never came. It seemed to me like Viza was smacking my face with her wing after I'd barely closed my eyes.

Get up!! Tanks in the city!

I leapt up, grabbing my sword and shield, and

looked around.

The fuck did she mean, tanks?!

You can thank me now.

Viza flew in a circle just under the ceiling, then landed on my shoulder.

Meanwhile, I'd more or less recovered and remembered who and where I was. I almost felt back to normal.

The smoke had completely dissipated, and the palace had taken on the deceptively peaceful look I'd first encountered when I came through the portal.

"You check for stashes?"

Yep. Nada.

Oh well. Though to be sure, I'd still have to check all the nooks and crannies. But first, I had to eat. The healing and potion had completely fixed the nausea and injuries, but the fierce hunger that came after such a crazy battle and the wild expenditure of magic energy hadn't been satisfied.

I spent the next 20 minutes fighting hard against it, and probably set a personal record for food eaten in one sitting. Well, so what? Viza had said there were no enemies here. And I'd digest as I walked around here.

After lunch, it took some effort to get up. First, I turned into the corridor where all the mummies had been. About half of the bodies were lying in the room. They were either burnt or sliced up. But the bodies in the corridor had clear traces of Viza's attacks. And I had to admit, she was a lot neater than I was, and killed mostly by tearing the monsters' heads off.

We'd handled an approximately equal number of monsters, but I was troubled by the thought that if I'd been here alone, I most likely wouldn't have survived. For some reason, this time the system decided to go all out.

Why could that be? Any reason, really, starting with it noticing my pet and ending with the fact that, when choosing a level of difficulty, it had considered my free body upgrades, skills in totality, and the elixirs I'd drunk. Or, it could be that what Visilius had mentioned was already starting: the system sensed something special in me.

Well, in any case, it was a good lesson. I knew I still had to accept any exclusive dungeon quests I was given, but I'd be more careful from now on. I'd gotten too relaxed lately.

I went through all the rooms on the first floor as I mulled this over, and finding nothing, I took the wide staircase to the second floor.

There was one large hall upstairs, and right in the center was a three-foot-tall golden pedestal. On a special stand, a short, bright green sword shone, clearly made for a halfling.

Shame it was only a quest item.

I walked up to the pedestal and took the weapon, not without some trepidation.

Congratulations! Exclusive quest: Find the Sword of Fate. Complete.

Your stamina has increased.

You are now the owner of an item that both the Rogues' Guild and Champions' Guild are in-

terested in. You can give it to them for a big reward and reputation, or keep it yourself.

Congratulations! You've reached level 11.

Your luck has increased.

You've received one skill point.

I paused and reread the system message a few times. What the hell was this? I'd never heard of anything like it before. Maybe the complexity was higher precisely because it was a nonstandard quest? Well, what did it do?

Sword of Fate: Level equal to that of the owner. The size changes depending on the owner's race. +1% to skill strength and efficiency for each level.

What the fuck?

I had the burning desire to turn into a human and see if the sword would actually change, but I couldn't do that. The dungeon might reject it and kick me out or even kill me. It wasn't necessary, anyway. There was no reason not to believe the description.

This sword was clearly inferior to the level 10 Mercenary Sword for now. Except that one only increased champion skills, and every level upgrade cost a ton of money. But this sword worked for any race and class, and would get stronger for free.

As far as I knew, items over level 15 could only be wielded by elite, and very rich, warriors. And level 20 items were rare throughout the entire kingdom. But I was holding one in my hands, and a two-for-one at that, both for champions and rogues...

It was so incredible that it was hard to wrap my mind around. But that didn't matter.

The main question was: what the hell was it doing here? On the first level of the Rogues' Guild dungeon? The exact thing I needed most...

There was only one answer: the system had singled me out, and as a final test had given me a fatally dangerous quest that I could only complete if I had superpowers. And I'd completed it...

So, what next? Whatever I wanted. I just had to hope that the system knew my level and wouldn't throw anything supernatural at me for now, but would let me grow. Especially since global events were heating up in Shrinanth.

Hm... Giving this treasure to someone was an amusing suggestion. Give it away, come on... Ha! It wasn't the key to an apartment where lots of money was hidden. Well... Of course I was keeping it! There was nothing in the message about protective runes that would give the game away. But I had to remember that if I was found out, my head would roll in an instant.

"What do you think?" I turned my head to look at Viza, who was sitting on my shoulder.

You could sell it and use the money to buy yourself a count's title and land with 10,000 servants...

"And drink their blood all my life?

Just a suggestion.

"No... I'm not going to look a gift horse in the mouth."

Then why'd you ask?

"I'm just so worked up, it was hard to hold it

in."

I put the sword away, looked around the hall just in case, and went back down the stairs. It was only when I put my foot on the first step that I remembered I'd also gotten level 11. Hm... I'd figure out how to use my skill points later, after I'd gotten another one for getting first rank in the Rogues' Guild.

*   *   *

I took my time getting back. I couldn't leave the guild's campus anyway. Plus, there were monsters here, albeit weak ones, and the experience was minimal, but still a trickle.

Viza seemed to get into the spirit of things, or she'd just decided to actively grind, and for the first time, she took it upon herself to actively help me. She acted both as a scout and a full-fledged combat unit.

In the end, five hours later, we'd destroyed 300 monsters. We didn't find any more stashes, though.

"Alright, I'm done," I mumbled, barely able to lift my arm to cut the head off another lizard. "Let's go back."

*   *   *

The medics met me at the entrance and, surprised I didn't need any help, told me where to get the reward. The assistant was in the same room as at the Champions' Guild.

"Let's have it!" the wrinkled, aging hobbit said in place of a greeting.

"Here."

I dumped out a dozen flowers, just under a hundred plums, and two rare vegetables the size of an average beet.

"Good!" The hobbit considered the loot. "What else?"

"That's it," I said, spreading my hands. "I got carried away and forgot to dissect the bodies."

"If you took some, just say that. It's not forbidden. Hand over your belt."

I gave him the belt with the experience counter. Oh, shit! If it showed the experience for the exclusive quest, that could raise some unpleasant questions... Ah, hell with it. I'd talk my way out of it. At the end of the day, selling loot outside the guild wasn't actually prohibited. And as rogues, it was pretty much approved. The ability to earn money was valued here more than with the champions.

The hobbit attached the belt to the ball. Then he took it off, turned it around in his hands, and attached it again. After which he knocked it on the table and tried again.

"Did I break it?" I asked as innocently as possible.

The halfling jumped and stared at me. It looked like his eye twitched.

"How many monsters did you kill?"

"I wasn't really counting... Maybe 400?"

Now his eye was definitely twitching.

"In the far area?"

"Yeah."

"Hand on the ball!"

Congratulations! You've received First Rank in the Rogues' Guild.

You've received a skill point.

Without saying another word, the assistant counted out my share of gold for the flowers and fruit, then nodded at the door, showing me I was dismissed.

As I left, I was well aware that the matter of my performance in the dungeon was far from over.

* * *

I was right. As soon as I finished dinner, Berins came into the canteen. He scanned the sprinkling of diners, saw me, and waved for me to follow him.

Ten minutes later, we were sitting in his office. From what I could tell based on his sharp temper over the last three days, there were rarely students here. The office also revealed that he really loved himself. Every item, from the chairs to the inkwell, was expensive and clearly custom-made. Absolutely everything had an image of crossed daggers on it, the logo of the Rogues' Guild. On top of that, the long shelves held a variety of trophies, statuettes, pictures in gold frames, and other things that were clearly rewards for some achievement or another.

"Where are you from?" Berins said right off the bat.

My sixth sense told me that, in this case, the story Visilius and I had thought up wouldn't work. This acerbic man wouldn't be satisfied with a vague answer about a remote village in a faraway land. I had to set boundaries right away and see if it landed. Either he'd accept it, or I'd get out of here in a flash.

"I'm the illegitimate child of a... member of the Rogues' Guild." I inserted the pause to leave space for the word "high-ranking" to be implied. "He prepared me especially for admittance. I can't say anything more."

"You killed over 400 monsters in eight hours. That tells me you're at very high level for your age, have good artifacts, and you've used a lot of enhancement elixirs."

Berins wasn't asking. He was stating facts. Just in case, I exhaled and nodded in confirmation.

"And you've been actively trying to stand out from the very beginning. Why?"

An important question. There was clearly something shady here, and they might be afraid someone was planted. That was probably why they filtered out humans as much as they did. But I was a hobbit, and I had a pretty good answer.

"I want to become a great warrior in the shortest amount of time."

I leaned forward and lowered my voice.

"I can't sit around here for years with this weaklings."

"Your skills will lag behind..." Berins said,

squinting.

"They haven't so far. I even have a solid supply. I've done all this in less than a year with elixirs, regen artifacts, and magic. I've been training for 18 hours a day and plan to keep doing so."

When I finished talking, I stood up, my face proud. I knew he could sense evasion and falsehood in my words. But he definitely wouldn't catch what they were, especially since the general sentiment and some of what I'd said were true. Most likely, he was thinking that I was a single-minded, brazen, self-centered natural (read: douchebag). I hoped they needed people like that.

Berins's face became even more pensive. He looked at me for a long time, drumming his hairy fingers on the top of the desk.

"And why do you want all that?" he finally asked, crossing his arms over his chest.

"What do you mean?" I asked, surprised. "I want to be the strongest hobbit ever!"

Another pause, though I could see from his face that he liked my answer.

"But that's not your ultimate goal, is it?"

I knew what he meant, but the character I was putting on likely wouldn't. Sorry, Berins, I'd have to spoon-feed it to you.

"Meaning what? If you mean money, that's not — "

"To hell with money." He screwed up his face.

"I don't have any trouble with women, ei — "

"Damn it!" Berins shouted. "Alright, I understand. I'll try to think of something to speed up your progress. We need strong, driven hobbits. Dismissed."

He didn't shake my hand.

I left the office. Once I was outside, I let myself smile. Everything had gone to plan, which was indirectly confirmed by the bell I'd heard during our conversation. It couldn't be anything other than leveling up my ability to lie. I'd shown myself to be strong and stubborn, but not very smart. And theoretically...

Willing to bet my house that I'd have a friend here in the very near future. More specifically, a "friend" sent by a wise mentor.

Chapter 22

WHEN I WOKE UP THE NEXT MORNING, it took me a minute to remember how I'd made it to bed. Oh, shit! The empty vial on the floor told me I'd managed to find the strength to rub ointment onto my exhausted muscles. That I felt incredible confirmed it. Well done, me!

Okay, I still had 15 minutes. I had to decide what to do with the three skill points I'd accrued.

I looked at what I could level up.

Cat Burglar (level 1, passive).
Eagle Eye (level 1, active).
Acrobatics (level 1, passive).
Quick Reflexes (level 1, passive).
Deft Legs (level 1, passive).
Deft Arms (level 2, passive).
Perfect Balance (level 3, passive).

Speed (level 1, active).
Soft Landing (level 0, passive).
Rain of Arrows (level 0, active).
Dagger Fan (level 0, active).

There was something to think about here. All my passive skills had been helpful. They made me permanently stronger. But in battles, the most useful skills were active, like Eagle Eye and Speed. Rain of Arrows and Dagger Fan would be especially good in battles with a group of enemies.

And I couldn't forget that the camouflage branch would unlock soon... Most of the skills on that branch required level 3 of Acrobatics. Well, why not level that one up? It made you more acutely tuned into your senses and gave you better control of your body, which indirectly influenced everything from battles and running to knife throwing and archery.

Okay. I'd leave the camouflage branch for later. That would most likely be the main reason for me to use my hobbit form. But first, I had to set myself up well for it. So I'd throw two points into Acrobatics, and use the last one for Rain of Arrows. I likely wouldn't be able to use it very effectively, but at least I could learn about it, and I'd be able to practice.

That was what I did. Then I quickly washed up and ran to morning "warm-ups."

Book Two

* * *

Berins acted like nothing had happened, and classes went as usual. But at breakfast, my suspicions were confirmed. A friend appeared. A female friend, specifically.

After the previous day's huge energy expenditure and level up, my appetite was record-breaking, and I arranged my tray to fit as many plates next to each other as possible, taking a separate tray for two mugs of kombucha. As I was carrying them to sit down, I noticed a young hobbit sitting at my table.

She was probably pretty for a hobbit (otherwise, why would she have been sent?), but not my type. She was small (like all of us) and plump, with a sizeable chest, round face, gray eyes, and light hair woven into a thick braid. Basically, nothing special.

I wasn't racist, of course... But I still couldn't imagine her in my bed. Well, maybe for an elixir, and even then, I'd have to get pretty drunk first.

"Hi!" I said as I sat at the table. "I'm Ilyenis."

"Hey! I'm Brenna," she replied, smiling in what I assumed was meant to be a seductive way.

Since I wasn't looking for friends, I wasn't going to take the initiative. I just pulled plate with four large chicken legs towards me and bit into the first one, almost taking a piece of bone with the meat.

"Berins asked me to help you."

I nearly choked, and had to wash down the piece of chicken with kombucha. I'd expected the introduction to be much less direct. Alright then. The main thing was just to remember that I was a wealthy, self-centered fool.

"You?" I shot her a doubtful look. "And what is it you can help me with?"

"Pretty much everything." The genial expression remained plastered on her face. "I'm a fourth-rank rogue. And I've already completed a year of fifth-rank studies."

As proof, she put out her palm and showed me the crossed daggers, glowing orange.

Fuck, I was going to get myself caught someday for not being able to determine how old hobbits were. On the other hand, it was often impossible to figure out whether human women were 80 or 30, too. Anyway, my new friend had to be at least 21, possibly older.

"You look young," I said, trying to smooth things over. "But I still don't understand how you can help me. Classes are taking up all my time."

"Are they?" Brenna said with a laugh. "Berins said you train for 18 hours a day. What you're saying now somehow contradicts that."

I lowered my voice so we wouldn't be overheard at the neighboring tables. "I don't have elixirs and magic now. Anyway, enough beating around the bush. What are you offering? I'll do anything to level up."

"We-e-ll," she said, drawing out the word, "that's a completely different matter!" She grabbed a carrot from one of my plates and bit into it noisily. "Here's the plan..."

The plan was sensible, and I was immediately invested.

I was dismissed from warm-ups in favor of independent training, as well as from all theory classes. Brenna would have to compensate me for the latter during our lunches together. And for all of my free time, as well as a few hours before bed, she'd tighten up the skills I was lagging in, but which were crucial if I wanted to gain ranks quickly.

"When do we start?" I asked, pushing the last empty plate away and finally feeling my hunger subside.

"Right now, of course." She grinned and stood up. "Our task is to make you eat even more at lunch. By the way, today's combat training will also be with me."

* * *

We headed for the furthest end of the arena, where my individual training with a high-ranking rogue would take place. We were allowed into one of the special pavilions without any questions. It appeared to be a round, isolated room about 30 feet across, its wooden walls covered with weapons of various kinds, as well as all kinds of gadgets and targets.

"Which skills do you have level 3 in?"

For the first time, the smile left her face, leaving a woman focused on business in front of me. But the plumpness preventing me from taking her seriously hadn't gone anywhere.

"Archery, using slashing and stabbing weapons, and Stealth. Maybe something else. I'm not completely sure."

"Well, let's find out." Brenna walked over to the wall will the dull training weapons and shields. "Take everything and put it into your inventory. You'll take out what you need on my command."

I did as she said, and soon we were facing each other in the center of the pavilion.

"Spear," she commanded. "Attack however you please. Your goal is to hit me. Don't hold back, and don't be afraid of hurting me."

"Okay."

I raised the spear and thrust it at her side. Her shield easily repelled my attack.

"I said, don't hold back!" Brenna growled. "If that's all you've got, I'll tell Berins to remove you from the special group."

To set the tone, she took out her own spear and drove it at my shoulder with all her strength. The long practices with Nikos were the only reason I was able to dodge, and the blunt end of the spear just grazed my jacket.

"Come on!"

I pulled myself together and started stabbing as hard and fast as I could. I didn't hit her once.

"Alright! Do the same with your left hand."

By this point, I was completely wrapped up in the thrill of the moment, no longer hitting from one place, but jumping like there was a fire under my ass, making deceptive maneuvers and being as crafty as possible.

In the end, I managed to land two (out of fuck knows how many attempts) glancing blows.

"Sword!" Brenna commanded, apparently deciding to see if I could do *something* at least.

I convinced her, hitting her regularly, and twice almost causing serious injuries.

"Okay, I believe you've got level 3 there," she said, rubbing healing ointment on her right arm with a barely perceptible smile.

Then she started laying into me with all kinds of different weapons, and I tried to defend, frequently unsuccessful.

After that, we switched to knives. We started with knife fighting, and then I threw them at the targets.

Later, I climbed the wall and jumped around on it using protruding rods and hooks, as well as almost unnoticeable ridges and recesses.

She tested all my capabilities, which turned out to be meager in comparison to hers. By my estimation, she had to be at least level 15. And most of her skills were level 4. Just what I needed in a sparring partner and personal tutor.

"Not too bad, overall" giving her assessment once we'd put the weapons back on their stands. "Your endurance is especially impressive. That'll help you level up the rest quickly. But I still don't understand how you killed so many monsters yesterday."

Well, yeah. She didn't know about my magic or Viza. I had to take the opportunity to tell a small lie. Berins and anyone else at a high level would have caught on, but it should slide past her.

"I used a few potions that temporarily increased my dexterity, strength, and stamina. I wanted to take advantage of the moment and get more experience."

"Ah," she said, drawing out the word. I thought I saw something like animosity pass over her face.

It was quite possible. I was playing the role of a driven hobbit, but still a silver-spooner. And a fabulously rich one at that. One who had an unfair advantage against the others.

Of course, if that really were my background, I'd eventually lose that advantage, and grinding abilities and skills would be the top priority. No one had enough money to drink elixirs all their life.

"Alright, let's go to the dungeon. We'll see what your rogue-specific skills are like."

The lower levels turned out to have some small areas for individual practice, too. About 50 square feet, dim like everywhere else here.

"Let's split up. We'll turn away from each other and use Stealth," Brenna explained. "We'll start looking for each other after a minute. Of course, I'll find you faster since I'm at level 4. But I won't hit you. I'll remain concealed. Your main goal is to sense me. Listen, smell, notice any changes in the air. This'll grind your Detection ability. A lot of folks forget about that one, since it's hard to create training conditions for it. We have those conditions here, so take advantage of them. Only use your sword when you 100% sure."

She was right: I had to work on this ability whenever I could. While we were playing hide-and-seek, I only heard the bell sound that indicated a level up once.

"Let's begin."

Brenna clapped her hands, and we turned towards opposite sides of the arena.

A minute later, I turned around and, naturally, saw no one.

I roamed around the empty arena like a blind kitten. For a while, I held out a little hope that Brenna couldn't see me either, but it evaporated when something lightly touched my back. I turned around, but only caught a shadow, which disappeared in an instant.

After 10 minutes, I realized it would come to nothing at this rate, and I kept my eyes open, but focused in on my other senses.

Progress was slow, but right at the edges of my perception, I caught a light rustle. I turned towards it. Another 30 seconds later, I felt a change in the air. I took a step forward and glimpsed the shadow again. I tried to follow, but lost it.

That was okay. I understood the idea, and was now starting to notice faint traces of someone more and more often.

This went on for another hour and a half. I tried out various tactics, but I couldn't catch Brenna.

I sensed movement again, but this time I didn't

rush after it, just slightly changed direction. The movement was accompanied by a faint smell and vibration in the air. I pretended to stretch my stiff neck, and when I turned my head a little, I saw the shadow clearly. I leapt towards it and swung.

The gloom lit up with the sparks of two blades meeting.

"Not bad," Brenna said as she emerged from the darkness. "Time for theory. Let's get food from the canteen and go to your room."

"Hey," I said as we headed for the dungeon's exit. "How do you have so much patience? I know I'm grinding, but you just circled me for an hour and a half. Seems boring."

"Good question." She turned to me, a sly smile playing on her face. "It's boring if you're just walking around. But if you're walking around naked while staying right at the edge of someone's perception... That provides a certain thrill."

She turned around again and left, her wide hips swaying. I stood with my mouth open in the middle of the dungeon for a few seconds, regretting for the first time that my night vision didn't work here.

As a hospitable host, I let Brenna have the small table and put my own tray on the floor.

"So," she started, dipping a spoon into her soup, "let's begin."

For the first hour, she covered some really useful things. The best combination of hobbit skills, and the standard classes like archer, knife specialist, assassin, and safe cracker.

I listened intently, taking in all the new information for later reflection.

In the second hour, we finally started on what I'd been expecting for a long time.

"So, where are you from?" Brenna asked, changing the subject.

That was more or less the introduction I'd expected, and I was able to get my bearings and answer quickly.

"From Krinb... oh. Damn it... From near Krinberg, basically. But let's not talk about that. What difference does it make?"

"How do I explain this...? It matters because... Hobbits born here, as unfortunate as it is, are often different from the ones born in our homeland."

And now we'd arrived at the part I was most interested in.

Since I'd been at the guild, I'd taken in everything that had reached my ears, storing the information with what I'd learned earlier and analyzing it all together.

There was a margin for error, of course, but so far, everything indicated that something was brewing here at the Rogues' Guild. Tension hung in the air. The anticipation of something people were whispering, exchanging glances, and dreaming about. I could always just ignore it and get out, having gotten what I'd come here for. But... My spidey sense was tingling, telling me it could be something critical both in general and for me personally.

Basically, I'd decided to try and infiltrate, and

the perfect chance had just appeared. Brenna had asked just the right question.

"Listen..." I started, stretching the word as if I was reluctant to say this. "For personal reasons, I don't want to disclose who I am and where I'm from... But just so you completely understand..." I sighed. "I'll swear a system oath to answer some of your questions, but you have to promise we'll never talk about this again."

Brenna's eyebrows shot up, and she even stopped chewing for a few seconds. Not surprisingly. System oaths were rarely used, since they were truly unbreakable. More precisely, anyone who used it for deception or decided to break their word later doomed themselves to a minimum of lifetime of substantial curses, and often death. Just stumbling or slipping up in the wording was enough.

Visilius had probably broken one of these in his time. But I was well-spoken, and I'd already rehearsed what I wanted to say.

"Well, if you're sure..."

"Yes, I'm sure," I said, grimacing. "I just understand how my secrecy comes across from outside. This should help."

"Okay..."

Brenna put down the cutlery and put her hands on her knees, making it clear she'd stay that way until I was finished.

I opened the menu. A warning popped up three times, and I confirmed each time that I did actually want to swear an oath. Then a system message appeared.

Begin when ready!

I was enveloped in a yellow glow.

"I swear to the system that I first stepped foot in Shrinanth less than three months ago, and if I met any Shrinanthian before that point, I didn't know where they were from."

When I finished, I tapped End Oath.

The glow around me turned green, confirming what I'd said.

"Something like that."

"Where did you spend your whole life," Brenna started, staring at me in a daze, "if you can say under oath that you'd never met a Shrinanthian before?"

Now that I wasn't threatened by the system's punishment, I could lie from the heart.

"I've been special all my life. I was hidden away in a house and spent my life preparing for initiation there. And when it happened, I trained around the clock. And I didn't say I'd never met a Shrinanthian. We just didn't talk about those we knew in Shrinanth and their lineage."

"Wow..." She exhaled, grabbed a pie from her plate, and started gnawing on it.

While she was thinking, I decided I'd eat, too. I'd already finished everything I'd taken from the canteen, so I had to go into my inventory. Thankfully, I knew my body and had enough extra food to feed an ordinary man for a month. Well, it would last me five days.

"To be honest, I don't know what to say..."

Brenna finally said. "Let's get back to this at dinner."

Having said this, she stood up, picked up her tray, and walked to the door.

"Meet at the canteen around 9?" I said.

"Sure!" she answered, and the door closed behind her with a thud.

I leaned back against the bed and stared at the ceiling.

Time to take stock.

Berins had sent Brenna to me. First, she lowered my guard by showing how she could be useful to me, and then she cautiously began leading me to a key conversation. Based on her reaction, my oath had eliminated her main questions, and now she'd be running to report to Berins.

Well, alright then. In that case, I'd go to the dungeon with a group in half an hour. And ideally, I'd get new information over dinner or afterwards, if all went well. For now, I'd try to guess what she'd be like, and fashion a response.

Chapter 28

AFTER THE EXAM, there were 17 hobbits left in the special group. But there were still at least 20 in every class. As far as I could tell, it was the high-ranking students who needed more experience in one aspect or another of training who joined us.

When we went to the lower level of the dungeon this time, it was to a different area, and we were given the rules for a new game. It would also help with Stealth and Detection.

We were sent into a shadowy labyrinth again. But now we weren't fighting each other; we were fighting artificially generated monsters.

There were two types. One was passive, roaming around using stealth while we hunted them. The other was aggressive, and they were hunting us.

I was most interested in the traps, though.

They were completely harmless. When activated, they just threw pebbles at us, and the mechanisms to disable them were levers and buttons disguised as parts of the landscape. Just like the thread, invisible to me, that Viza pulled in the guild dungeon. Finding them helped with the Detection ability.

"Go!" Berins barked, and I entered the labyrinth.

There was no need to hurry. My task here wasn't to show off and prove to the others that I was better than them. They already knew that. I had to practice my intuition, instinctually sensing and hearing what was hidden.

It would probably be smart to keep my eyes closed to work on listening, smelling, and touch, but you wouldn't do that in a real scenario. So I dismissed that idea.

I sensed the first threat after only 30 feet. The changes in the air gave it away. Taking a step to the side, I swung the training sword and struck.

The wolf-like body fell to the ground soundlessly. Hey, I got a predator right away! Not bad.

I could just make out a rustle on my other side, and I quickly retreated. A shadow darted past me. Another hit, and a second wolf was neutralized.

Not bad at all!

I pressed myself against the wall and waited. It seemed like the coast was clear. But I still moved forward with extreme caution.

I wandered around the labyrinth for 10

minutes, then noticed that the wall in front of me was somehow different. I examined it. Yes... The terrain had changed. A trap, maybe?

If so, the disabling mechanism should be nearby.

I stood still, examining first one wall, then the floor, and then a second wall. Something lit up faintly, and I took half a step forward. Yes! One of the stones was flickering slightly.

I put out my hand, but then heard movement behind me. I turned and slashed without aiming. The dull blade collided with something, and one of my classmates crumbled to the floor.

He shouldn't have been stomping around like an elephant!

Checking to make sure there was no one else, I pressed the button. Something rustled, and the flickering stone changed shape and became an ordinary part of the wall.

I was even a little sad that I didn't know what kind of trap I'd disabled. Well, somehow I'd survive without that valuable information. Most likely, if this were a real-world setting, it would probably just have squashed me against the other wall.

We strolled around the labyrinth for four hours. Despite having our Stealth levels equalized again, I only got caught four times. Twice in a trap, and a third time when I ended up in the same place as another hobbit, a wolf, and a sheep. A wolf who came into the area last won. Towards the end, I was just tired and collided head-on with a class mate, and in that moment, we were attacked by two of the ever-present wolves at once.

* * *

Brenna was already waiting in the canteen. I grabbed some food, and we went back to my room. From the expression on her face, I could tell she had something to ask me.

I was right. As soon as we started eating, she got right down to business. But she started from a distance.

"What do you think about the last war with the orcs?"

"I try not to think about it..."

"And?"

"We got screwed."

"And yet, you're here..."

"So are you."

"Have you forgiven them?"

"Who? The humans?"

"Yeah."

The main thing here was not to overdo it so she didn't get the impression I was telling her what she wanted to hear.

"I barely interact with them, but as far as I know, not all of them supported the decision of that assh — uh... Our emperor..."

"What about elves and dwarves?"

Hm. I wondered what she was looking for.

"I don't think anything about them. They live and let live."

"Right..."

Brenna fell silent, lost in thought as she picked at the cutlet she'd barely started on. Either she didn't have much experience recruiting, or I'd said something wrong.

I decided to give her a nudge. "Why do you ask, anyway? Because the orcs are close? Well, our council is wise, and we won't step on the same rake a second time."

"That's true," she said, then suddenly seemed to come to her senses. "Ignore me. All this news from the wall is just bringing up lots of different thoughts. For example... What would happen if the orcs got into the Central City? Or... If Shrinanth fell completely? You haven't thought about that?"

"Hm..."

She'd thrown the ball back into my court, and I had to think carefully. Thankfully, her question didn't need a quick answer.

I picked at my roast, looking out of the corner of my eye at the young halfling who could probably give me at least some answers about what was going on in the world. I had to choose the right words.

"Well... I mean, if they even get here, it'd be bad," I finally muttered. "A lot of our people are here... A lot of money and goods... And the guilds, of course. It'd be better to stop the greenskins at the wall... or... Let them get in."

There. I'd said the biggest thing. There were three ways the game could go now.

First: They wouldn't trust me.

Second: They'd trust me, but they weren't actually planning anything, and this was just a conversation between two young hobbits.

Third: They'd trust me, and there was a conspiracy.

"Yeah... I think about that sometimes, too," Brenna said, nodding, and tore off a piece of her cutlet. "It's a shame none of this depends on us. Well, anyway. While we finish eating, why don't I give you some theory? Then we can continue our training."

We didn't touch on any other slippery subjects that evening. During and after dinner, Brenna told me about the specifics of choosing weapons and armor for the various classes of rogues. Then we went to the training grounds, and she spent a few more hours teaching me knife fighting.

* * *

The identical days started flowing together. Training in the special group, and personal classes with Brenna.

She didn't start any more conversations about the place of hobbits in this world, but she took advantage of any opportunity to ask my opinion for any reason.

The most unpleasant thing, though I couldn't say for certain that it was happening, was the either she was putting together my psychological profile, or I was just paranoid.

As for my progress, it was clear as day.

Within two weeks, I'd gotten level three in

Knife Throwing, Quiet Steps, using stabbing weapons, and using a shield, and I was probably close with ambidexterity. I'd also leveled up Detection, Rock Climbing, and Night Fighting to level 2.

And thanks to the constant heavy training and acrobatic exercises, I'd continued to improve my natural strength, dexterity, and stamina.

We rode horses for an hour every other day. Well, not really "rode"... We did our usual training, only on horseback.

I also learned how to make a quick-and-dirty small dexterity and focus potion from the grass that was growing everywhere under our feet.

There was no news from the city, but from snippets of conversations, I gathered that there were fierce battles being fought almost the entire length of the wall. Shrinanth was sending all its forces there, but the forecast was grim.

I couldn't be sure... Maybe I was getting too worked up and anxious, but it seemed to me like the people here were eagerly awaiting this grim news about the expected imminent breakthrough...

Well, and most interesting of all these days was the organized visit to the guild dungeon, which took place a week after the second course started.

I admit I accepted an exclusive quest with a certain amount of danger...

Take the Scarlet Flower from the highest tower in the abandoned city.

Reward: A free body upgrade.

The Last Portal Jumper

It took me about two hours to get to the tower, waging war on all the local fauna along the way, and occasionally hitting the flora with fireballs by accident.

The base of the tower was 15 feet wide, the tower itself almost 70 feet tall. It was built from large stones with two rings of darkening windows, or embrasures, to be more precise.

In theory, there were plenty of places to put your hands and feet on the outside. Sure, in the worst case scenario, you could fall quite a ways, hitting the hand and footholds on the way down.

Of course, I was a prudent man (well, hobbit) and had brought ropes, hooks, and crampons. Except my goddamned inventory stopped working as soon as I got within 30 feet of the tower and saw the system message that I'd reached the right location.

But what bothered me most was that my weapons were still active, which meant that enemies could show up at any moment.

"Maybe we should just forget about it?" I turned my head to look at Viza, who was sitting on my shoulder.

Speaking of whom, she'd finally gotten into her groove and a taste of freedom, and this time she almost killed more monsters than I did.

Chicken?

"I'm not chickening out... I'm just exercising sensible precaution."

Read: sensible, precautious chickenshit.

"You got it, clever boy. I mean, clever girl! Fly

in circles and cover me until I get the scarlet flower. If you stay hidden, that means *you're* chickenshit."

Oh, here we go...

"Chickenshit!"

Okay, alright! Crawl on!

Viza took off and sped to the top of the tower in a spiral. I followed her with my gaze, got a rough idea of my route again, and walked up to the wall to put my foot on the first stone.

Danger always looks bigger through the eyes of fear (and little experience), but my body was another story. I had a significant advantage with the passive skills Cat Burglar, Acrobatics, Perfect Balance, Deft Legs, and Deft Arms, as well as my body upgrades, so the climbing itself was easy. But I remembered the last exclusive quest, and had a growing suspicion of some kind of setup.

Ilya! Ilyaaaa!!

"What?!"

I froze and equipped my sword, balancing on a small protrusion.

Nothing! Just being supportive!

God damn it...

I looked at the first embrasure about 3 feet above my head. It was 30 inches high and eight inches wide. A large beast wouldn't be able to come flying out, but it depended on its capabilities. Just in case, it'd be better to crawl between two neighboring embrasures. There was about a foot between them.

I put my sword back into the Quick Access

menu, shifted a little to the left, and kept climbing.

Seems like there's no one here... Viza said uncertainly, hovering outside of one window. *I'd go inside, but my wings won't — SHIT!*

I heard the sound of membranous wings beating the air rapidly, and then a howl came from inside the tower. Well, that made sense. They hadn't been expecting someone to slip through. I clambered up two steps and got into position on rocks protruding most from the wall, where my feet could fit comfortably and I could hold on with my free arm.

My head was almost spinning as I swiveled it from side to side, trying to figure out where the mystery beast howling angrily would finally pop out from.

They didn't pop out — they flew out. From both sides at once. And it was clear from their appearance that this would be a real mess.

They resembled dachshunds, their bodies about the size of the embrasures, but... First of all, when the monsters leapt out, they immediately spread their three-foot-long wings and looked significantly larger... And secondly, they were hovering within 10 feet of me, their while bellies beginning to inflate. A second later, spikes began growing rapidly from them.

I didn't need fine-tuned senses to understand that those spikes were about to come flying at me.

The fingers of my left hand were clinging desperately to a stone sticking out of the wall, so I couldn't take out my shield. It wouldn't have covered my whole body, anyway. Jump? It was an option. The height wasn't fatal yet... I might not even break my legs.

Naturally, I didn't jump. As the possible ways this situation could develop flew through my mind one after another, I put up a fire shield and took out a throwing knife.

Precise shot!

The blade sunk into the direct center of one of the beast's chests, and it plunged downward squealing. An instant later, a second one seemed to explode, and the spikes from its belly flew towards me... and burned up against my fire shield. The monster lurched to the side after attacking, but my second knife landed, and it followed its predecessor to the ground.

Two more monsters appeared on opposite sides from behind the tower. I put up another fire shield and got ready to face the nearest one, but a black shadow flashed before me, and the spiked beast was split in half. I turned towards the next one, but Viza killed it before it could get close.

"What took you so long?!" I shouted, looking around me.

There were three of them on the other side!!

"Okay then... Can you grab my knives?"

You want me to chew your food for you, too?

"Where did you learn that language?!"

From a camel, damn. One sec.

I barely held back a smile when Viza brought me the knives I'd thrown, vigorously flapping her wings and trying to fly vertically.

"Get on my shoulder!"

I took out an egg and showed it to her... Barely a millisecond passed before it disappeared into her insatiable belly.

Why do I feel like that was a trick?

"I can't get inside," I said, nodding towards the nearest embrasure the monsters had come out of.

Aw, come on! Try to stick your head in. If it fits, the rest of you will...

Not bothering to react to Viza's joke, I climbed towards the embrasure and positioned my shoulder so it would be easy for her to get into the tower.

Slave driver...

Her mental grumbling didn't stop her from darting into the tower.

Ugh, it stinks. And it's as dark as a —

"You should be able to see well in the dark!" I shouted from the embrasure.

Just stating facts. Hey!

"What?!"

I winced at the sharp change in Viza's mental tone.

There's a button and an inscription here... One sec, I'll get closer.

My heart was racing.

"Well?"

Hang on... It says... The chosen...

There was a pause.

"What?!"

The chosen... Ilya... Should buy a lip-sealing machine.

"God damn it!!"

Book Two

A comedian pet was a disgrace to the family. I'd never heard mental laughter before... Well, however she wanted to amuse herself, she did help me in battle.

Alright, don't yell. There's a little ring...

She appeared in the opening, a ring sparkling on her lower fang. It was the same one I'd found in the previous exclusive quest.

Small Trickster's Ring. Rogue branch skill efficiency: +5%.

Hm. Well, it was better than nothing, especially since I hadn't expected it.

I took it and put it on. It might not be much to improve all my specialized skills, but it would help in the immediate future.

Of course, I'd have loved to take a rest inside the tower, but there was no way I could get in, so I'd have to keep going. Thankfully, my body was more than capable of handling the exertion.

I got to the next ring of windows without any incident. For some reason, when I got close, I decided to look down.

Shit!

The ground was 50 feet below, and the bodies of the monsters we'd killed looked so far away...

"Do you think you could..."

I wanted to ask Viza, who was sitting on my shoulder (and making it difficult to climb), if she could hold on somewhere else, like the back of my neck, but I didn't have time. The sound of my voice was cut off by the familiar shriek of the tower's inhabitants as they came flying out.

The Last Portal Jumper

There were twice as many this time, a second monster following each one. But we had some experience now.

I quickly climbed to the nearest embrasure, slashing at the first monster and the one right behind it on the way. Then I threw three knives in a row, hitting another two monsters. The next one shot out spikes, but my fire shield held, and the beast plunged downward a second later, my fourth knife in its chest. Viza took care of the rest.

She showed off her incredible flying skills and, having taken a decent loop, flew into the embrasure at full speed, folding her wings at the very last moment.

There's a button with an inscription here! Want me to read it?

I burst out laughing and almost fell off the wall.

"Anything else?"

Nooope, sorry.

"Okay, let's keep going."

We were still about 20 feet from the top of the tower, where the roof narrowed steeply. At the very top, I discovered something like a nest, and...

Quest: Find the Scarlet Flower. Complete.

The flexibility of your joints has increased.

I also learned that the nectar from this plant was highly valuable, and I'd get at least 50,000 gold for it at the market. I could give it to the Rogues' Guild for 40... But why would I? I didn't need reputation here.

Getting down was much easier. Once the quest

was complete, my inventory unlocked, and I could use all the gadgets I'd brought.

Of course, I took my time leaving the dungeon, and killed monsters until my arms couldn't lift a sword properly anymore.

* * *

Everyday life dragged on again, consisting only of grinding, grinding, an hour and a half of theory, and more grinding. By this point, I almost believed I was just paranoid...

But the night before the exam for second rank, Brenna, instead of sitting down for dinner, leaned close to my ear and whispered:

"Berins is expecting you in 20 minutes."

As I watched her leave, I realized this would be the moment of truth.

Chapter 24

BRENNA DIDN'T COME into Berins's office, and the two of us sat alone in the light of the single candle burning on the table. He didn't even offer me water.

"Ilyenis, we need people like you..." Berins was starting to get on my nerves, drumming his fingers on the desk. "The orcs have almost broken through the wall."

He stopped and stared at me.

Well, I was supposed to be stupid. I had to figure out how a stupid hobbit would react to misinformation like this. I couldn't come up with anything, and just looked at the instructor, smiling.

"The orcs will soon be in the Central City."

"Do we need to leave?" I asked after a pause.

"The ones who need to will leave." He nodded, confirming I'd guessed the right answer. "But a lot of people will stay and help the orcs."

My stunned face wouldn't give me away here. Shock would be an appropriate reaction from both a young halfling and the human Ilya from Earth, since... Really?

Just like that? So direct! How could you know who to trust with this information?! Fucking hell, that was bad! He clearly had some kind of trump card to be speaking so openly... Alright. I had no other options, so I'd keep playing.

"Help how?!" I whispered, looking down and staring at my hands.

"Don't worry, Ilyenis! There are a lot of us, and like you, we want the empire of Shrinanth to fall! That's what you want, right?"

"Well... Yeah, but they're..."

"Strong?"

Berins leaned back in his chair and laughed loudly.

"Yeah..."

"Not anymore, Ilyenis! Not for a long time." The hobbit slammed his fist on the desk so hard, the inkwell jumped, and the candle's flame flickered. "Shrinanth was weakening even under the last emperor, and the current idiot... You know how he treats us and everyone else! This fucking empire is only holding on because of the victory in the last orc war, which WE gave them!"

"Us?"

It was so strange, I couldn't help myself.

"Yes, US. Hobbits and elves! Without us, they never would have won, even with those northern bastards and the Ziranians. There would be orcs sitting here now!"

"That's true," I said, taking advantage of the short pause.

"And now it's time to take what rightly belongs to us!"

God damn... I probably should have kept my mouth shut, but I couldn't.

"What?"

"What do you mean, 'what'?!" Berins hopped up, his spittle flying towards me. "Our honor! The money that bastard's held onto from the last war with the millions in interest he's underpaid all these years. Good gods! Have you never learned any history at all?!"

Well, not really, to be honest.

Berins's face was so distorted with hatred that it took some effort not to pull out my sword, my mental cursor hovering over the icon.

"Pronzel and Grondin, cities we built! They're rightfully ours. Why the hell are they part of Shrinanth?!"

Oh shit, right! I couldn't remember the details, but Visilius had said that under the current emperor's grandfather 70 years ago, a large portion of the hobbits' land was given to humans after a short war.

Well, the general idea was clear. Time to get into the details and remember that I was a cool, promising douchebag with my own views on life.

"Do we have a shot?" I raised my head and looked Berins in the eyes.

"Victory is guaranteed!"

"The orcs'?"

"Ha!" Berns grinned and sat down. "The orcs can't settle here. But it's too soon to talk about that... I need to know if you're willing to join us."

"Yes!" I squared my shoulders. "What do I need to do?!"

"Ha!" he said again, more relaxed this time. "Nothing at all. Everything is already done. We're recruiting people like you for the future."

"Ah," I said, drawing out the word and genuinely disappointed.

"Don't worry! You and your peers will build our new future when Shrinanth falls! Right now, we're laying the groundwork for a new world."

I had nothing to say, so I kept quiet. Good thing, too — Berins got down to business.

"All candidates have to pass a test. We have to make sure you're one of us. Are you ready?"

"Yes! What do I have to do?"

"Ha! Nothing too difficult." He winked at me and leaned on the desk. "Just kill a human."

Just like that...

"Are you ready?" Berins repeated when I hesitated.

"Yeah... But if people start dying in the city..."

"They won't!" He laughed again. "You'll do it tomorrow. During the test in the dungeon!"

For the first time in this conversation, I felt like things weren't going to plan. But I wasn't sure of the extent yet. I had to keep playing the role.

"The system won't let me..."

The Last Portal Jumper

I knew what he had planned was impossible. If one participant suddenly killed another, he'd be marked and get a major debuff until the end of the subsequent trial. It was so harsh that he often wouldn't be able to walk on his own. And the trial judge would be the system itself to prevent any set-ups... At least, that's what I'd thought until now.

"In the dungeon, that's true." The smile fell from Berins's face. "But not on exclusive quest grounds. The system only keeps track of who goes in and out."

Holy shit!

"And?"

"And tomorrow, you'll have to kill a human."

"Why make it so complicated? We might not even get an exclusive quest. It'll be risky. Suspicious. Wouldn't it be easier to just do it in the city?"

"It would be easier, but... Well, first of all, we're certain he's a spy," Berins said, sitting motionless. "And secondly, we need to test you. You're good, but you're slippery."

"Me?" I exclaimed.

Knowing full well what he was referring to, I realized something terrible. Despite calling him a "spy," this human would probably die exclusively so these bastards could test my loyalty.

"You," he nodded. "We don't even know where you're from, who you are..."

"I..."

"Close your mouth, and let's cut to the chase." A formidable-looking shortsword appeared in his hand. "We need good, young warriors, but we don't need impostors. You either do what we ask, or you go on your way..."

"I..."

Berins's sword flew up. My chair was thrown to the side, my own sword shining in the light of the only candle.

"I understood, but why the fuck are you acting like this?!" I said, preparing to attack.

"Hm..." Berins looked me over, also standing. "My apologies..."

His sword disappeared, and he righted his chair so he could sit.

"Go on." I wasn't going to put my sword away, and I took a step back, too. "So far, this all looks like bait, like you're identifying hobbits who aren't loyal to Shrinanth and handing them over to the Emperor."

"Bah!"

The hobbit's eyebrows flew up. He gave me a long look, then burst out laughing. He roared so hard that I couldn't doubt the sincerity of his laughter. Moreover, I clearly heard him say something...

"Am I an idiot?" I asked, continuing to play my role.

"Who the fuck else?!" he said, wiping tears from his eyes and stammering. He pointed to the wall. "See that stone?"

"Yeah."

"Press it."

"You press it."

I took a few steps to the side.

"You're good."

The hobbit stood and pressed on the stone that was sticking out of the wall.

Right between us, in the middle of the dark room, a glowing yellow portal appeared.

"Follow me."

Without looking at me, Berins went into the portal.

Son of a bitch!

I glanced around the office. I didn't have long to think... I knew that since this asshole had started being so forthcoming, he had an ace up his sleeve. Which meant I couldn't leave, and he seemed to be a natural. Which meant I had to try to untangle this knot... I unequipped my sword and followed him through the portal.

It didn't close, and lit up a room with... Jesus Christ! There were dozens of dead people chained to the walls. Most of them had died from torture, and some, judging by the skeletal bodies, of hunger.

"Enough?" came Berins's voice from behind me. "Let's go back."

I turned around, but I couldn't make out the hobbit in the bright yellow light from the portal. I grit my teeth and took a step forward.

A second later, the office — and Berins — appeared. He came out from the side in such away that if I'd tried to attack him, I would have missed. But, of course, I didn't do anything.

"Now, to the main order of business..." Berins

sat down again, a smile playing on his lips. "As I'm sure you understand, we don't show these things to, or have these kinds of conversations with, just anyone."

Spit it out!

I kept quiet and pretended to be a startled young hobbit. It wasn't hard, since inside, I was a no less startled human.

"So... Down here," Berins said, indicating somewhere under the desk, "is a powerful artifact. When you came in, it made a connection to your head. And on my command, it'll erase all your memories of this conversation. Got it?"

"Yeah."

"There are two options here," he said, grinning. "You say that everything you've seen is incomprehensible and uninteresting because you don't want to join us, or you think we're working for the emperor. It doesn't matter which. After this, you'll leave and be done. You'll just forget everything and be the student you were before this. You'll pass the exam, and that's it. Or... You're with us. You'll keep your memory, and tomorrow... and after... you'll do what I say without any questions. Decide. You have one minute!"

He stopped, and I stood there in complete shock.

This was the kind of scenario where you'd get your memory erased... And when these things... If I were the ordinary guy I was playing, there wouldn't be any problem... But I was actually a double agent (put here by myself), and the information I'd received was worth quite a lot. And if I wanted to remember it and keep playing this game... I'd have to kill a human tomorrow... It was highly unlikely they'd trust my word and just release me in the dungeon with the proposed victim... where we could come up with something together...

"Time's up!"

"I agree!"

"Wonderful!" Berins smiled. "You'll be dismissed from the first part of the exam. Come here at 8:45. You'll receive further instructions then."

Having said this, he waved his hand, letting me know I could go.

As I left the office, I shuddered internally, afraid my memory would be erased, but it wasn't.

I still remembered everything Berins had said, and the room with the bodies of humans chained to the walls.

* * *

"We're conducting an experiment!"

Berins was sitting behind his desk, a quartet of students standing in front of him — three hobbits and a young human man. Condemned to death. I'd arrived early so Berins could bring me up to speed on the plan, and now he was telling the others the story.

"Billings," Berins said, pointing at one of the hobbits, "came to us fairly recently, but he's 24 and already level 11. Sincher's also a latecomer to the rogues, and he's already level 9. Ilyenis is the best in the class, and Green's a human. According to our estimates, if the four of you go to the far area of the dungeon, the aggregate stats of your group will trigger an exclusive quest to destroy a monster. That will give each of you a body upgrade... If you survive. Participation is voluntary. Now is your last chance to decline."

Berins paused and gave us a long look, drumming his fingers on the desk. No one declined.

"The risks are high, since if you get a quest, the monster will be strong," he continued without waiting for comments. "So we'll give you potions, supplies, artifacts, and everything else you'll need..."

He fell silent again. I cast a glance at the doomed man. He looked self-assured. He was looking at the instructor silently. Was he a spy? Or was that just thrown at me yesterday? Who knew? But we'd find out very soon. Probably...

*   *   *

This time, the party leader wasn't me, but I knew immediately that the plan would work.

ATTENTION: A new exclusive group quest is available: Kill the Ape Warrior.

Reward: A free body upgrade for each participant.

This offer will be active for one minute.

...

I didn't accept it this time.

Your group has accepted an exclusive quest.

The most challenging thing for me on our way to the entrance of the quest location was just not revealing my full capabilities (which Berins didn't know about, either) while still acting natural and trying to figure out what kind of companions I'd been given.

That morning, Berins had let me know in private that the two other hobbits were in on the plan and would be witnesses to the upcoming event. He also told me about the possible bosses we'd face, and the monkey was far from the best option.

We were expected not just to kill Green, but to make good use of him first. Ideally, we'd first cripple the boss, then I'd handle the human (before killing the boss so the experience would be divided among the three of us).

All night, I'd searched for a way out of the setup.

One option was to escape before the exam. But I wasn't that naive, and I knew my room was being watched. So the chances of escaping alive were slim to none.

Of course, I didn't intend to kill the human, either, and I'd thought up an idea.

The belt each of us were given before entering the dungeon would serve as proof of the target's death. I had to take it from the dead body and bring it back.

There were serious holes in the plan. First and foremost, what to do with the hobbits. Kill them?

That was an option, but only as a fallback. I had too little information about them, and about what was happening... Although the dead humans in the room reeking of decay made that possibility quite likely.

Second question: what to do with the human? I was counting on the cooperation of the champions here. Or rather, on being able to turn the issue over to them. For now, I'd brought a lot of food with me so Green could survive here comfortably for a week or so.

But there was a third problem: Berins and the other high-ranking hobbits who, if they weren't going to meet me at the dungeon portal, would be expecting a visit from me as soon as I left. Considering the interesting mental artifacts they used, it'd be best to avoid that meeting. And on top of that, I definitely needed to get a skill point for second rank. I didn't need to be Miss Cleo to know they wouldn't let me onto the grounds of the Rogues' Guild anymore. Same for the Central City.

"Air!" Billings shouted, and I instinctively grabbed my bow and shot down a diving eagle.

"Not bad..." the second hobbit, Sincher, said with a nod.

He'd raised his bow, too, but didn't have time to loose the arrow.

We'd been walking for about an hour already, and a few oddities had started catching my eye.

Sincher seemed to be really weak. He may have been level 11, but he clearly didn't have many skills, his abilities were mediocre, and by all appearances, he'd never drank an enhancement elixir in his life. Not much of a problem, basically, in contrast to Billings.

He was leading the group and rarely participated in battle himself. But even the few times he did were enough to make me suspect Berins had been lying...

He at least tried to hide it, but his reaction speed and strength were clearly higher than mine, to the point that it was impossible that we were both at the same level. Or at least extremely unlikely.

"Careful! Looks like a snake!"

Billings once again showed that his powers of observation were incredible and indicated a wall that was blocking our way. And when I looked closer, I saw that the long, completely unassuming vine hanging in the shadows wasn't actually a vine, but a monster.

No. Before the main event, my suspicions had to either be confirmed or proven wrong.

I had gloves on my hands, and aside from providing protection, they also functioned as camouflage. There was no reason for everyone to know about my rings, especially the gold signet I'd taken from the last of the Count's soldiers I'd killed.

Ring of Revelation, level 8. Number of charges: 4/10. When activated, allows the wearer to see hidden enemies and the true identity and level of those around. Duration: 30 minutes.

I was covering for my companions, and since

they were just finishing off the snake, they weren't paying any attention to me.

Activate!

Their appearances didn't change, but red letters and numbers flashed up over their heads.

Green (human), level 5.
Sincher (hobbit), level 9.
Billings (hobbit), level 25.

There it was. What did that mean? It meant that Billings wasn't just an observer; he was a supervisor.

Berins didn't know me, which made him wary. He wasn't going to risk just taking me at my word, so he sent a halfling capable of making quick adjustments on the spot, if necessary. So, if I didn't do what I was supposed to, he could neutralize me.

And considering his high level, the powerful artifacts and good consumables he probably had with him, it was unlikely I'd leave here alive.

Which meant that the monkey boss, if it was based on the average level of the group, would be incredibly strong.

"Ilyenis! What're you standing there for?"

Green and Sincher had already jumped over the stone wall, and Billings was sitting at the top, waving his arm to tell me to hurry up.

Hm... The evening was finally getting interesting.

The monkey boss, the level 25 hobbit following my every move, the halflings at the exit from the dungeon, and the critical information I had to get to the champions at any cost. My little "task." On the other hand, whatever doesn't kill us makes us stronger. Now I just had to not die…

"Just adjusting the Quick Access menu," I answered, and hurried after my companions.

Chapter 25

I WENT INTO THE PORTAL FIRST, and soon it closed behind Billings.

The location looked different from the abandoned city. It seemed like we'd been transported somewhere on its outskirts. It had the same sky with its perpetually low-flying clouds, but the buildings here had been hit much harder; there wasn't a single intact structure. At their essence, they were ruins overgrown with grass and shrubs.

The borders weren't marked, so we could go wherever we wanted. It soon became clear why.

"Your task," Billings declared, holding an expensive-looking bow, "is to distract it without breaking your legs jumping over rubble. I'll kill it systematically."

Sounded solid...

Not for the first time, the thought popped into

my head that Green's accidental death would solve all my problems, but I pushed it away again. First of all, they'd just think up another challenge right away, and there was no guarantee it'd be easier. And secondly, he could really work for the champions, and it'd be nice to talk to him first.

"Ready?" Billings asked.

I nodded, took out my own bow, and went first according to our prior agreement.

King Kong seemed to erupt from the ground 50 feet ahead of me. I couldn't think of any other name for this 25-foot-tall gray gargantuan. He was shaggy, with a deafening roar, arms like tree trunks, and claws, each of which could impale three people.

He had also started throwing the stone rubble that was plentiful here.

I felt like the hero of an ancient *Donkey Kong* game. Though, in that case, I'd be dodging barrels. But then, my current skin did bear a strong resemblance to the hero of that arcade game.

I waited a moment, and when a stone shot from the gigantic paw, I leapt to the side, taking cover under a low wall. There was a crash above my head, and pieces of stone showered over me.

I darted out and shot an arrow into the monster's face. He roared, and I had to leap back again immediately after. Damn it! The most important thing here was not to overdo it with magic. Meaning nothing that would draw attention, otherwise I might get myself killed by accident.

On the other hand, that would automatically

solve all my problems.

I darted out again, and this time ran without shooting. The next two volleys from King Kong were launched at me again, and then he turned his attention to one of my companions. I shot another time, hitting him in the eye, but he didn't fall.

I shot a quick glance back at the rest of the party. My temporary allies were doing pretty much the same thing I was, except that only Billings was using fire arrows. Not with any apparent effect, though.

Wait — that wasn't true. There *was* an effect!

All of a sudden, the boss squatted down and sprang... For some reason, directly at me! I managed to dodge and take cover again, but when he landed, his massive frame shook the ground tremendously.

Without turning around, I darted out and jumped again. The burst of air I was caught up in confirmed that the monster's fist had landed far too close. Only after another vault did I allow myself to turn around. Just in time, too. The beast was holding a stone in his huge paws, and he launched it at me a second later.

Were the others doing anything at all?!

Luckily, I was right next to the three-foot remains of a wall, and I was able to dive behind it.

The wall exploded with a thundering crash. A few razor-edged shards flew towards me, burning up in the fire shield I created at the very last second.

Well, fuck it. It would give my capabilities away, but I'd survive... It wasn't easy to see the shield, anyway, unless you were standing close.

I took off running again, but the ape apparently thought I was done for, and turned to the others.

I looked around as I ran and realized that I could shoot at the monster from behind forever, but it wouldn't do any good.

Two explosions in a row interrupted my train of thought. It was Billings, finally remembering that killing the boss was a required condition for a successful mission and using one of the resources he was given: fire grenades.

The first of them just scorched the hair on King Kong's leg, but the second exploded at his belly and knocked the giant off his feet.

A suicidal thought flashed up in my head. I could rush over to the monster now as he lay on the ground and plunge my spear into his eye. Fortunately for me, though, I hadn't lost all my marbles yet, and I continued to move further away, fully aware of what was about to start.

And start it did.

The infuriated behemoth leapt back to his feet, roared something that could only have translated to, "You motherfuckers!" and jumped. Away from me, luckily.

Luckily for me, but not for Sincher. The hobbit tried to dodge, unsuccessfully, twisting his ankle instead and falling out of my view. A moment later, the boss's enormous fist came down in the exact same place. Then it rose again, and the previously gray hair was now stained red.

The fist came down and back up again. And again. The blows were accompanied by crunching sounds, and the fist became enveloped in scarlet.

"Throw some grenades, for fuck's sake!" I shouted.

I had grenades, too, of course, but they were weak, and I only had two of them.

Billings stood about 20 yards away, and as far as I could tell from that distance, had been shaken to the core. But my shout brought him back to reality, and he stopped being so precious with his resources, immediately launching seven grenades.

The series of explosions knocked the behemoth back. Right back to me. Shit! This time, I didn't hold back. Taking advantage of the boss's lucky fall, I threw my own grenade directly into the muzzle of the temporarily disoriented monster.

To incredible success. He had just started to lift his head when the grenade exploded. His head jerked back and hit the ground again.

I was already rushing forward, and pushing off from the remains of another wall, I soared through the air, equipping my spear mid-flight.

The red, burning eyes of King Kong opened wide. He lurched away as I got close, but that only helped me, and the tip of my spear sank right into his eyeball.

It plunged into his brain, giving us the victory... Only in my fantasies, unfortunately.

The anatomy of high-level system monsters

was completely different from that of common beasts. I'd pierced the eye, but my spear hadn't gone any further.

I saw a giant fist flying towards me, and had just enough time to jump off the ape's head. There was a splat, and then silence. My eardrums ruptured, and blood was flowing down my neck.

The only good thing was that a blow to the head like that could cause a concussion, assuming the beast had a brain.

Meanwhile, I was already hurrying away from the boss. As soon as I saw something suitable for cover, I dove into it and cast Healing four times in a row.

The first sounds that got through to my besieged ears were the rumbles of explosions. Billings finally realized that the boss had to be taken down before Green and I could be dealt with.

I stuck my head out and assessed the situation. Hm. Blinded in one eye and being pelted with grenades, King Kong was already back on his feet, firing stones like nothing had happened.

The spectacle cast doubt on whether the hobbits who'd sent us here had calculated correctly.

In any case, I couldn't just sit around. Once the monster killed my allies, he'd take care of me.

I exhaled and charged forward, but I didn't make it in time. The enormous bastard turned out to have excellent hearing, and he whipped around to face me. Fuck! I was out of options, and after launching my last grenade in the direction of his head, I started running.

There was an explosion, then a howl... Victory? My ass! The boss, blinded by fire, went berserk and started grabbing and throwing stones even faster.

I took cover again and watched for a minute as huge boulders flew over me. A few more explosions followed, then a horrible scream.

Horrible because of the words it carried:

"I'm out of grenades!"

Great. Fucking great!

I leaned out briefly, then ducked back.

Billings's last volley, to be frank, had done fuck all, and aside from a few more scorched areas and becoming even more frenzied, I saw no changes in the ape's condition. On top of that, I had a terrible suspicion that he would quickly regenerate. And that spelled death for us. If he healed, then, considering our lack of grenades, we were toast.

Okay... I had no choice. Time for plan B!

I darted out and charged at the boss again. Distracted, he let me get within 20 feet of him, then turned around... and got a fireball to the face.

It wasn't a fireball like the ones I'd eked out at the very beginning of my magical training. It was a buzzing, concentrated mass of destructive firepower the size of a volleyball.

King Kong roared, started smacking his burning face with his paws, and stumbled back.

I'd expected all of this, and kept rushing forward. I jumped onto the hairy body, ran to the head, and drove my fire-enchanted spear into the writhing beast's throat. It almost broke through... I swung again, gritting my teeth in pain.

The spear sunk halfway into the ape's body.

He threw up both his paws, and I leapt away. They fell back down, hammering the spear in as far as it would go, and I ran across the ground, trying to get as far away as possible.

All of a sudden, something hit my shoulder hard. I rolled on the grass and hit my head on a rock.

My vision blurred, but through the shroud, I saw the silhouette of a hobbit approaching. He was holding a shield — the same one he'd just attacked me with.

"Who the fuck are you?!" Billings shouted.

"I saved your life, asshole."

I took out a healing potion, but only managed two gulps before the hobbit kicked it out of my hands.

"What's going on here?!" came Green's voice from behind the hobbit. Billings whipped around and hurled a dagger.

End of Book Two

Want to be the first to know about our latest
LitRPG, sci fi and fantasy titles from your favorite
authors?

Subscribe to our **New Releases** newsletter:
http://eepurl.com/b7niIL

Thank you for reading *The Last Portal Jumper!*

If you like what you've read, check out other sci-fi, fantasy and LitRPG novels published by Magic Dome Books:

NEW RELEASES!

The Selected
A LitRPG Action Adventure Series
by Vasily Mahanenko & Yuri Vinokuroff

The Afflicted
A LitRPG Apocalypse Adventure Series
by Konstantin Zubov

The Dark Summoner
A Portal Progression Fantasy Series
by Andrei Tkachev

The Banned
A LitRPG Adventure Series
by Michael Atamanov

The Order of Architects
A Portal Progression Fantasy Series
by Oleg Sapphire & Yuri Vinokuroff

The Hunter's Code
A Portal Progression Fantasy Series
by Oleg Sapphire & Yuri Vinokuroff

The One Who Changes the Future
A Dystopian Portal Progression Fantasy Series
by Boris Romanovsky

An Ideal World for a Sociopath
A LitRPG Apocalypse Adventure Series
by Oleg Sapphire

The Healer's Way
A Portal Progression Fantasy Series
by Oleg Sapphire & Alexey Kovtunov

How I Built a Magic Empire
A Portal Progression Fantasy Series
by Konstantin Zubov

The Dark Healer
A Historical Progression Fantasy Series
by Alex Toxic & Nadya Lee

Lord of The System
A LitRPG Progression Fantasy Series
by Alex Toxic & Furious Miki

A Shelter in Spacetime
A LitRPG Apocalypse Series
by Dmitry Dornichev

The Coming of God of Death
A Portal Progression Fantasy Series
by Dmitry Dornichev

The Village
A LitRPG Progression Fantasy Series
by Dmitry Dornichev & Alexey Kovtunov

Condemned (Lord Valevsky: Last of the Line)
A Progression Fantasy LitRPG Series
by Vasily Mahanenko

Living Ice
A Portal Progression Fantasy Series
by Dmitry Sheleg

Ghost in the System
An Apocalypse LitRPG Series
by Alexey Kovtunov

Crossroads of Oblivion
A Portal Progression Fantasy Adventure Series
by Dem Mikhailov

The Goldenblood Heir
A Portal Progression Fantasy Series
by Boris Romanovsky

More books and series are coming out soon!

In order to have new books of the series translated faster, we need your help and support! Please consider leaving a review or spread the word by recommending *The Last Portal Jumper* to your friends and posting the link on social media. The more people buy the book, the sooner we'll be able to make new translations available.

Thank you!

Till next time!